# "Where to?"

Wyatt and Cricket stood midway between the elevators and the outdoor deck.

"My suite?"

"Sure?"

She nodded.

He kissed her lightly, quickly. "I need to get that wine."

She held him even as he tried to make a break for it. "That's what room service is for."

"Is that all?"

"For now," she said, pulling him along until she could hit the button to go up. His arm slid just above her waist, his fingers gliding on her bare skin.

She shivered at the feeling, and when she opened her eyes, he was staring at her with so much longing it stole her breath away...

Dear Reader,

After writing over sixtysomething books for Harlequin, here it is, my very first Superromance. I have to say, it's been a total joy to write. I loved delving so deeply into the relationships, fell madly in love with Wyatt, wanted to be just like Cricket, and I absolutely want to move to Temptation Bay...this week, please?

I got so involved in this story that I dreamed about these characters, thought about them at inconvenient times (while watching a movie— that I actually liked) and now that I'm not writing it anymore, I miss them like crazy. I keep calling my dog Baby Girl, have made myself a lobster roll because I couldn't bear not to and, well...I truly do hope you enjoy Wyatt and Cricket's story.

All my best,

*Jo Leigh*

# JO LEIGH

—

## The Navy SEAL's Rescue

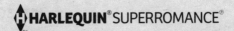

**HARLEQUIN**®SUPERROMANCE®

Recycling programs
for this product may
not exist in your area.

ISBN-13: 978-1-335-44907-8

The Navy SEAL's Rescue

**Printed in U.S.A.**

www.Harlequin.com

**Jo Leigh** is from Los Angeles and always thought she'd end up living in Manhattan. So how did she end up in Utah in a tiny town with a terrible internet connection, being bossed around by a houseful of rescued cats and dogs? What the heck, she says, predictability is boring. Jo has written more than sixty novels for Harlequin. Find her on Twitter, @jo_leigh.

### Books by Jo Leigh

#### HARLEQUIN BLAZE

##### *NYC Bachelors*

*Tempted in the City*
*Daring in the City*

##### *It's Trading Men!*

*Choose Me*
*Have Me*
*Want Me*
*Seduce Me*
*Dare Me*
*Intrigue Me*

To my editor, Birgit Davis-Todd.

We've been partners in this journey since 1997, and we've worked on Temptations, Blazes, Intrigues, special series, online reads and now Superromance. She's been my advocate, my sounding board and my trusted advisor, which makes me the luckiest Harlequin writer ever!

# CHAPTER ONE

"Ms. SHAW, YOUR weekly delivery is here. Should I send Arnold to your office?"

At the sound of Felicity's voice coming from the intercom Jessica looked up from her laptop. Ignoring her assistant's blatant attempt to get a rise out of her, she said, "I believe you still have tip money in the envelope I left with you."

"I do. So would you prefer he leave the flowers with me?"

Jessica sighed. "Please." A headache threatened from reading briefs most of the day and she wasn't in the mood for her assistant's teasing. Not just that, but encouraging Arnold in any way wasn't a good idea. Ever since he'd become Jessica's regular deliveryman, he'd had a crush on her. If you could call it that—the guy had to be in his late twenties. It hadn't turned into anything...it wasn't as if he was stalking her. But six months of trying to engage with her was too long.

A few minutes later she heard a light knock at her door.

"Come in, Felicity." Jessica stood and moved last week's flowers off the corner of her desk.

The door opened and the young woman entered, holding a glass vase filled with cheery yellow daffodils and pale green chrysanthemums. Huh. Interesting choice for the middle of June in Chicago. It did the trick, though, and boosted Jessica's spirits.

"Sorry about earlier," Felicity said, setting down the bouquet. "I shouldn't have been joking around today of all days."

"Why? Because I had only four hours sleep last night and I'm cross-eyed from reading briefs? Or did something happen that I don't know about?"

"No." Felicity smoothed her blue skirt. It was unusual to see her without a blazer. She tended to mimic Jessica in her manner of dress and hairstyles: conservative suits, hair pulled back in a neat twist or upswept. The staff often referred to her as mini-Jessica, only Felicity was a blonde and Jessica had dark hair. "It's been raining steadily since this morning. You're usually in a funk on gloomy days."

"Am I?"

"Maybe subdued is a better description." Felicity shrugged. "I've always assumed it made you a little homesick."

Jessica supposed that was partly true, although the weather in Rhode Island could get cold and nasty in the winter. Still, the pleasure of growing up with sand between her toes, the sun's warmth on her skin and the tangy smell of salt in the air wasn't something one could easily forget.

And her dad of course... Ronny still lived in the old beach shack they'd shared for ten months out of each year until she'd left for college. As long as the surf was up he was out there on his board, along with his groupies who worshipped him. To pay the bills he gave surfing lessons to tourists or took groups out on fishing charters. But only when he absolutely had to. He was a true free spirit, her dad. For him, there was no place on earth that could top Temptation Bay. Some days she tended to agree with him.

The moment she sat down, her gaze caught on the wastebasket under her desk, where just this morning she'd dropped the invitation to her fifteen-year high school reunion. She regretted making the decision not to attend the event. She'd vacillated for over a month about whether or not to go. Most of the girls she'd hung out with at Roger Williams Prep had gone off to college, then moved on just as she had, and she would've loved to see them. Catch up on what everyone was doing with their lives. But in the end her workload had made the decision for her.

Her career ran her life. Not that she was complaining. Being recruited by a prestigious firm like Burrell, Scoffield and Schultz right out of law school had been crazy lucky as well as a personal victory.

"So…" Felicity nodded at the flowers Jessica had moved to the credenza. "Are you going to take those home? They still look fresh and pretty."

Jessica laughed. How many times had they done this dance? "Take them," she said.

"Excellent." Felicity scooped up the vase quickly. "By the way, still no card."

Jessica already knew that, and the tiny amused satisfaction she got out of keeping the secret that she sent the flowers to herself wasn't a big deal. In fact, the truth was so much more mundane—she loved getting flowers so it was a treat she indulged in. When the office staff assumed she had an admirer, she'd let them.

Felicity shook her head on the way to the door. "You'd think just knowing you have a secret admirer would be enough to discourage poor Arnold."

"Hey, about that…" Jessica picked up her mug, then remembered she'd thought about getting a refill an hour ago. "Don't tease him anymore." She held up a hand at the first sign of protest. "I know you don't do it openly, but I don't want this thing with him escalating."

Felicity nodded thoughtfully. "May I get you some coffee? I can make a fresh pot."

"Thanks, but I need to move." She arched her back and glanced at the time. "Oh, great, I missed lunch."

"I have some yogurt in the fridge."

"No thanks." Stretching her neck from side to side, Jessica followed her assistant out of the office and headed for the break room. She hadn't actually felt hungry until she realized she hadn't eaten. If she could manage to leave at a decent hour—anytime before seven would do—she'd pick up dinner from Max's Take Out.

The whole floor seemed quieter than usual. Which was saying a lot. At least now she'd acclimated to the atmosphere at the firm. Being one of the top fifty law practices in the country, the attitudes and mores of the senior partners were still nestled in the stuffy long ago. Which included not rubbing elbows with the lowly associates.

At first she'd been put off. After all, she'd graduated third in her class at Yale. She was a damn good contract lawyer. Despite her skill and commitment, moving up in the firm was a slow and opaque process. But all in all, she liked it here. Everything was very…tidy. Organized and compartmentalized.

"Hey, Jessica."

Grant Herbert, who was a junior partner and quite a few rungs above her on the ladder, called out from his office, and while he wasn't actually her boss, she often worked on projects for him. Grant was a friend. Sometimes a little more than that. And he had an amazing office with a window view of Lake Michigan. While it wasn't the Atlantic Ocean, it made her think of home.

In fact, her gaze was drawn instantly to the glorious reds and oranges of the late afternoon sun, fighting to make it through the dark clouds coming in from the lake. She let out a breath, and felt her mood lift just looking at it.

"Someday, you're going to come in here and look at me the way you look out that window."

She smiled, knowing he understood that at work, it was all work, and nothing more.

"You wanted to talk to me?"

"I was about to call you," he said, leaning back in his leather chair, looking a little too handsome with his shirtsleeves rolled up on his toned arms. His dark hair could have been longer, but at least the top was at the stage where she could tell he'd been running his fingers through it. "You working late?"

"I was hoping to leave before seven."

"How about we order in some sushi? I'd like to talk to you about Burbidge."

"Has something happened?"

He nodded. "And it's a doozy. You want your regular?"

"Sure. Anything else going on? It's too quiet around here."

"Big meeting upstairs."

"Ah." She should've guessed. The top floor was occupied by the senior partners and two conference rooms that looked more like penthouses. "I'm surprised you aren't up there."

"I was." Looking grim, he rubbed a hand over his face. "How long before you finish up?"

"An hour?"

"Good. I'll have Gretchen order the sushi now before she goes home."

Jessica hurried back to her office, her curiosity flying high. Their client, Alan Burbidge, was one of their biggest assets. His billable hours made up a large percentage of the firm's income. He dealt primarily in real estate, although he owned over a dozen companies, from manufacturing to insurance to media outlets. A good deal of Jessica's workload consisted of reviewing contracts and cases for Burbidge, her current focus on a lawsuit that was pending over a violation of Title II of the Hart-Scott-Rodino Antitrust Improvements Act of 1976. It was interesting, and had led her to a great many precedents for both sides. But it was hard to believe anything could be a doozy about this particular case.

Yet Grant had looked worried, even though he didn't rattle easily. So something was definitely brewing. Having landed Burbidge's subsidiary accounts had put Grant on the fast track to senior partner.

After forty minutes she called it quits, too jumpy to stay focused. She quickly cleared her desk and headed back to Grant's office. The scent of soy sauce and vinegar hit her before she stepped inside his office, making her stomach rumble.

"Hope you don't mind but I need to take a few bites," she said, grabbing her bento box before she sat across from him. "I haven't eaten today and I'm starving. So, what's this all about?"

Instead of answering her, he got up and closed his door. Unusual. When he took his seat, he opened both bottles of Kirin beer. "Burbidge Jr. has done it again."

Jessica moaned. "Oh, God. What this time?"

Grant's expression told her this wasn't just another DUI. "He's been accused of rape."

She set down her dragon roll. "No. Please tell me Burbidge doesn't want us to make this disappear."

"He does. And he's adamant about it. Threatened to walk away from the firm if we don't provide a winning defense."

"I'm surprised he isn't demanding we get the charges dropped."

"Oh, that's his first preference."

Losing his business would be a huge price to pay, but letting a rapist off the hook, especially one with money, happened far too often. To be any part of that kind of travesty was unconscionable. "I don't know how I feel about this. I mean, the poor girl—"

"He's still entitled to a defense."

"Do you—does anyone know if he actually did it?" She studied Grant's face, but couldn't read him. "Personally, I think the kid is narcissistic and stupid enough to admit it if not brag about it...at least to his daddy's attorneys."

Grant shrugged. "If it's at all possible there's DNA evidence, he'll claim it was consensual. I'm not a defense attorney, but that's how I'd advise him."

A chill ran down her spine. "You were, though. Early on."

"Yeah, for about a year after I passed the bar. That's it."

"Who's being assigned as lead counsel? David Crawford?" Jessica didn't care for the newest senior partner, mostly due to his reputation for being ruthless. But with his win record, he seemed the logical choice.

"Look, Burbidge isn't being entirely rational at the moment. He seems more concerned that Sanford is going to be branded as a rapist."

Jessica searched Grant's eyes, wondering if he'd purposely ignored her question, which wasn't like him. "Great. That means he'll do anything to avoid a trial. Has he suggested paying off the victim yet?"

"I understand this is a sensitive topic. Just don't forget we're still his attorneys. It's not our job to pass judgment. Innocent until proven guilty, remember?"

"Not having to work with rapists is one reason I never wanted to be a criminal attorney. And we both know he's got the wherewithal to manipulate anything that can be bought."

"There's no wiggling out of that. Two witnesses have come forward. Money alone won't let him walk."

"So, what then?"

"Burbidge is handpicking a legal team that he thinks can pull this off."

"Wait. You mean, personally? He's choosing who'll be—"

Grant nodded. "I told you he isn't being rational."

"You've known him for a long time. Can't you reason with him?"

Grant set his beer down and leaned forward. "He wants both me and you as co-counsel."

Jessica lurched back in her chair. "That's not funny."

"It's not a joke. He specifically asked for you."

"What part of me not being a criminal attorney doesn't he understand?"

"I'm not one, either. But he trusts me. And he insists on you."

"Well, you'll just have to work harder to get him to see he's being an idiot."

Grant's temper bled through, but only for a second. "Naturally we won't tackle this alone. Crawford will be lead in every way that counts. And Lister and Ulrich are joining the team."

Jessica stared at the man she thought she knew.

Did he really think she'd want any part in this? "Why on earth would Alan Burbidge ask for me? I've hardly had any personal interaction with him. But I have dealt with Sanford Burbidge a number of times, as you know. What I haven't mentioned is that twice he's bordered on inappropriate."

"Well, damn." Grant stared blankly past her for a long while, then he leaned forward, his elbows on his shiny teak desk. "Alan thinks you've got the right stuff to handle a jury. Possibly because Sanford put a bug in his ear, but that's immaterial because he's already hired Roger Eastman—arguably the best jury consultant in Chicago—and they came back with a profile that fits you to a T."

"I understand why they'd want a woman at the defense table for a rape charge, but it's a moot point, anyway. The prosecutor's office would have a field day with me at the table. For God's sake, I'm a contract attorney. Even if I did agree to join the team, I'm not equipped for the job. There are excellent women criminal lawyers in the firm, so asking me is ridiculous. I'm not getting on board with this, Grant."

"I hear you. I do. I told Crawford you would strenuously object, but he wasn't particularly interested in your moral objections to the case."

"That's too bad. I won't do this."

Grant pushed his uneaten sushi aside before he got up so he could sit in the second visitor's chair. He caught her gaze and held it. "I'm having to do a lot of thinking about this myself. But the reality is, Burbidge is going to get what he wants, even if it means finding another firm. And if he walks over this, you and I will be out on our asses. No question."

"I can live with that."

"Really? Just think. It would mean giving up everything you've been working for since you started here. You're a step away from junior partner. You know this would do it. Having Burbidge request you personally is huge. The partners would owe you big-time. It could mean the difference between a good career and sky's the limit."

"And it wouldn't do you any harm, either."

He didn't even blink. "True. It's a lot to consider. You won't walk away with sterling references either. You'll be considered a problem, not a team player."

"It sounds as if you've already made a decision."

"I've got a lot of years and sweat invested in this firm. Not to mention the chunk I fork out for child support and alimony every month. I know it sucks, but part of this job means representing causes that aren't our own."

"I'm not judging you," she said, although she was disappointed. But she did understand. Her own predicament was less clear-cut. "So I'm not only supposed to help the bastard get off scot-free, when I'm not even qualified to be anything more than window dressing, but be blackmailed into doing it?"

"The partners have to protect the firm's reputation. They can't let Burbidge jump ship. If he goes, that will send a signal to other clients. Major clients."

She felt sick. The scent of the sushi was making her stomach churn. It would be a crushing blow to lose this job, to get a bad name so early in the career she'd worked hard for, but how could she do anything else?

"Listen," he said. "I know your reunion is coming up this weekend."

"I'm not going."

"I think you should. Get out of here. Take a long weekend. Think it through. You know I'll stand behind you on this, whatever you decide."

"Will you?"

"I won't throw you under the bus. But this is too important not to consider all the angles. Take my advice. A break would do you good. Think about your options. I'll get the firm to pay for the weekend."

"No, you won't. I don't want their money, not for this." She stood up. "Keep me in the loop, Grant. Seriously. I'll need to know if anything changes."

"Of course."

She turned to go.

"Don't forget your food."

"I seem to have lost my appetite," she said and didn't look back.

# CHAPTER TWO

"SEASIDE ON THE BLUFF, eh?" Joseph, the white-haired cab driver, asked. They'd just left the airport, and Jessica was still in the midst of a silent battle between ethics, duty and career. "It used to be a small hotel, nothing like the fancy resort it is now. Back then Temptation Bay was just a small village of fishermen that had sprung up in the 1800s. They caught and sold fish from one generation to the next, that's it. Until two brothers—Angus and I forget the other one's name—they hated fishing and got tired of seeing so many tourists bypass the village to go to other seaside towns like the Cape, so they built the hotel sometime in the 1920s."

She sighed. It was clear the taxi driver had a spiel he always gave, probably had one for each of the key destinations along the Rhode Island coast. It was clever, though, a way to entertain the tourists for extra tips. Of course she could recite the entire story of her town and then some. In fact, she knew the second brother's name was John. But frankly, she preferred to let the driver gab for the next ten miles, so she didn't have to talk.

"Some folks thought the brothers were crazy, but I think they were smart." Joseph touched a finger to his head. "Temptation Bay has everything Cape Cod has and more. Like the sunken pirate treasure off the shores south of the village. Some people don't believe there were any pirate ships that sailed up this far but no one knows for sure. Anyway, the brothers built their little hotel on the bluff and suddenly tourists started coming to Temptation Bay."

Well, Joseph had gotten most of that right. At least that was the story she'd heard from Ronny and the fishing families. As for the treasure, that had been causing arguments since she was a little kid. Everyone seemed to have a great-uncle or cousin who had found booty washed up on shore.

"Eventually, some big-shot investor bought the hotel and turned it into a five-star resort and the village expanded with lots of fancy shops and seafood restaurants. A few are rated five-star, too. Some people come here just to eat. How about that?"

"Huh." Jessica made the appropriate noise, not surprised he'd left out the part that all wasn't smooth sailing in Temptation Bay. The village had also transformed into a thriving art colony, with pricey cafés and upscale shops. Not everyone wanted to share their slice of paradise with outsiders, and the beautiful beach town quickly became divided into the old and new. And while a few more hotels and B&Bs had sprung up, thankfully, the shoreline remained mostly pristine.

The cab stopped in front of the towering resort where a uniformed attendant was quick to open Jessica's door. "Good afternoon," he said with a friendly smile. "Welcome to Seaside on the Bluff."

"Thank you." She paid Joseph with an extra ten for the tale, and grabbed her small carry-on and leather garment bag before climbing out.

The young man looked alarmed when the cab pulled away from the curb. "Don't you have more luggage?"

Shaking her head, she inhaled the familiar scent of the ocean, felt the salty breeze stir her hair. "Just these."

Another employee hurried over with a large cart and she let him take both bags from her. She could've easily carried them herself, but she didn't like denying them the tip. On the other hand, maybe she wasn't doing them any favors.

Tourist season was in full swing. Three cabs had lined up at the curb and most of the other carts were loaded down with luggage. She'd been lucky to get a room at the last minute. It was a pricey suite she wouldn't necessarily have booked, but she had to admit, the idea of getting a massage and soaking in a jetted tub sounded like heaven.

"I'm Hector," the husky young man told her

and started pushing the cart toward the glass doors. "Are you here for the reunion?"

"Yes, I am." She glanced around at the busy port cache and dug into her purse. "Look, my bags are light, and I see you're busy. I'll probably end up bumping into people and—"

Ignoring the five-dollar bill she tried to give him, Hector shook his head. "For you, I have all the time in the world," he said, his grin growing wider as he gestured for her to lead the way through the open glass doors.

She didn't know what he meant by that, but she preceded him into the stunning, open lobby with a killer view of the ocean. It had been updated since she'd last seen it, although the same beautiful hardwood floors were polished to a shine, and the stark white reception desk with the old-fashioned wooden pigeonhole room slots was still there. The furniture was more elegant—suede chairs and couches, all variant colors of the sand and rock of the landscape, were placed in perfect groupings with convenient, antique tables and plenty of room to maneuver. Stunning bouquets led the eyes from one gorgeous view to the next.

Most of the chairs were occupied with people sipping cocktails and chatting away. She assumed a number of them were here for the reunion, though she hadn't recognized anyone yet.

Luckily, only two guests were waiting at the front desk. Jessica's gaze returned to the blue sky and even bluer water, and she had the sudden urge to kick off her flats, make a dash to the shoreline and dig her toes into the warm sand. Soak up enough sunshine to get her through a Chicago winter. More than once Ronny had told her the ocean flowed through her veins. And that she'd be back sooner than she'd thought...that she'd always come back.

By the time she turned to Hector he'd passed the cart to another bell attendant and was holding her things in his large, tanned hands.

"So I'm guessing you're from Temptation Bay," he said. "Went to school here." It was a statement, not a question. "Your family, did they live at Waverly Hills?"

Jessica laughed, unsure if she should be insulted. But in truth her bloodline extended to both sides of the track. Her dad's clan were townies, less charitably known as the *fish people*. Ronny came from a long line of fishermen who'd settled on the coast generations ago. The *hill people* were newbies, relatively speaking, and consisted primarily of wealthy tourists who'd bought prime land atop the bluffs and built second homes.

Ultimately, some of the families made Temptation Bay their permanent residence. Jessica's grandparents might've followed suit, if their only daughter hadn't announced that she wanted to marry Ronny, a local surfer, who, despite his two championship titles and his big heart, they could never see as anything but a beach bum.

Much as Jessica adored her dad, she knew her grandparents hadn't been completely wrong. The next week they'd sold their gorgeous vacation home sitting high on the bluff and returned to Connecticut. Of course that hadn't stopped their headstrong daughter.

At eighteen, Victoria Danes had returned to Temptation Bay two weeks later, on her own for the first time, armed with determination and confidence born from a healthy sense of entitlement. The next day she and Ronny were married on the beach, the water lapping at their bare feet. By most accounts Jessica was born eight months later, give or take. The marriage had barely lasted two years after that.

Noticing Hector's odd look, she pulled herself back to the present. It took a moment to remember his question. "Any chance you know a local surfer named Ronny? He has a shack on the beach near the old docks."

"Sure, I know him," he said, grinning. "Everybody knows Ronny."

"He's my dad."

Hector's dark eyes nearly bugged out of his head. "No kidding."

"No kidding." She moved closer to the front desk when she realized a couple had slipped in ahead of her because she hadn't been paying attention. "What about you? Your family lives here?"

He nodded, still looking puzzled. "How long have you been away?"

"Hmm…" It wasn't a simple answer. Home every summer while she was in college. Three years of law school hadn't given her much leisure time. Then while waiting to take the bar, she'd spent a month abroad with her mom and husband number four. "Not counting visits, about ten years." Jessica wondered if he could hear the defensiveness that had crept into her voice. Probably not. Although Hector had somehow managed to identify her as a local in a matter of minutes, whereas Grant knew so little about her that he'd had the gall to ask her to help free a rapist.

Generally she wasn't quick to judge someone. But after being subjected to Sanford Burbidge, she wouldn't put anything past him. The guy was a sociopath. She pitied his defense team. Which would not include her and she sure as hell didn't need a weekend away to think about it. Although, the idea of starting over with a tainted reputation sticking to her like a shadow made her want to cry.

Luckily, that didn't make her any less glad to be here. She hadn't realized just how much she needed this trip home.

"So, you must surf, right?"

"I used to." She'd been pretty damn good, too. "But like I said, it's been a long time."

"I bet once you get back on that board you'll rock."

Jessica laughed. "I doubt I'll be putting it to the test," she said, estimating Hector to be in his midtwenties, about ten years younger than herself. So it wasn't a surprise that she didn't recognize him. It still made her a little sad, though. It wasn't so long ago that she'd known just about everyone who lived on the other side of town.

She stared past him at two women across the lobby waving frantically at her. The glare was awful with the bright sunlight flooding in. Perhaps she wasn't the intended…

*Ginny?*

"Oh, my God, it's Ginny Landry," Jessica murmured, waving back.

Harlow was with her…a little slimmer, quite a bit blonder. At least she was pretty sure it was Harlow, another member of their high school gang—the Fearless Four as they'd called themselves. But Ginny was the only classmate Jessica had seen since they'd graduated because Ginny still lived in Temptation Bay. Ironic since of all of them, Ginny had been on the fast track to become a concert pianist just like her late mother. But life often didn't turn out as expected. Jessica could attest to that.

It was her turn at the front desk. She stepped up

and motioned for Ginny and Harlow to wait, just as a woman dressed in a black uniform brought them drinks.

Check-in went smoothly, and when Hector told her he'd leave her bags in the suite so she could meet her friends, Jessica was grateful he hadn't ditched her when she'd given him the chance.

She tipped him well, and was about to veer toward the bar, but curiosity stopped her. "How did you know I'm from here?"

"Easy," Hector said, grinning. "You've got that laid-back beach vibe."

Jessica laughed. "Boy, would my coworkers disagree."

Of course the reunion was a big clue. He'd probably used the line on all of the attendees to boost his tips.

She sighed at her own cynicism. Laid-back. Right.

Ginny and Harlow were waving again, as if she hadn't seen them. The lobby and bar were really jam-packed. Not a single empty table or seat, except for the one Ginny had a chokehold on.

Jessica wove her way through the crowd, smiling and nodding, recognizing a few faces but unable to come up with names.

"I should've known I'd find you guys near the booze," she said as she reached them, momentarily losing her breath when Ginny abandoned the chair and pulled her into a huge hug.

"I'm so glad you're here," Ginny said. "I couldn't believe it when I got your email yesterday."

"Ditto for me. Now, quit hogging her." Harlow was the athlete. Always in motion and winning awards. She'd almost made it to the Olympics before her life had been hijacked by injury. Clearly, she hadn't let it stop her from staying in great shape.

Jessica grunted. "Okay, you have to let me breathe," she said when they locked her in from both sides. "Seriously."

Laughing, Ginny backed off first. "We better grab our seats. Where's Ronny? Did he just drop you off and leave?"

"He had a charter today. Some guys hired him to take them past Block Island to fish for marlin." Jessica smoothed her white linen slacks before sitting. "I didn't want him to lose the business. He had an accident that put him out of commission for a couple weeks, so I took a cab."

"What happened?" Ginny asked, sinking onto her chair.

"It was a loose board on the old dock. I've asked him a hundred times to get the harbormaster to make some repairs."

"I thought he might have cracked up the Jeep again."

"He had a car accident? When?"

"Maybe four months ago? I ran into him at

the drugstore. He was filling a prescription, but I don't think he was hurt too badly."

"So why didn't he tell me?"

Ginny gave her a sympathetic smile.

"Don't look at me," Harlow said. "I just arrived from LA this morning. Oh, hey, there's our waitress. Cricket, what do you want?"

Jessica stared at her friend, then burst out laughing.

The other two exchanged puzzled looks. "What?"

"No one's called me Cricket in a really, really long time."

Harlow frowned. "What are we supposed to call you?"

Jessica thought back to when she'd gotten the nickname, well before she'd started kindergarten. Maria and Stella had sold their husbands' catches every morning, come rain or shine. They were always first to set up at the fish market and had bonded over both being married to men named Jimmy. Since Jessica had just seen *Pinocchio*, she'd thought they were talking about Jiminy Cricket, and she'd gotten all excited, hopping around in her tie-dyed sundress, barefoot as always, and that was it. Cricket had followed her onto the beach and into her classrooms. Even her mother, who was mortified at first, had come around when she realized how much it suited her. Although once Jessica had gone to college, she had let go of bare feet, high school mischief and her nickname.

"I have to admit," Ginny said. "The first time I read one of your emails I thought who the hell is Jessica?"

Harlow nearly spit out the sip she'd just taken. "Jessica? Yeah, I kind of remember a teacher calling you that once." She shook her head. "Sorry. Not me. I can't call you that. Too weird."

Jessica grinned, feeling truly at ease for the first time in forever. She'd needed this break. She needed them.

"To the resurrection of Cricket," Ginny said, holding up her glass.

"Ditto." Harlow held up her drink.

Jessica—no, Cricket let the name sink in deeper. Since she had only a white napkin sitting in front of her she waved it over her head like a flag of surrender, though she would've preferred a drink. "Cricket it is."

WYATT COVACK HEARD his phone beep and hoped like hell it was part of a dream. He grabbed the extra pillow and just as he was about to put it over his head he heard the second ring. Cursing, though not loud enough to drown out the third beep, he opened one eye. The alarm clock was a red blur but he finally made out the three and the one. That's all he needed to see to make him want to punch the wall.

Who the hell was calling him? Just about everyone he trusted with his cell number knew he'd worked until 5:00 a.m. and then hadn't hit the sack until eight. The bar had closed at one but trying to win his two hundred back from that lousy cardsharp Bobby Cappelli had been damn hard work, and Wyatt dared anyone to tell him otherwise.

He'd left his phone on the kitchen counter, all the way on the other side of the cramped apartment. The place wasn't very big, but trying to navigate past all the crap he'd left lying around was like crossing a minefield. Maybe worse.

As if the universe decided to prove the point, his bare right foot landed on something sharp. A pain shot up his leg. Dammit to hell. One of Josh's Lego pieces. He swore the kid was out to kill him. Nerve clusters made the bottom of a person's feet vulnerable. A ruthless target if you needed to extract information without leaving obvious marks. Made it a popular torture technique.

Wyatt winced. He hated that he knew that, and a lot more, all remnants of his former life. He'd heard time would eventually blunt the memories... reduce the flashbacks. If guilt didn't punch his ticket first.

Before he made it to the phone the caller was sent to voice mail. He squinted at the call log. Sabrina. Oh, man. If she was calling in sick again, he was gonna...

He actually didn't know what he was gonna do.

Sabrina was his backup. None of the other waitresses could handle running the bar in his absence. Most of them were kids who attended the local community college, a couple considered themselves artists and sold their work at street fairs. But waiting tables paid the bills. Especially during tourist season.

Most nights he was behind the bar, pouring drinks and filling pitchers, occasionally breaking up fights, and making sure last call didn't stretch past one o'clock. But there were times when he had to just plain get away. Away from people. From responsibility. Get away from himself when he could manage it, which usually meant getting shit-faced. Other times he borrowed Marty's chopper. Flying into the clouds had a way of letting him feel weightless and unburdened. And then there were those times when Becky needed him to watch the kids. Sweet-tempered, obedient Rose and Josh, the little terminator.

He rubbed his gritty eyes and waited for his vision to clear. Next he'd probably get a text from Sabrina. Best-case scenario, she'd be late. Worst-case? She was sick, again, and didn't know how long she'd be out. He was beginning to think he should have a little man-to-man talk with her worthless boyfriend. Wyatt got the feeling the dumb bastard was responsible for most of Sabrina's absences. That wasn't what bothered Wyatt the most. Normally he wouldn't think of butting into someone's private life. But she was a nice girl who deserved a lot better than an abusive drunk.

On cue his cell signaled a text.

Just as someone knocked at his door.

"Are you kidding me?" he muttered and threw in a curse.

Another loud bang.

"Hold on, for crying out loud," he yelled and glanced at the text, then searched the floor for his jeans.

When he'd bought Sam's Sugar Shack two years ago, he'd left everything intact—the funky decor, the staff, the pseudo uniforms, which amounted to very short denim cutoffs and a cropped T-shirt with the bar's logo. In good conscience he had offered to get rid of the Hooters look, but the waitresses shot it down. Better tips. Who was he to argue?

Hell, he'd hadn't even changed the name of the place, which every local seemed to have a strong opinion about. The purchase price had included the apartment above it. Never having had a conventional job before, it seemed like a major win.

Big mistake. It made him too accessible.

He couldn't even get away with turning off his phone. If he didn't answer, someone always came knocking. Usually over something stupid. Civilians were a bunch of damn crybabies.

He pulled on his jeans and opened the door.

"Hey, boss. Sorry to bother you but—" Tiffy's gaze froze on his bare chest. He was pretty sure she wasn't admiring his pecs, although he did keep in shape. She was staring at the scars left by a pair of particularly nasty knife wounds.

He rubbed his stubbled jaw, using his arm to obstruct her view. "You were saying?"

"Oh, um, right. We're really getting slammed downstairs and Cara and Viv are both late. Well, we knew ahead of time Cara was going to be late because she has an appointment with—I guess it doesn't matter. Anyway, if you could come in early that would be totally awesome."

"Early?"

"Yeah, um, like now?"

Wyatt sighed. "I gotta take a quick shower and I'll be right down."

Tiffy was still staring at his chest as he closed the door.

## CHAPTER THREE

CRICKET STOOD ON the balcony of her suite, inhaling the salt air and feeling it cleanse the body and soul of Jessica and her problems. At least for the moment. This far up the coast you couldn't smell the fish market. As a kid she'd rarely minded the odor, though sometimes if the temperature climbed too high in the peak of summer, the stink could get to anyone.

One of the advantages of the resort sitting on the bluff was being able to look down at the clear, beautiful water. She could make out the green roofs of the bungalows that had been a recent addition to the resort. Her first choice would've been to stay in one of them so she could be right on the beach. But there were only a half dozen available and they'd been booked quickly.

She glanced at her watch, startled that a whole hour had slipped by. With barely enough time to change her clothes, she had fifteen minutes to meet Ginny at Sam's Sugar Shack.

After hurriedly changing into tan capris and a casual blouse, she rode the elevator down to the "beach and pool level" below the lobby, hoping she wouldn't run into anyone. Something was clearly bothering Ginny and they didn't need old classmates inviting themselves along. After all these years and having seen each other only twice, Jessica was glad her old friend felt she could confide in her.

The second before she hit the beach, she kicked off her sandals. Feeling the warmth of the sand and the cooling breeze made it a whole lot easier to shift gears now that everyone would be calling her Cricket. She'd laughed when she picked up her nametag earlier. It had been a hard transition in college becoming Jessica, but since she'd decided early that she wanted to study law, she needed a serious name. But nobody here knew her as an attorney. Even her dad called her Cricket occasionally, but mostly he called her Baby Girl.

After a ten-minute walk, Sam's came into view. Shading her face from the bright sunlight, she saw Ginny standing at one of the tall umbrella tables outside, wearing a green sundress, which showed off her stupidly perfect arms and the legs that had made half the boys in school walk around with books in front of their jeans. When a couple leaving the bar caught Ginny's eye, she waved and disappeared inside. The place was probably as packed as the resort bars. Cricket quickened her pace. Hopefully Ginny was able to grab a table. It would be more private and comfortable talking inside.

Removing her sunglasses, she hesitated at the door, letting her eyes adjust to the dimmer lighting.

"Over here."

She followed the voice and saw Ginny sitting at a small table for two in the corner. It was slightly out of the way and couldn't be more perfect. All except for the donkey piñata hanging over the wicker chair Cricket sank onto. No, not wicker, more like straw, firm enough to poke her behind. She doubted investing in a few cushions would've broken the new owner.

When she saw the pink-and-green Hula-Hoops hanging on the back wall, she grinned. "Oh, my God. This place hasn't changed one bit. I wonder if they still have Hula-Hoop contests for free drinks."

Ginny glanced up at the large piñata over Cricket's head. "I don't know if I trust that thing."

"So, you left this chair for me?"

"Well, yeah. I have a kid, you don't. And you're an attorney. You can sue without it costing you." Ginny barely got it all out without laughing.

They were both cracking up and pointing out the strange assortment of hanging decorations. Aside from piñatas of all types, there were also dangling skateboards, a couple of bikini tops, several license plates and a group of visors with dumb sayings. And then Ginny looked at the hula girl bobblehead sitting in the middle of their table.

With a flick of her long elegant fingers she set it in motion and they laughed until they both had to wipe away tears.

Sniffling, Cricket moved in for a closer look at the hula girl. "Is that thing glued to the table?"

"I think so."

"For God's sake, who would steal that?"

"Oh yeah, you've definitely been away too long."

Cricket glanced around, saw the coast was clear and bowed her head to use the hem of her shirt to dab at her nose and eyes. "Do not make me laugh like that again."

"It felt good, didn't it?" The trace of wistfulness in Ginny's voice didn't go unnoticed. "Look, I'm sorry for pulling you away from everyone," she said. "It isn't fair, I know, but I figured it would be harder to find time toward the end of the weekend."

"Oh, please. There's nothing to be sorry for." Cricket did a quick survey of the place and thought she recognized a woman in an absurdly short skirt downing shots at the bar. "Could just be me, but I have a feeling we're going to be pretty sick of some of these people by Sunday."

"It's not just you." Ginny's smile softened the worry lines between her brows. "Does everyone drink so much at reunions?"

"Beats me. I've never been… You must've come to the ten-year. It was at the hotel, wasn't it?"

"I'd planned on it but Tilda was sick and I didn't want to leave her alone."

"Isn't your dad—?"

"Tilda and I are living in the family home. He's still in his apartment in Providence." Ginny shrugged. "It's for the best. He'll never accept Tilda or forgive me for not wanting to spend my life playing a piano."

"It must hurt, though."

"No, actually, I've let it go. I don't think he ever recovered from my mom's death, and he never will. It's sad, and if I thought I could help him I would. But honestly, I think there's a part of him that blames me. After all, she died giving me life."

"Of course he doesn't blame you." Cricket knew Ginny's dad. Robert Landry was a well-known attorney, and not just in Rhode Island. "That's completely irrational."

"Oh, and you have two perfectly rational parents?"

Cricket let out a strangled laugh. "Good point." She reached for a glass that wasn't there. "Did anyone ask if you wanted a drink yet?"

"They probably figured we've had our limit."

"Probably." She leaned to the side, scanning the room for a waitress. And found someone so much better. "Oh, hello. Did you see the bartender? Nice. Despite the fact he looks as if he just rolled out of bed."

Ginny looked over her shoulder. "Despite? I think he looks yummy just as he is. I wonder if he's the owner."

"Why do you say that?"

"I'm guessing he's midthirties? Most of the employees are barely legal drinking age."

"True. He's not messing around, either. He's really whipping out those drinks." She liked his lean, athletic build, the broad shoulders that filled out his wrinkled T-shirt. Even from clear across the room she could see the play of muscles across his back as he turned and grabbed a bottle off the shelf.

He startled her by swinging a sudden look in her direction. "Sorry," he called out. "Be right with you."

Cricket felt the heat surge up her throat to her face. How had he known she was—?

"Was he talking to you?" Ginny asked, turning her head for another peek at him.

"I guess so. Was I that obvious?"

"He probably thinks you're impatient for a drink."

Cricket could only hope. "Tell me what you wanted to talk about," she said, giving her complete attention to her friend.

"Actually, I need your advice on something."

"As an attorney or a friend?"

Ginny looked surprised, and Cricket couldn't

explain what prompted her to make the distinction. "Both I hope."

"Okay, I'll be happy to do what I can."

"It's about Tilda. Or more to the point, about her father."

"Wait. Is this a custody issue?"

"I'm not sure. Maybe." Ginny sighed. "I really don't know."

Cricket drew in a deep breath and leaned forward. "First off," she said, "you should know that family law isn't in my wheelhouse. But that doesn't mean I can't help in some way. Even if it turns out I recommend someone good for you to contact."

Ginny nodded. "I understand."

"Has Tilda's father been in her life at all?"

"No."

"Did you name him on the birth certificate?"

"Absolutely not."

"Does he even know she exists?"

"Not really."

Cricket leaned back and smiled. "You're going to have to tell me a bit more about what's going on. Does Tilda want to search for him? Is that what's bringing all this up?"

"No, but I expect she will soon." Ginny shrugged. "If for no other reason than she's getting to be at that age, you know?"

"How old is she now?"

"Fourteen. I have pictures if you want to see them later," Ginny said, grinning proudly.

"Your daughter's a teenager? How is that even possible?"

Ginny chuckled. "You never were very good at math."

"All right, come on, let's see the pictures." Cricket thought back to her first visit home after graduating from college. She'd run into Ginny at the local supermarket. It had startled her to discover Ginny had a kid, which certainly explained why she'd left Julliard. All Cricket had been able to think was how horrible it must be for her. Her friend had shown so much promise. And Ginny was a smart girl, it seemed impossible that she'd have unprotected sex. Yet she couldn't have planned the pregnancy either…

Ginny handed over her phone. "Scroll through as many as you want. I've got a million of them."

Cricket smiled at the dark-haired preteen striking a goofy pose. The girl didn't resemble Ginny, but maybe the father. "She's a doll," Cricket said, continuing through the photos. "She seems to have such a sweet disposition."

"Ah, you must be looking at the ones before she hit puberty."

"Ha. I bet she's not half as bad as we were."

Ginny sniffed. "As you, maybe. I was a good kid."

Cricket glanced up and glared. Then she sighed. "Okay, you're probably right."

"Probably?"

"All right already." Cricket couldn't resist a few more pictures as it occurred to her that she was actually feeling a twinge of envy. Where was that coming from? She hadn't thought much about kids, not for a while. That's why she'd been okay hooking up with Grant. Her whole world was her job, although that might be changing in the very near future.

Just as she was about to hand over the phone to Ginny, a deep, raspy voice stopped her short.

"Sorry for the wait, ladies. What can I get you?"

Cricket looked up into a pair of gray eyes. He was even better looking up close. His jaw was dark with stubble, which normally would've been a turnoff for her. But with his lean, tanned face and firm mouth, faintly curved as he held her gaze, he was the best-looking man she'd seen in a long time.

Ginny cleared her throat. "I'll have a frozen margarita, easy on the salt."

He turned a smile at her. "Got it," he said before looking back at Cricket. "And you?"

"Um, I guess the same."

His sudden frown came out of nowhere. He whipped a look toward the entrance. "Hey, what are you doing here?" he barked at two young kids who'd just stepped into the bar. "Back up. Now. Both of you."

"Mom said you're supposed to watch us." The boy tilted his head back and stared at the ceiling, his gaze bouncing from one colorful papier-mâché animal to the next. He pointed at the blue pig. "Is that *pintana* new?"

"That's not how you say it," the little blonde girl, who looked to be about seven or eight, told the boy. "It's called a *pinta*."

"Rose, Josh…" The man gave them a stern look. "What did I just say?"

"That we can have an ice cream cone?" The girl flashed him a dimpled smile that he seemed to be having trouble ignoring. Guess who had Daddy wrapped around her little finger?

"If you're good, and you listen, then maybe." He gestured toward the door. "Now, scram."

Josh wrinkled his freckled nose. "But…"

"I mean it. You go around to my office and stay there till I tell you otherwise. Nothing less than a real emergency, like we talked about." He swore quietly under his breath. "Damn kids… I'm gonna lose my liquor license."

"What's a licker li—"

"Come on, Josh." A waitress cut him off and grabbed his hand. "Rose, you, too, let's go," she said, leading them outside.

"Thanks, Tiffy," he called after them, then rubbed a hand over his face and sighed. Just as he turned back to Cricket and Ginny, a tall, slim woman with strawberry blond hair rushed in.

"Oh, my God, Wyatt, I'm so sorry. We were on our way over and I turned my head for only a second—"

"It's fine, Becky. I know how it is. Tiffy is taking them around to my office."

"I saw her. Look, I'll only be gone a couple of hours…" She trailed off, studying his face. "Did you forget? You did, didn't you? You said you'd keep an eye on them while—"

"I didn't forget," Wyatt said.

Cricket was willing to bet the farm he was lying, but he was damn good at it, she'd give him that.

"I thought you were off today," the woman, probably his ex-wife, looked confused.

"I was. We got busy. Don't worry about it. I'll make sure they have dinner."

Becky made a face, clearly not thrilled with his offer.

Wyatt gave her a wry smile. "Believe me, I'm not gonna do that again. Now, go." He turned to Cricket. "Sorry about all this. Tell me again what you wanted. It's on the house."

At this point she wasn't sure she remembered. "Tell you what," she said with a slow smile, "why don't you surprise me?"

He raised a questioning brow. "You sure?"

"Positive." His dark good looks accompanied by that sexy rasp in his voice were enough to send a little shiver down her spine. When was the last time that had happened? God, she really hoped Becky was an ex.

"Uh-oh. That sounds too much like a dare," Ginny said, laughing. "Bring her a margarita. You can surprise her another time."

Cricket glared at her. "What are you, my mother?"

"I know you, Cricket. We have a function to attend tonight, and you aren't weaseling out of it. You promised to be my date."

She knew what Ginny was getting at. Frank Geary, who had more money than brains—or anything else including class—was one person neither of them wanted to see. As luck would have it, he was hosting the welcome reception in a couple of hours and Ginny didn't want her using the excuse she was sick.

"Cricket? That's your name?"

"No," Cricket said and Ginny said, "Yes."

"Interesting." He extended his hand. "Wyatt."

Cricket responded in kind, liking his firm grasp, then felt greedy and petty when he let go to offer his hand to Ginny. It hadn't even occurred to Cricket that her friend might share an interest in the guy. Although she seemed to have a lot on her mind concerning her daughter. And here Cricket was flirting instead of being the friend Ginny needed.

"Coming right up with those margaritas," Wyatt said, and turned with a grimace at the high-pitched voice of the kids coming from somewhere in the back.

"Hubba hubba," Ginny said, the second he was out of earshot.

"Are you interested?"

Ginny frowned. "I meant for you."

"Are you seeing anyone?"

"Nooo…" Ginny shook her head. "I have enough on my plate."

"Yeah, let's get back to your custody question. Look, you don't have to tell me who Tilda's father is… Or you can. I won't lie, I'm curious as all get out."

"You don't know him."

"Okay, that helps." Cricket smiled sheepishly. "Me anyway. But you're probably wondering if he has any rights."

"He can't prove anything without a DNA sample. Do you think the court might compel me to provide one? I mean, he can't just make demands because we had sex a couple of times." Ginny worried her bottom lip. "Right?"

Another high-pitched screech cut through the bar noise. It sounded like Josh again.

Standing behind the bar making the drinks, Wyatt just shook his head.

Ginny chuckled. "Aren't you glad you missed all that?"

Something twisted inside Cricket. "You say that like I'm over the hill. I might still have kids."

"Really?"

"You never know." She shrugged, shocked to realize it wasn't just envy niggling at her. Much worse, longing tugged at her from both sides.

# CHAPTER FOUR

AFTER KEEPING UP with a steady crowd all evening, Wyatt was ready to sit down with a cold one himself. In between mixing a Long Island Iced Tea and a gin and tonic, he looked over at table seven to see if the preppies were still there. If they were still called preppies. Brand-name clothes, tidy hair and smug laughter spelled prep school at the very least. The short guy wore a designer golf shirt and loud pants. Yep. Reunion attendees, all three of them, products of Roger Williams Preparatory Academy. He'd bet his lucky charm on it, or had he lost that to Bobby last night, too?

Huh. Sounded familiar.

Checking his pocket, he felt the Leatherman tool. Hell, maybe he'd be better off getting rid of it. His life had been anything but lucky in the last few years. Although the fact that he was still alive might be argued as a win, but not by him.

Slamming the brakes on his dark thoughts, he set the finished drinks on Lila's tray, and took a moment to rub his gritty eyes.

She stopped flirting with the old guy at the end of the bar and swept up her order. "Thanks," she said, giving him a sexy smile and a toss of her long blond hair. "After I deliver these, you want some help behind the bar?"

He shook his head. "I'm good. Just worry about your tables."

"I only have three, so I can easily cover the beer tap, too."

"No thanks."

Her lips pursed in a pout, a very fetching pout. But no way he was going anywhere near that. Not just because she was an employee. Sexy, persistent Lila was built like a wet dream, but being in the vicinity of twenty-two, she made him feel a hundred years old. Hell, being with anyone that young would just exhaust him.

On the other hand, looking wouldn't kill him. He watched her curvy hips sway in rhythm with the jukebox music as she made her way around a rowdy group of surfers from Australia.

"Hey, Covack, you up for another game later?"

He turned just as Bobby pulled out a stool and dropped his car keys on the bar. "You've got a lot of nerve showing up here, Cappelli."

"What? You don't honestly think I cheated." Bobby chuckled. "Come on. Why would I waste the energy?"

Ignoring him, Wyatt wiped down the bar. Arnie was sitting two stools down, crying in his beer over his lousy morning catch. A lot of the older fishermen frequented the bar when there weren't too many tourists crowding the place.

Arnie glanced up and pushed his empty mug forward.

"You got a ride home tonight?" Wyatt asked him.

The old man nodded. "Left the truck with Thelma."

Wyatt believed him and poured him a refill. Arnie was one of the more responsible drunks.

"The trouble with you is, you think you're good at poker," Cappelli said. "But you stink, and I don't mind taking your money while you try proving otherwise."

"Yeah, keep it up. Like I don't already wanna throw your ass out."

Grinning, Bobby pulled out a wad of cash, half of which had been in Wyatt's pocket last night. "Give me a Scotch," he said, peeling off a twenty. "In fact make it Glenfiddich. I'm feeling flush tonight."

Wyatt flipped him off.

Cappelli laughed and swiveled around to survey the room. "Dude, you need to do something with this place. It doesn't just look like it belongs in a trailer park, it would have to be a condemned trailer park."

Yeah, most of the piñatas were old and faded. He'd been told on more than one occasion the dangling bikini tops were offensive. Maybe. But most of the locals thought they were funny and part of the landmark bar's signature. "The place has character."

"Sure, if all you care about is the local crowd." Cappelli appeared to have caught a back view of Lila leaning over a table and suddenly he had no more opinions to share.

Good.

The newest hire, Shelly, stood at the end of the bar waving an order ticket. Wyatt nodded as he poured the jerk's Scotch. Not that he'd admit it, but Cappelli had a point. Wyatt had been thinking along those lines as he watched tourists and reunion people float in and out all afternoon. If he wanted to be a serious business owner, better yet, a more profitable one, he had to get his act together.

He should've contacted the hotel, or whoever was in charge of the reunion activities, to get a copy of the weekend's agenda. Figure out how he could attract the prep schoolers during the times they had no organized functions.

If turning a healthy profit was just about him, he wouldn't give a damn. But he had Becky and the kids to consider. They were the whole reason he'd moved here. To make sure they were safe and had everything they needed. Becky was certainly a smart, competent woman, but it was tough for her to work full-time with two little kids at home. The monthly widow's benefit she received from the government was decent but could only go so far. Adam's grandparents lived nearby and helped however they could, but they'd already gotten up in years when they'd raised Adam.

Jesus, someone must've just gone through a shitty breakup. Wyatt looked up from the Sex on the Beach he was mixing to see which idiot was playing "Un-Break My Heart" for at least the hundredth time. His gaze didn't make it to the jukebox. The brunette from this afternoon had just entered the bar, all dolled up in a short red dress that showed off long killer legs. He chuckled when he saw she was barefoot, a pair of five-inch red stilettos dangling from her hand. Man, he didn't think he'd walk barefoot on this floor, even though it was washed every night after closing.

Evidently she figured that out for herself. Her lips moved as she looked down at her feet and made a face. Grabbing the back of a chair, she quickly slipped on the heels, then glanced around.

It was a sure bet she'd join the Ivy League trio.

A bet he would've lost. The second she spotted them she turned her head, completely cool and collected, as she swept her gaze in the opposite direction while strategically arranging her long dark hair to hide the side of her face. She zeroed in on the empty barstools and headed toward them.

Wyatt didn't want her sitting anywhere near

Bobby, or Mad Dog, who was downing shots to Bobby's left. "Hey, Cappelli, move over three stools."

"What?" He glanced warily at the large, bearded biker. "Why?"

"Just do it."

"You're nuts."

"If you need a fourth, I'll play tonight. But you gotta move now."

"I'm holding you to it." Cappelli got up, stepped back and nearly plowed into the woman. "Hey, sorry, I didn't…" His voice trailed off as he turned, his eyes level with her chest. Bobby was short and she was wearing very high heels. He looked at Wyatt. "You dog."

"What?" Wyatt said, laughing. "Move and let the lady sit."

Bobby pulled out a stool for her. Then the jerk sat right next to her. That wasn't the deal.

"Am I chasing you away?" she asked.

"I should be so lucky," Wyatt said, shooting Cappelli a warning look. "Cricket, right?"

Her brows rose and she blinked at him.

"We met this afternoon."

"Oh, I remember," she said with a slow smile. "It's just… I haven't been called Cricket in a while and I'm trying to get used to it again."

"So, what should we call you?" Bobby was all teeth, his body twisted around, elbow on the bar, facing her.

Wyatt shook his head. "Ignore him. He'll go away. Now, what can I get you?"

She laughed. "I believe you're supposed to surprise me?"

"Right." Wyatt thought about it as he took in her manicured hands, neat, trimmed nails with a faint gloss, nothing flashy. She wore minimal jewelry, earrings and a watch, both classy but understated. No ring, and if she'd ever worn one, it had been a long time. "Did you drive?"

"I walked."

"You staying at the Seaside?"

She nodded. "Only ten minutes by beach," she said with the smile that had drawn him in the first time he'd seen her. "Did I pass? Do I get some alcohol now?"

"Sounds like you need it."

"Most definitely."

"Yeah, reunions must be a b—" He didn't finish.

"A bitch? Yep."

He'd already decided what to pour her. Nothing fancy, not for her. Figuring he'd start off with something as high-end as those earrings, he grabbed a glass and a bottle of his Lagavulin twelve-year Scotch, which he liked better than the Glenfiddich. Neat or on the rocks, he wasn't sure about that detail.

Wyatt went for neat. And was rewarded with another one of her gorgeous smiles.

So HE'D GUESSED she was a Scotch drinker. Wyatt was either really good at reading people, or Cricket hadn't left the no-nonsense image behind in Chicago like she thought. She watched him hesitate, probably wondering if she drank it on the rocks.

Seeing Ginny and Harlow had felt good, and it would be even better when they connected with Jade once she straightened out her delayed flight—she was hoping to arrive sometime around 2:00 a.m. Jessica—no, Cricket—hoped she didn't regret promising to wait up for her. Ginny had left the reception early to pick up her daughter from a party. Harlow had hooked up with a football player from back in the day, a guy Cricket barely remembered. They'd begged her to join them but she'd lied. Told them she had a headache and she still hadn't seen Ronny yet. That part about her dad was true.

They'd talked on the phone when he returned from the fishing charter. She'd just gotten to the reception and he'd had a long, taxing day and suggested she come over for breakfast tomorrow. Waiting for anything wasn't Ronny's strong suit, and after what Ginny had told her about his accident, Cricket hoped he wasn't avoiding her.

No, that was crazy. Ronny probably hadn't given it a thought. Nothing fazed him. It wouldn't have occurred to him that Cricket might be worried about his health.

She looked down at the Scotch the bartender slid across the bar to her. Neat. Perfect. She'd been surprised that he hadn't given her the Glenfiddich that was already down, but had gone for the top of the line. Trying to score points? When she took her first sip, she gave him a ten out of ten.

She heard the guy next to her sigh, and realized he'd been trying to hit on her, but she'd been lost in her own thoughts, and if there was one thing she'd learned how to do in law school, it was ignore distractions. Luckily his phone rang and he quickly got involved in the call.

"So, did I get it right?" Wyatt folded his muscled arms across his chest and leaned back. His gray eyes looked darker than they had this afternoon, his stubbled jaw, as well. And damn, he was still hot.

"Oh, yes." She lifted the glass in a salute, then took another sip. "But you would've been right with wine or beer, as well."

"Huh." He frowned. "What kind of beer? Specialty microbrews made in small batches, or…"

"Actually, I'm not that picky when it comes to beer. Lately I've been leaning toward Corona. Unless I'm having sushi, then it's…" She flashed back to the evening in Grant's office, and just like that her mood plummeted.

"Kirin?"

She blinked at Wyatt, and seeing curiosity flare in his eyes, she lowered her gaze and nodded.

"Got an order." The woman's voice came from directly behind her.

"Be right there," Wyatt said. "Hey, would you prefer something else? This being a vacation maybe you want something pink and frilly?"

"Don't you dare."

"Blue, then. With a couple of cherries, a matching umbrella?" he said as he drifted toward the end of the bar.

Cricket smiled, watching him take a slip from the blonde waitress who was staring at her. Wyatt said something to the young woman and she hurried around the bar to the beer tap. While he mixed drinks, she filled mugs. He didn't look too happy when she seemed to go out of her way to stand close enough that her hip rubbed against his thigh. But then maybe that was just part of the gig. Just because he'd flirted with Cricket didn't mean he wasn't playing with the Happy Meal toys.

Nope. He laid down the law. Cricket couldn't actually hear what he'd said but she was good at reading body language. Besides, the waitress hastily hopped a foot to her right and, stone-faced, finished filling three mugs. Maybe Wyatt wasn't just the bartender but the owner. Not that it mattered, at least not to Cricket.

She'd be here for another two days, spend some

time with her dad, catch up with old friends and acquaintances, and then return to Chicago and tell Grant she hadn't changed her mind. Sanford Burbidge could fry for all she cared. Yes, innocent until proven guilty—she got the concept, she even believed in it—but sometimes you just knew a person was evil and capable of doing evil things. She didn't have to be a criminal attorney to know that wasn't a rare experience.

But dammit, what if being true to herself really could torpedo her career? It was possible that Grant was using the threat to strong-arm her, just to placate Burbidge. She didn't want to think he'd do that, but making senior partner was singularly important to him. She had no illusions where his career was concerned. Still, the firm had other female attorneys much better qualified to defend the creep. All Cricket would be was a figurehead, a very reluctant, pissed-off figurehead. How would that help anyone?

Grant wasn't stupid. Quite the opposite, in fact. And he knew her better than anyone at the firm. Surely she could convince him to talk Burbidge out of it, reason with the partners and smooth any ruffled feathers…perhaps even without letting them know just how vehemently she opposed being placed in such an untenable situation.

"You're away from work, sitting in a bar on the beach, drinking good Scotch…"

She looked up. Wyatt was back, leaning against

the counter behind him, those tanned muscled forearms crossed again and he must have known how much that stance complemented his strong, broad chest. His snug T-shirt hid nothing.

"So why look as if the world is about to cave in on you?" he asked.

"Um, maybe because it is?"

His mouth twitched into a wry half smile, as if he didn't believe a word. "You sure? The mind is a dangerous place to be roaming around this late."

"Amen to that." Cricket let out a soft laugh, then drained her Scotch.

When he picked up her glass and raised his brows, she nodded.

"Hey, if you need an ear…" He shrugged. "I'm a bartender, it's my job."

"You're so full of shit." Bobby or Billy—she'd forgotten—was off the phone and snorted like a pig. "Anyone tries to unload on you and you tell 'em to go find a damn shrink."

Wyatt pinned him with quite an impressive glare. "I'm selective," he said, and grabbed the Scotch.

After he poured her drink and corked the bottle, something behind her caught his attention. "Excuse me," he murmured, suddenly preoccupied. "Sabrina." He stepped to the side and motioned. "You okay?"

"Fine," a woman's soft voice replied.

"What are you doing here?"

"I came to work. I'm really, really sorry I'm late, Wyatt. Please don't fire me. I—I couldn't help it."

"I wouldn't do that," he said, then muttered a curse. "What happened?"

Cricket sat up straighter, fighting the urge to turn around. Something about the way Wyatt looked stirred some instinct that lifted the fine hair on the back of her neck. If she hadn't seen him with the children earlier, the hard edge in his eyes would've given her a completely different impression of him. She couldn't resist a brief peek.

The bruise on the young woman's face was impossible to miss, even though she'd tried her best to hide it with her long auburn hair. Cricket's chest tightened at the sight. At what it so clearly meant. The woman, who couldn't have been more than twenty-five, and Wyatt were speaking quietly, their conversation not meant to be overheard, but Cricket couldn't do anything about it, short of getting up and leaving.

"It's fine, Wyatt. I promise. Can we drop this?"

He took so long to respond, Cricket stole another quick glance. The hardness was back in his eyes. "Don't worry. Take the rest of the night off."

"Thanks, but I really need the money."

His jaw clenched. "After we close, you can stay upstairs if you want."

"That's okay. I've got it covered."

Wyatt didn't move for a while, but Sabrina did, slipping quickly behind the bar.

Cricket couldn't help but think about how Wyatt was still watching the woman. No, not just her. He did a scan around the bar, and she had the feeling he knew exactly who should be there and who shouldn't be in the crowded room, before his protective gaze returned to Sabrina. Cricket's esteem for him went up, way up, along with her curiosity. So far, he'd surprised her twice tonight, three times if she counted this afternoon.

Interesting. The guy next to her? He was like a bottle of wine. The label might be enticing, but when you got up close, he was bland and boring.

Wyatt, on the other hand, had something going on inside, in addition to the tantalizing label. She was trying to remember if she'd met anyone who had ever stirred that particular feeling in her before. Although she didn't know this man. He could be a wild card. A complication she didn't need.

"Hey," Bobby said, loudly in her ear. "He forgot your drink. I can get it for you if you want."

"That's okay." She gave him her patented not-interested look, then glanced behind him to focus on Wyatt as he filled drink orders on the other side of the bar.

Then her phone rang. Small mercies. She pulled it out of her bag. "Jade. Where are you?"

"I'm here. Five minutes from the resort."

"How?"

"I used my incredible charm."

"Right. You bulldozed somebody into giving you a seat."

"What's the difference?"

Cricket laughed. Some things never changed. She hadn't seen Jade since the day they'd graduated but they'd kept in touch through Facebook and Cricket knew she was working for some giant perfume company in New Jersey. "Where do you want to meet?"

"Is the hotel bar okay with you? I want to check in and dump my stuff."

"Sure," Cricket said, glancing at Wyatt.

"Say, fifteen minutes?"

Bobby leaned in and waved at her. Cricket turned on her stool, ignoring him.

"Okay," she said, but Jade had already disconnected. It was probably going to be a late night, and she doubted she'd be back to flirt with Wyatt, but that couldn't be helped.

She left a twenty on the bar, figuring it should be enough with tip, and walked to the door. Before she left, she turned her head, just in time to catch him staring right at her. His eyes narrowed and she wondered what he saw, but then his eyes widened, his brows raised in an obvious question.

She gave him her most enigmatic smile. At least she hoped so. She might just look like an idiot.

When he grinned back, she still wasn't sure.

# CHAPTER FIVE

CRICKET'S PLAN HAD been to walk to Ronny's shack. But staying up until two thirty this morning put that idea to bed. Which she wished she had done for herself, instead of taking a cab the sinfully short distance to the place where she'd grown up.

She couldn't complain too much. Harlow had joined her and Jade after ditching the football player, and they'd laughed themselves silly in the hotel bar, and then after it closed, out on the deck. The talk had been about the past. She knew her reasons for not telling her friends about what was happening in her life now, but she also knew they'd all fess up soon enough.

Thoughts of Wyatt had floated through her brain all night. Just images, stray thoughts. She'd slipped once about him, and the others had glommed on to it like leeches. After that she'd been careful not to mention the bar. They all knew it. And soon enough they'd all be checking him out.

As the taxi pulled up on the beach road, she smiled at Ronny's sky blue shack, the only one like it on this stretch of the best surfing beach for miles. The city had tried to make him change the color back when she'd been a teenager, but they'd given up eventually. That house was as much a landmark as anything in Temptation Bay, and surfers came from all over to meet Ronny, in his fifties, and still a legend in his own right.

She gave the cab driver too much money, then slipped off her sandals to walk the familiar sand, clean and cool in the early morning air. She'd worn one of her old sundresses, something she'd taken with her to Chicago out of nostalgia more than anything, but hardly ever wore. Last time had been on her last visit… God, three years ago already. How had that happened? She needed to come more often. He missed her. A lot. He'd promised to make her favorite breakfast, chocolate chip pancakes, and swore his groupies, the surfers that swarmed in the summer and made his shack their headquarters, were banished for the day.

She hadn't the heart to tell him she hadn't liked chocolate chip pancakes since high school. It didn't matter. She'd eat whatever he had. Guess she missed him just as much.

The front door was open, but she stopped on the second step up to the porch. The board had been replaced recently. Unfortunately, the other two hadn't, and it was evident that they'd already started rotting.

But that was her dad. Fix what's broke. If it's

not, why bother? There were waves to catch. Fish to fry. Books to read. He'd always been like that. It had driven her mother nuts, and as Cricket had grown up, it had bothered her, too.

The whole house was in need of repairs. Shingles missing on the roof, one window broken, fixed with duct tape, the paint was peeling, and she was pretty sure the whole place was leaning a little to the left.

"Well, are you coming in or what?"

She grinned and trotted past the porch, straight into his arms.

"Oh, Baby Girl, it's been too long. And you're too skinny."

She leaned back, studying his face. Wow, she'd never thought it would happen, but he was looking his age. "Look who's talking. Hasn't anyone been feeding you?"

"I'm not an invalid. I take care of myself just fine." He pulled her tight again. "Besides, being lean is good for longevity. I'm thinking of going macrobiotic. I read a really interesting book about it."

"You'd blow away in the wind if you lost more weight," she said. "I'm actually surprised that you and this old shack didn't get flown to Oz during that last big northern."

"That's the beauty of the Bay, my girl. We're protected here, just like the pirates."

"Oh, for… You know the cab driver from the

airport was talking about that stupid treasure on my way here. I can't believe it hasn't been completely debunked by now, and what's that smell?"

"Goddammit." Ronny abandoned her to the kitchen, where at least one chocolate chip pancake had become a lava cake.

"It's all right," he said. "I mixed up plenty."

He always had. Burning meals was another Ronny specialty. Which was troubling. Although she wasn't going to say anything yet. Not until she found out more about the Jeep accident and the fall on the dock.

"How's the coffee?" she asked.

"Like always. Tastes like motor oil, keeps you up as long as you need to be."

"Tell you what, just for a change of pace, I'll fix you some a little milder." Anticipating his protest, before he opened his mouth she said, "I'm not throwing away your tar. You can heat it up later. But I need coffee that's not ninety-four octane."

"Be my guest, Baby Girl. There's OJ in the fridge, too."

Butter sizzled on his old cast-iron grill while she busied herself with the beverages, pouring them both a glass of juice as the new coffee brewed.

"What do you hear from your mother?"

"She's good. Still living in Paris with the judge."

"That's number four, right?"

"Yep. But she likes him. He's got hobbies."

"Hobbies. So she can shop all she wants without him tagging along?"

"That's right." Cricket grinned. "And they like taking river cruises. I think the last one was from Budapest to Amsterdam."

"Huh. I'm glad she's happy."

"She asks about you, too, you know."

"What do you tell her?"

"That you're forever Ronny. That you don't have a new woman in your life. Or has that changed?"

"Nope. I'm forever me. How about you? Got yourself some hot prospect?"

"I'm too busy working to have any kind of prospect."

"That's a shame, Baby Girl. I'd like you to fall madly in love with a good man."

Cricket smiled. That didn't surprise her. Ronny had always had a romantic soul. "Well, that's not exactly off my wish list. Just not in the immediate forecast."

"Put a couple forks on the table, huh? The food'll be ready in a sec."

She did, along with the juice. His old coffeepot took forever, but that was okay. "How's the charter business going?"

"Good. You know summer's always busy for me. Lot of tourists wanting to catch their trophies. I had one guy wanting to know where he could get a baby marlin stuffed. Got all upset when I told him we had to throw it back, that it was below the limit."

"What about your regulars?"

"Yeah, yeah, I get enough repeat business to pay the bills, but the extras help out for the winters. With the crazy weather patterns now, you never know what to expect." He brought two plates over, each one pretty much covered in a giant pancake. "There you go, Baby Girl. Your favorite."

"I see you didn't forget the butter and the syrup."

"Nope. Never will." He sat down across from her, at the table he'd had as long as she could remember, made from driftwood by a local craftsman. It was really ugly and wobbled, but it went with the rest of the decor.

Almost everything in the shack was roughshod and the style could only be labeled as beach bum. There were still a couple of lamps that her mother had added, both classic and traditional. Also, the painting above the long couch that had to be worth a lot by now, although she doubted her dad had done much to preserve it. She couldn't remember the artist's name, but he'd been renowned back in the day.

"About those charters," she said, "you are insured, right?"

Ronny stopped eating to stare at her. "Insured?

Why would I need that? You're an attorney. Anything happens and I get sued, you'll take care of it."

She dropped her fork. "Are you crazy? The only thing I'd be able to do is visit you in prison."

A smile with lots more lines crinkling his tanned face made her roll her eyes. "I'm insured," he said. "Very well, in fact. Both the business and the house."

"Speaking of, what happened with that fall on the dock? And also, how come you didn't tell me about crashing the Jeep?"

"Lousy gossips in this town. The Jeep was nothing. A fender bender. I needed three whole stitches. Jeez. As for the dock, it was slick and I fell, that's it. It happens."

"Was it the dock or your personal slip?"

"I don't remember. Does it matter?"

"Of course it does. You're responsible for your slip. Before I leave, I'm going to the dock to make sure it's not a hazard, talk to the harbormaster if need be. Even with insurance, if someone breaks their neck and they can prove maintenance wasn't kept up, they can sue the pants off you."

"Honey, I hate to tell you, I've been without pants on that dock plenty of times before."

"Ew."

His hearty laugh hadn't changed a bit. "Eat your pancake. If you finish it all up, I'll make you another."

"Oh, Ronny. I'm not twelve anymore. All this sugar is going to keep me wired all day."

"And you turned your nose up at my coffee."

She laughed and ate, enjoying the cloyingly sweet chocolate and syrup despite herself. It reminded her of home, of such happy days. Even when Ronny and her mom fought, they must've been civil, because she didn't remember any of it. After they split, her childhood spent mostly with her father was a collage of shining memories, filled with an ease she rarely found outside the Bay.

"How's Eleanor and Oliver?" They were his longtime neighbors. Oliver was a retired fisherman and Eleanor worked at the library part-time. They'd watched her often when she was growing up.

"Oliver's getting old. Can't walk too much anymore. Working on the sea takes it out of a person. He's got arthritis so bad his hands are almost useless. Eleanor still goes out to the library three times a week, though."

"Do they still argue like street fighters?"

"Yeah, but it's better now that Eleanor doesn't hear so great. Oliver spends most of his time yelling at the kids who come around here." Ronny shrugged. "It's okay, though. A man like Oliver needs something to be angry about, other than his own body."

"And how's your body?"

He looked wounded, and honestly, she hated to even bring it up, but there was something off about him. His eyes still made him seem young, and his floppy hair, permanently sun streaked and brushing the neckline of his T-shirt, had grayed some, mostly at his temples. It wasn't that, though. His movements were somehow more careful. Even when he walked the short distance from the kitchen to the table. "I'm not that old."

"I know. That accident? Whose fender was the bender?"

His guff of air was a warning, but she wasn't about to back off yet. "Mine, okay? I got distracted. What, that's never happened to you? I'm fifty-eight years old, and I've had exactly two car accidents. Both of them minor. I think my record is pretty damn good."

"When was the other one?"

He didn't answer.

"Could vertigo be the problem?"

"No."

"What about surfer's ear?"

"You think I wouldn't know if I had surfer's ear?"

"Have you checked?"

"Yes."

She was about to ask him another question, but reconsidered.

His stare made her feel awkward, something she wasn't used to. Ronny wasn't just a community legend, he was her own personal hero. His kindness had always been unfailing, and she'd known many boys turn into good men because they'd hung out with her beach bum dad. "Isn't that famous coffee of yours done by now?"

"Yes, it is." She got up, took her empty plate into the kitchen, which was really just on the other side of the standing counter, and poured them both a cup. Despite his complaining, he'd always liked the way she made it with a pinch of cinnamon.

"Tell me what else has changed," she said, setting his cup in front of him. She kissed his forehead before sitting down.

There was the smile that she loved. "Every damn thing. Except the surfing and the fishing. Some company offered me a fortune to buy the shack, and my slice of sand."

"Really?"

"Of course I told them no. I'm never leaving this place. I want you to have it after I kick off. Besides, this old thing survived Hurricane Sandy, the town council and five mayors."

"Even you have to admit it could use a few repairs."

"I'll get to them before winter hits, how about that?"

"How about you hire someone before winter?"

"Why? I'm perfectly capable—"

"I'm not saying that. But come on, why should

you? You already do too much. Tell you what. Now that I'm a rich attorney, let me do this for you. I didn't get you anything but a card for your last birthday."

"Absolutely not. You put that money into savings. Jeez, I want you to retire early so you can come back home where you belong. This town needs a Cricket. Bad."

She reached over and took his hand. God, his skin was dry and spotted. So much exposure to the sun. His words, though, they brought a small lump to her throat. "Okay. We'll discuss the repairs later. Right now, I want to ask you something."

"What?"

His eyes had narrowed, and Cricket immediately put off the question she'd been about to ask him. "Do you ever go up to Sam's Sugar Shack?"

"Yeah, sure."

"You know the new bartender?"

"There's a new bartender?"

"Maybe not new," she said, realizing it had been three years. "Tall, lean, muscular build—"

"Oh, you mean Wyatt?" Ronny frowned and turned to the window. "Why, is he here?"

Her throat tightened and she almost took a look outside, herself. "Are you expecting him?"

"No," Ronny said. "I figured you must have seen him on your way over. He runs most mornings, past here, to the fish market. Sometimes he likes to hang out here or at the market, just to shoot the breeze."

"Does he own Sam's?"

Ronny nodded as he sipped his coffee. "Yeah. For a couple years now. Good guy." A smile tugged at Ronny's mouth. "As long as you don't bother his waitresses or get rowdy. He doesn't care if you're a local or not, you have too much booze and act up, he'll put a stop to it. Always calm, but tough. Like you know he could kick your ass, so you just might as well walk it off."

"I'm sure that's never happened to you."

Ronny laughed. "I have many sins, Baby Girl, but overindulging in alcohol isn't one of them."

"I suppose that doesn't go for the recreational weed I can still smell in the rugs?"

He laughed again but before she could tell him she wasn't calling him out on his habit, there was a knock on the door. A banging, actually.

"Dammit, I told you guys to stay away today," Ronny yelled, and goodness, his voice hadn't weakened a bit.

"Ronny," some guy yelled back. "Don't be like that. Hector said your daughter's hot. We want to meet her."

"Beat it!"

"Besides, there's a sweet two-foot swell coming in, and you'll be sorry if you miss it. Come on, man."

"You want to escape, now's the time," Ronny

said, inclining his head. "I bet you can still crawl out through your bedroom window."

Cricket grinned. "You knew about that?"

His look told her more than words.

"No. I'd actually like to meet these young hooligans. Make sure there are no unsavory characters."

"Except me?"

"Except you."

The front door, never locked to her knowledge, squeaked open. "So, it's okay if we come in? It's just me, Ted, Igor and Wendy. The rest of the guys are still out there."

Cricket mouthed, "Igor?"

Her dad just laughed as the door opened farther. "Ronny?"

"Fine. But you don't touch. Anything. Especially the fresh coffee. You want some, you heat up the stuff in that pot by the microwave."

The boys and Wendy came in a rush, as if they'd all been huddled by the door. Wendy was a pretty girl in a very small bikini top and boy's trunks. Her long hair was pulled into a braid down her back, and she was tan with bright green eyes and the pink lips of a teen. There had been a time when Cricket had looked a lot like that. Not the eyes so much as the innocence.

The boys were a range of heights and ages. One kid looked no more than fourteen or fifteen, and one might have gotten into the bar without a fake

ID. But they all looked like surfers, as close to the California stereotype as they could get without a Malibu tattoo. It felt as if they'd all looked like that, from the time she'd learned to surf herself, at the tender age of nine.

Someone whistled. "You are hot."

"Thanks. Also, too old and wise to get mixed up with surfers."

"Hey." That came from a chorus of voices.

"Besides," she said, finishing her coffee. "I've got to get back to the hotel and meet the gang."

"Who came?" Ronny asked.

"Everyone but Meg."

"Jade?"

"Yeah. Even Jade. It's great. Anyway, I'll come by tomorrow, if you don't have any charters or surfing lessons."

"I've got an early evening charter, other than that I'll be here." He stood up and wrapped his arms around her again. "You be careful with those hill people, all right?"

She refrained from reminding him he'd married one of them. "I'm always careful."

"Don't go yet," the taller surfer said, moving in closer. "We haven't even been introduced."

"Let me guess. You're a surfer from New York or New Jersey who'd heard about the great surfing at Temptation Bay, and about Ronny Shaw in particular, and this is your first season on the beach, probably sharing a room at the motel with three or four of your new friends?"

"How'd you know I was from Jersey?" he said, in an accent so thick it could paint walls.

Cricket smiled. "You take care of him," she said, nodding at her father. "And listen to what he says." It was time to get away. Now, before the rest of them screwed up their courage. She wanted to take her time walking back to the hotel, and with any luck, she just might run into Wyatt.

# CHAPTER SIX

WYATT WOKE WITH a start, his hand reaching under his pillow for a gun that wasn't there. "Shit," he said, his mouth dry and his eyes blurry. It was later than he normally woke, but now, as thoughts started forming, he knew exactly why he felt like a war was at his door.

It was Adam's birthday.

He needed coffee. After throwing off the sheet, he stumbled to the coffeepot that had been programmed to brew three hours ago and managed to pour himself a mug. He put it in the microwave and hit the button before he went to the bathroom. After he'd splashed his face with ice-cold water and taken care of business, he retrieved the blessedly hot coffee. Leaning his hip against the counter, he sipped from the mug, hoping his head would clear some more before he made any decisions.

By the time he finished his second mug, he knew he was going to have to go for a run despite the late hour. It was already hotter outside than he liked it, but there was no getting around the fact that he'd think more clearly after he'd done a few miles. He'd stayed up till three listening to Sabrina, while trying to hide just how much he wanted to beat the crap out of her worthless boyfriend. Luckily, Tiffy, who also knew the problem, had stuck around and offered Sabrina a safe place for the night. No denying she'd go back to the bastard. She always did.

Wyatt pulled on a pair of running shorts and a T-shirt, then stuck his key in his pocket, grabbed his cell to put in the other one, but stopped as he noticed the text message.

It was from Peter, Adam's grandfather. Wyatt didn't need to open the text to know what it was about. They wanted him to come to dinner tonight. To celebrate.

He put the phone in his pocket and left his apartment, stopping when he saw Becky halfway up the stairs.

"You're going running now?"

He nodded. "Got up late. Bad night."

"Sorry about that." Becky looked polished, as if nothing could possibly be wrong with the day. Her strawberry blond hair was up in a neat twist, her dress a pale floral, sandals with a moderate heel. Of course, her makeup was perfect for a Navy officer's wife. Except when she got close, he could see that even makeup couldn't quite hide the red tinge along her lower lid. "I'm sure they've called already."

"Texted."

"They're learning. They want to be experts by the time the kids are old enough to have their own phones. Or at least can spell."

"Josh can spell."

Her anxious expression needed no translation.

"Hey, he writes his name like a champ."

"You don't have to go tonight," she said softly. "Unless you've said something to the contrary, I've already told them you have to work."

"Do you want me to go?"

Her shoulders drooped. "*I* don't want to go. But the kids do. They like that there'll be cake and ice cream. In fact, I'm on my way to drop them off. They get to help with the frosting and decorations."

"And what about you?"

"I'm going to spend some quality time by myself, doing nothing. I haven't had that in a while. I'll join them later." She turned to stare out at the sea. "It always starts out as a party but then... well, you know. It's more like an annual tribute now. I mean, not that I begrudge them. But every holiday it's the same."

"I know. It's hard."

"The family is wonderful, and I love them all so much. But it's almost three years now, and I worry that at Peter's and Yvette's ages, hanging on to the grief will hurt them."

"Those kids of yours help keep them going. And you're like one of their own."

She looked at him again, her blue eyes welling. "So are you."

His breath caught. "They've known me a long time."

"Anyway, go for your run. The car's going to get too hot to leave the kids in it. And yes, smart-ass, all the windows are open, and they're drinking their juice boxes."

He took the next three steps to get close to her. "I never doubted it for a moment."

His hand went to her arm. "Look, I'll go tonight."

"No. Absolutely not."

"I promise it won't kill me."

Becky shook her head. "I think it's good to start weaning everyone. Next holiday we'll just do a pop in, or something."

"Are you sure? Because I can—"

"I'm sure." She nodded, turned and hurried down ahead of him.

Watching her, the way she straightened when she got near her SUV, hearing Josh say, "Mom, guess what?" made Wyatt ache. He'd never get the hang of the different holidays. But Adam's birthday was the worst. It always felt as if Wyatt were intruding if he went, that he was just a terrible reminder of what everyone had lost.

Maybe even worse, was that he'd never wanted Adam's grandparents to think he was trying to be a substitute. Even if he wanted to be, he'd be lousy at it. Adam had been a great husband and father. Wyatt had been told several times that he was a nice guy, but a lousy boyfriend. And as a husband? A dad?

Hell, now he wasn't even the good son.

That got him moving, racing down the stairs straight past the already-open bar to the sand. It really was late. He'd have to dodge people. Not that he minded. He needed his mind to be on his gait, his time. No one but him gave a shit, but he liked to beat his best time once a week. He'd already done that two days ago, but who cared.

In this heat, it would be difficult. He wanted difficult.

Even with hustling, his thoughts couldn't stay just on his pace despite the rhythm he worked to establish. He kept thinking about Peter and Yvette, and how they would decorate the house with a banner they kept, and how Adam's pictures would be all over the mantel and the walls, and in the kitchen, and in the hallway. Interspersed with photos of the grandkids and wedding photos. But Adam's portrait was the only one with a black ribbon around it.

How they loved his friend. The two of them used to gorge on Yvette's packages of cookies and candy whenever they knew where the unit was going to be. She'd always sent double, knowing Wyatt would steal half, and borrow the extra socks.

His mom had sent stuff, too, but she'd never been extravagant. Not with food or supplies, or letters for that matter. Too busy being an officer's wife. With the Marshes, including Adam, family always came first. In Wyatt's family, it was duty.

"Hey, what are you doing here so late?"

Wyatt recognized the voice before he spotted Delia, who was standing at her stall at the fish market. How was she already almost sold out? He checked his watch. Damn late. And nope, hadn't broken any records. Down by six seconds. It didn't matter.

"How are you, Delia?" he asked, slowing to a crawl, wishing he'd brought his water bottle. He rarely forgot it.

"You're sweating like a pig. You want some water?"

"Yeah, thanks. That'd be great."

The stands were cooled very pleasantly with misters and fans, and the ice that was constantly replenished under the morning's catch. He could see from the scarcity that the local chefs had been by, not just for the restaurants, but for the hotels and B&Bs, and then there were the locals, who knew when to show up. He'd often gone home with a fish so fresh it'd barely stopped wiggling. One of the great joys of living near a fishing village.

"So this reunion, huh?" Delia said. "Damn prep school a-holes."

"They're not all a-holes."

"No. That's 'cause some of them come from the south."

She meant the fish side of town, he knew. That rivalry wasn't going to be over anytime soon.

Delia had to be over sixty-five, but she was out here every day until most of the catch was sold. During tourist season, that was pretty early. Today, she'd be wrapping things up soon. He thought about buying some fish but he wasn't finished running, and it was too hot to lug a striped bass home. "But they pay a pretty penny for seafood."

"Damn straight they do. I see 'em coming, I put out the other prices."

He'd known that for a long time. It had been almost a year before she gave him the local rate. "That's wicked smart, Delia," he said, using his best Rhody accent. "Say hi to Fred, would ya?"

"Your accent's still crap, you know."

"I'll keep trying." Instead of running back to the bar, he was going to go to the hotel, find out what the schedule was for the reunion crowd. He knew there was a big dinner tonight, but he might let a few of the bell staff know he'd have a special going on.

His trip had nothing to do with hoping to see Cricket. Nothing at all.

CRICKET FOUND THE gang in the perpetually crowded bar off the lobby.

"I ordered a pitcher of sweet tea," Jade said, just as Cricket sat down between Harlow and Ginny.

Harlow grabbed the small menu displayed in the middle of the table. "Guess who's here?" she said, glancing at Jade. "Fletcher Preston."

"So. What do I care?"

Cricket and Harlow laughed. Ginny only smiled. She looked tired. Cricket wished she had more time here. To go see her, to meet Tilda. But she was leaving Monday morning, and God, she didn't want to think about that. Not when her nights had been crowded with worry.

Jade checked for the waitress, then pushed back her flowing copper hair, the hair she'd hated in school because the boys made fun of her. She wore tamer makeup now, and curled her hair, and wore nail polish that wasn't black. Getting away from Temptation Bay had done wonders for her, although she was still Jade. Ready to stand up to anyone.

"You were hot for him all of junior year." Harlow sat up taller, smiling as the pitcher arrived at the table.

"At least you're not denying it," Ginny said once they were alone again, and Jade was pouring. "Did he ever ask you out?"

"No." Jade grunted while taking her first sip. "Men are dopes."

Cricket smiled.

Ginny and Harlow grinned. "Not all men."

"Most men."

"So, you're not seeing anyone, I take it?" Cricket said.

"Nope."

"What do you do about sex?" Harlow asked, not in the least abashed by her question.

"That's what one-night stands are for," Jade said. "No fuss, no muss and no disappointments. Except when they're…" She held up her hand, index and thumb two inches apart.

"I've missed you, Jade Kelly," Ginny said, laughing. "A lot."

Jade gave her a look. "What about you? Living here and all. You getting any?"

"With Tilda around? God, no. I don't even remember getting any. I think I'm actually a virgin again. Technically."

"Oh, honey." Harlow covered Ginny's hand with her own. "That's what reunions are for. You have a babysitter, right? Tonight's your night. We'll all help you find someone decent."

"Someone from school? No, thanks."

"A stranger, then. Honest. There are lots of guys here, and if it's someone on vacation or here just for the golf tournament, you never have to see them again. It's perfect."

Ginny blushed, but grinned. "I did shave all the important parts."

"That's the spirit." Harlow drank some more,

looking around at the packed tables. "I wouldn't mind a dip in the water myself. Although, I don't know. There's someone in LA that I've been kind of seeing. No one special, though. Another teacher. Science and math. You'd like him, Jade."

"Just because I'm a chemist doesn't mean I instantly bond with all other science nerds. Especially the men, superior jerks. When I open my store, I'm only hiring young women who are interested in STEM, and I'm going to mentor my ass off."

"Wait?" Cricket put down her drink. "Opening your what?"

Jade grinned wide. "I'm going to open a perfumery. Nothing huge, but I'll be making personalized scents. Tailoring them to people's chemistry. I've already set up a website, even though I can't start yet, not until I'm out of contract, which won't be for another five months. And I have a partner. She's a professor from Berkeley and she's financing the whole thing, because God knows I'm still in debt up to my eyeballs, but she thinks we can really do a lot with this. Kind of like what they're doing now with DNA. Getting saliva samples from people via the mail, then I do my magic, and give them a scent that's unique to their body chemistry. I'm wearing one of mine right now."

"You smell delicious," Harlow said, leaning in for another sniff. "I noticed when we hugged."

"I know," Cricket added. "I noticed, too. But it's not the same as last night, and I told you how amazing that was. Are they both yours?"

Jade nodded.

"I'll spit on whatever you want," Harlow said. "Please."

"Good. I'll send you all kits. You can be guinea pigs for my questionnaires."

Cricket held up her almost empty glass. "To new adventures and tremendous success. Jade, you'll kill it. You'll absolutely kill it."

"I'm glad you think so," Jade said, clicking her glass with the others, "because I'm totally going to ask you for help drawing up the legal stuff."

"Of course."

"You'll be paid, don't worry about that."

"I'd do it anyway. You know that."

They drank, and then Jade leaned in, her eyes shining with mischief. "Did you guys see Winnie this morning? What the hell has she done with her hair?"

"Oh, yeah." Harlow shuddered. "She looks like Billy Idol. I mean, with her coloring, those platinum spikes? Honestly, what in the world?"

"God, she was such a bitch," Jade said. "Thought she was all that, so I made a point of looking at her current bio. She's divorced, two kids, ex-husband's in insurance. She lives in Nebraska. Remember how she was going to take New York by storm?"

"She used to call me a grotesque giraffe," Harlow said. "When she couldn't even make the cheerleading squad."

"Better than telling me every single day that I stunk like fish," Jade said. "I mean, every day? Waving her hand in front of her face when I'd walk by. God, I hate her."

"Now this is like old times," Ginny said. "Remember Tommy Zico? That pervert? Is he here? I didn't see his name…"

"I bet he's in jail." Harlow shook her head. "At least he should be."

"Well, how about that?" Ginny said. "Cricket. Check out who's at the activity board."

Jade followed Harlow's gaze and said, "I'll take him to go, please."

Cricket turned around. It was Wyatt. Looking even scruffier than he had last night. Wearing a sweat-stained T-shirt over running shorts, his stubble darker, his hair a mess, and she felt her insides melt.

"Wait a minute," Jade said. "Cricket? He's so not your type."

"You don't even know what my type is."

"Uh, corporate. Silk neckties. Penthouse apartment. Drives a Porsche."

"Stop it." Cricket flushed, although not about Jade's comment, even though she'd almost described Grant to a T. "I'm versatile."

"You sure?" Harlow said. "Maybe we could

Rochambeau for him? I'll be paper, you can be rock."

Cricket polished off her drink and dropped her napkin on the table. "Don't get into too much trouble while I'm gone."

"Why, you hogging him all for yourself?"

"Very possibly." She tugged her dress down, then headed over to him.

WYATT THOUGHT ABOUT what kind of special he could offer, but gave up the idea when he saw there would be dancing after the dinner. That gave him only an hour window before the law made him lock up. Besides, it was a dumb idea. These people didn't care about specials.

"See anything interesting?"

He jerked at the voice, recognizing it instantly. Cricket was standing a little to his right. "Hey. I didn't even notice you here."

"I could tell. It's okay. I was with my friends. Gossiping. It was great. We all still hate the same people."

He laughed as he followed her gaze to a table of women, who were all staring straight at him. Three of them waved. One of them gave him a thumbs-up. Embarrassed, he looked back at the board as he realized he hadn't thought this through. Hoping to see Cricket was one thing, but he smelled and looked like hell. Thank God he'd brushed his teeth. Nodding at the board, making sure his arms stayed by his sides, he said, "You guys actually have a party tomorrow at the yacht club. How rich are you people?"

"Shut up," she said, laughing. "It wasn't my idea. And I doubt I'd be welcome."

"I think you'd be welcome anywhere."

"Oh, my, you aren't from here. There's definitely a caste system coming out of our prep school." She lifted her brows at his slow smile. "Don't get me wrong, it was a very good school and helped get me into Yale, but I wasn't actually part of the 'it' crowd."

"Thank God."

"Oh, really?"

"No," he said, "Actually, I don't like to be that way. I had damn good friends who were well-heeled and loaded."

"I know. Me, too. Although not that many from those years. It was pretty awful for us fish people."

"Excuse me?"

She sighed. "I grew up on the south side of the tracks. Surely you're aware of the tension."

"I didn't know where you were from, but yeah."

She stepped in closer. Brave. "I was sorry I had to leave last night. My friend had arrived, and I'd promised to meet her. We ended up having a late meal and talking until the wee hours."

"I understand. I was up late, too." He almost

told her why, but that was Sabrina's business, so he left it.

"I like Sam's Sugar Shack, but I can't imagine how exhausting it must be to run the place."

"Something tells me you're one of the people who don't think it's an institution and should be preserved like Mount Vernon."

She laughed again, and oddly that sound made him itch to touch her skin. Especially in that strappy dress. She clearly worked out. Her arms, which weren't normally a thing he thought about much, were nicely toned. He'd already noticed her legs. Stellar. And the rest of her was pretty sweet, as well. He wasn't one of those men who insisted on huge breasts. He liked all kinds, and Cricket's looked just fine.

"I don't know. If your trade is mostly local, I suppose the decor is perfect."

"Even if politically incorrect..."

She smiled. "I'm staying out of that discussion."

"Actually, with the hotel so near, I've considered making it a little nicer. Still a dive bar, though. Just fewer piñatas and bikini tops."

"What a party you could have taking those piñatas down."

"Now that's an idea. Ah, on second thought, I'd be worried about the contents. If it's candy, who knows how old it is. I'd hate to kill everyone. That might be bad for business."

"Might be, yeah."

"So, the dinner tonight. Sounds fancy. A professional DJ? From New York? What, there aren't any in Rhode Island?"

"They probably weren't prestigious enough. I told you."

"Prep school."

"Right," she said. "Speaking of, um, if you don't have to work tonight, would you have any interest in being my date for this fancy dinner? I promise no rubber chickens. In fact, the food is known to be exceptional."

Well, that was a shocker. Hell, he didn't know what to say.

"You'd have to change, though."

"But this is my formal running gear."

"Rules are rules."

"We're not talking tuxes, are we?"

"Some of the more clueless people will be in them, but the people you'd be hanging out with won't. It's not formal, honestly. And with dancing, it gets hot, so you wouldn't want to wear, say, wool."

"No sheepskin then."

"No."

He looked at the schedule. "It starts at seven."

"I probably won't go down till seven thirty."

"Ends at…"

"Midnight." She smiled, and it was a little flirty. "Or whenever you want to leave."

"You have anything going on before this shindig?"

She shook her head. "Or after."

Interesting. "Well, sure. I can make it. And I promise not to embarrass you with my attire. I'll even shave."

"Don't on my account."

That surprised him. "Seriously?"

She blushed just a bit. "Whatever makes you comfortable. That's great. Although be prepared. We're all gossips and we are merciless. On the plus side, most of the people we'll be talking about don't live here."

"Too bad. Gossip is a hobby of mine. Why do you think I bought a bar? You know how people open up to us bartenders."

"I don't believe a word of it." Her gaze caught on something behind him, and her smile vanished. "Grant? What on earth are you doing here?"

## CHAPTER SEVEN

LOOKING PALE AND overdressed in his gray suit, Grant smiled at her as if he were meeting her for a lunch date. She really wasn't ready to see him, and to surprise her like this?

Wyatt stepped a little to his left, his arm brushing hers. She didn't move, just stared at Grant. "What's going on?"

"You invited me. Tonight's dinner dance?"

"What? Are you—?" Cricket darted a glance at Wyatt, and saw him tense. "Wyatt, this is Grant Herbert," she said, struggling to keep a smile in place. "He's a colleague of mine. This is Wyatt."

"Nice to meet you," Wyatt said, his expression neutral. "I'd shake your hand but I've just come back from a run…"

Barely sparing him a glance, Grant just nodded. The self-absorbed prick.

Wyatt didn't smile until he turned to Cricket. "Rain check?"

She hesitated, knowing there was no way in hell she'd be going anywhere with Grant. But the situation was awkward enough. "Absolutely."

Wyatt nodded and headed toward the beach exit.

She looked at Grant just in time to see him check out Wyatt and dismiss him. It didn't make her feel any more welcoming. "Now, tell me again. Why are you here?"

"We talked about it. You wanted me to come."

"Months ago, when I got the invitation."

"I got jealous, thinking of you out here in the sand and sun."

"Well, you're certainly dressed for it."

His laugh didn't make it to his eyes. "How about we get a drink? I sure could use one." He glanced over at the crowded lobby bar. "Someplace quiet. I had a crying baby to deal with on my flight."

She thought about the minibar in her suite, but she didn't want him getting too comfortable. "The Waverly bar should do."

He made a face. "Will reunion people be swarming the place? I don't want to be continually interrupted," he said, then caught her glare and changed his tune. "I want to be able to loosen up. I'm looking forward to tonight. We've never been dancing."

"No, we haven't. Come on." As she led him across the lobby bar, she realized she'd automatically become Jessica the moment she'd caught sight of him. Something about this impromptu visit wasn't sitting right. Why hadn't he called her? About the case, about coming here? Grant wasn't big on surprises. Giving or getting.

As they walked toward the restaurant bar, she glanced at the girls' table, and they were staring as if they'd never seen a man before. Jade was shaking her head, clearly preferring Wyatt's scruff. Harlow grinned and Ginny, well, she seemed awfully amused.

Making sure Grant couldn't see, she widened her eyes at them and dropped her jaw, a Cricket move if there ever was one, but she quickly reverted to Jessica as they walked around the corner. Grant led her to the last two seats at the bar, and put his bag by his feet. He sighed as he smiled at her. "This resort is great. I imagine you hung out here a lot growing up."

"Not really, no."

"The cab driver told me all about the alleged hidden treasure buried somewhere on the coast. From the view I had flying in, I could see how rocky it is, but the bay looks protected. Pity I can't stay longer. I'd have enjoyed doing the tourist bit, especially with you as my guide."

"The resort is probably the place you'd like best."

The bartender took their orders: she ordered a soda, and of course he got his extra dry martini with three olives.

After they were served and she took a sip, she decided the small talk was far too awkward. "So, anything new on the Burbidge case? I've checked my email, but haven't seen anything."

"Look, Jess..."

He'd never called her Jess. And any sentence that began with *Look*, wasn't going to be good.

"There's no way I can keep you out of this without tanking your career. If anything, Burbidge is even more determined to have you. Ulrich is adamant as well, and frankly, we've already discussed the repercussions of you bowing out."

It was all she could do not to throw her drink in his face. The fury rose up from her gut in a white rage. He couldn't have tried very hard, since it had been only two days since their talk. She doubted he tried at all. "You knew all along, didn't you? Before I even left Chicago."

He leaned back a little, which was smart, because she was spitting mad.

"You just figured I'd eventually cave, and that would suit you just fine. No risk involved. Hell, that's why you offered the company money to fly me out here, to soften me up. But this was always more about saving your own neck, not mine."

"That's not true. You know damn well Burbidge is pressuring the partners. They can't afford to have anything go wrong on this case. Surely you've thought about this while you've been gone." Pausing, he studied her closely. "Honestly, you can't be this naive. We don't get to pick and choose our cases."

"I can't believe you lied to my face when you said you had my back."

He looked away, but not soon enough for her to miss the anger that flashed in his eyes. After a deep breath, a couple of sips of his drink and another sigh, he looked at her. "I do have your back." His tone was gentle, as if he was trying to coax a feral cat into a box. Then he reached over, and put his hand on top of hers.

She whipped it out from under him, and he jerked so hard he nearly spilled his olives.

"Look, I know you're upset, but come on, let's try to have a nice time at this dinner thing. I'd love to meet your friends, and I've wanted to take you dancing for a long time. We can talk again in the morning."

Cricket knew no matter what he said, she wasn't going to change her mind. Maybe she didn't belong at such a prestigious firm. The ACLU could use a good contract lawyer, right? ...ould probably suit her better, and it wasn't as if she needed the Chicago lifestyle. The idea of giving up everything made her stomach clench. She'd worked so damn hard…

"I don't think so." She slid off her stool and looked at him. "If you haven't made a room reservation, you might want to head back to the airport. The resort and every other place in town is booked for the weekend."

"Jessica. You're being irrational. What are you

going to do with lousy references? You think any-one who's anyone will hire you?"

"My father's ill, and I need to make sure he gets some medical care. I'm not sure when I'll be back. It shouldn't be a problem, though," she added, just to let him know she wasn't going down without a fight. "I have a lot of vacation days accrued."

"Jesus, Jessica, don't do this—"

"Goodbye, Grant." Walking away in her best Jessica style, stiff back, head high, wish-ing she was wearing something else, she made her way out of the bar, straight into the elevator and pushed the button to her floor. As soon as the door closed and she was alone, she let it all drop: Jessica, her career and especially Grant. It felt tangibly lighter being Cricket. Although the last thing in the world she wanted to do was go to the damn dinner dance. Having her last hopes dashed to pieces was exhausting. She wanted to sleep for a week.

The walk to her suite was slow, and took all her failing energy. She didn't even bother to take off her shoes before she landed on the bed and closed her eyes.

Unfortunately, her plan to nap went to hell. Her friends would all be at the dinner. On the one hand, ditching them would feel like a betrayal, and besides, she loved those whack job friends of hers. On the other, they'd all have questions.

Then again, because it was a big event, she could probably get away with promising to tell them all the grisly details tomorrow.

Besides, she'd brought a knockout dress for tonight. Grant would have peed his hand-tailored slacks. But screw him, screw Burbidge, screw the partners…all of them could go straight to hell.

She had just enough time to wash the day off her before she could put on her chic, very expensive, sleeveless cocktail dress. It was gold and white, and hugged her body to its best advantage.

The shower was an elixir, especially wiping off her makeup. But when she sat down at the vanity, she knew tonight would be a challenge.

Of course, she was late. It wasn't until Jade texted her that she realized they were all waiting for her inside the banquet room. At least she wasn't the only straggler. She made her way to their table, wondering if it was Ginny's turn to get drinks, because there were two empty seats.

"Finally," Harlow said, her hair magically transformed from pale wheat blond to an astonishingly gorgeous rose gold that made her look like a princess in her sea green dress, tight on top and frilly on the bottom. "Some friend you are, keeping us all in suspense."

"Where's that hottie?" Jade asked. "Although I prefer the fabulous and scruffy Wyatt."

Harlow's hand went up when she practically shouted, "Team gorgeous suit."

That made Cricket smile, at least. "He's no one. Someone from work. With news that I don't want to even think about let alone talk about. Is Ginny at the bar? I need liquor."

Jade shook her head. "She can't come. Something's up with Tilda. She didn't get too specific, but she sounded upset."

"Oh, no."

"She said she'd talk to us tomorrow."

Cricket frowned. It probably had something to do with their discussion. She'd text her soon, see if she needed anything. "Well, where's the nearest bar?"

"I'll go," Jade said. "Harlow went last time. What do you want?"

Cricket didn't hesitate. "A double Scotch. Neat."

"Whoa, that must've been some really bad news." Jade walked behind her and gave her shoulder a squeeze. She also looked beautiful in her elegant blue sheath dress. "Hang tough. We'll keep you in Scotch for as long as you want."

"No, I need you guys to make sure I don't get sloppy. Two is my max. Seriously."

"Fine. But we'll keep my Sea Breezes coming. Don't say anything interesting while I'm gone."

Jade kept walking, and Cricket glanced around the room. Everyone seemed to be having a good time already. That could've included her had she come with Wyatt. At the thought, a wave of sadness washed over her. Dammit. She probably shouldn't have come. But she was made of tough stuff, so she put on a smile and sank onto her seat.

Looking over at the bar where Jade was in line, Cricket knew it would be a while until she came back, especially since she was talking to a tall, good-looking guy. "Wait, is that Fletcher?"

Harlow followed her gaze. "Yep. Odds are, he'll help her with the drinks, then come and join us. You know anything about him now?"

Cricket shook her head. "We all have to get together tomorrow for brunch, or, I don't know, something."

Harlow moved over to sit next to her. "Hey, you don't look so hot. Oh, wait. I mean, you look, wow. That dress is stunning. But something's off."

"I'm fine. Really," she said, catching sight of Lindsey McCarron, an old nemesis of Harlow's. That made steering the conversation away from Cricket a piece of cake.

In one second flat Harlow was off and running about "the prissy rich girl with a stick up her butt." Hard to believe it had been fifteen years since they'd graduated. A familiar face, a vague memory, it didn't take much to hurl them back through time.

When Cricket noticed the servers bringing out trays of food, she was actually hungry.

Jade and Fletcher joined them carrying all

the drinks, but they had to wait until the salads were served.

Fletcher, who'd grown into a real hunk, knew everyone so there was lots of chitchat, while Cricket nibbled on her salad and watched her tough-as-nails friend get dreamy-eyed. Yep, there was something going on, and she wondered if it would continue beyond the reunion. Probably not. The real world was rarely so tidy.

Damn Grant. She wished more than anything that she'd never started anything with him. She knew better than to mix work with sex. God, she was thirty-two years old, not some stupid little girl.

Between the salad course and the entrée, a choice of prime rib or a tuna steak, one of the guys who'd been flirting with Harlow joined them. Cricket had been told his name, but it didn't stick. He wasn't someone she'd known from school.

A good-looking man stopped to chat up Cricket, claiming he knew her from a biology class. She didn't remember him, though she could've been a little nicer about blowing him off.

Honestly, she didn't think her mood could get any darker. But she waited. Long enough to push her food around her plate so it looked as if she'd made a dent, and then waited for the plates to be cleared. Somehow, when she was included in the conversation, she was able to respond appropriately, although it wasn't easy.

It was past time to make her exit. Instead of just vanishing, she waited until Fletcher and the other mystery man left to get more drinks, causing a natural lull. If it had just been the girls, she would have stayed and milked her malaise for all she was worth. But she was glad they were all having a good time, which also made it easier for her to bow out. "You know what?" She put her napkin on the table and stood. "I'm really not able to enjoy this like I wanted to. I hope you understand it's nothing personal, but I'm going to go back to my room. Just, if you guys decide to do brunch in the morning, or whatever, text me, okay? I don't want to miss out."

"No, Cricket." Harlow was suddenly next to her, grabbing her hand. "Please don't go. You'll get drunk. We'll all get drunk, and dance and have a great time shaming ourselves in front of the Waverly Hills gang. It's our duty."

"Thanks. But I'm just not in the right space for that. Also, get extra desserts for me and Ginny, then each of you have some. It's crème brûlée, your favorite."

After two heartening hugs, she left, just as the desserts were being served, and Nia Quail—the scourge of anyone who wasn't rich, thin and willing to follow the leader—went onstage to the dais.

"Wait for us," Jade called out as Cricket crossed to the door. "Don't leave us with these people."

Cricket couldn't help laughing. Half the room could've heard Jade, but she didn't care. She hadn't changed a bit.

Out in the corridor, the quiet was an immediate relief. At least she'd showed up, and her friends kind of understood. On her way to the elevator, she texted Ginny for the second time to make sure she was okay, and let her know she could call if she needed anything. Then she rode up to her room, anxious to kick off the heels and get to bed, let sleep put an end to the awful day.

It was only nine by the time she got to her room. She went straight to the minibar, opened the little fridge and then closed it again. Dropped her shoes off in the closet, then went back to the fridge and got out a candy bar.

She almost tore into it, but it really wouldn't make up for the crème brûlée, so she put it back. Even the liquor didn't interest her.

All she could think about was how her life had spun out of control. After she settled on the comfy couch, she thought about getting up again and changing out of her dress. Instead, she turned on the TV. There was a Sandra Bullock movie on HBO, but that didn't hold her interest for long.

Dammit, Grant was such a bastard. She should have known better. Although he'd never been a real contender for anything serious, nothing more than a guy to pass the time with. He hadn't even been that great in bed, and besides, he spent longer than her in the bathroom. She'd never figured out what he did in there that took so long, although his skin was pretty smooth.

Had he really not known her well enough to think she'd be willing to do *anything* for the firm? It was just this kind of dilemma that made her forego criminal law. It was part of her job to keep contracts legal and binding, to warn her clients when other companies were trying to pull one over. She was great with the fine print. It was the reason Burbidge had noticed her in the first place. She didn't miss a trick.

She turned off the TV. A bath called, but she'd just keep thinking, and that would ruin the whole experience. Since she rarely had trouble sleeping, she had no pills to help her out, and the thought of drinking to oblivion alone in a hotel room made her sadder than ever.

She could call Ronny. He wouldn't be asleep yet. But then she'd have to explain about work, and she didn't want him worrying about—oh. God, she was dense.

Wyatt.

For heaven's sake, it wasn't as if he hadn't been lingering in the back of her mind all evening. In spite of Grant and all his bullshit.

Oh yeah, Wyatt was just the man she wanted to see. He was the perfect distraction. Sexy, rugged, mysterious—a cocktail she was more than ready to indulge in.

Besides, she had a legit rain check.

Before she could change her mind, she slipped on her heels, reapplied her lipstick and headed out the door.

As she walked down the hall, her mood lifted more than she thought possible. What was it about that enigmatic, scruffy man that had her smiling for the first time since Grant had dropped a bomb in the middle of her life?

# CHAPTER EIGHT

WYATT STOOD BEHIND the bar, his back to the customers and staff as he lifted his shot glass. "To you, Adam," he said softly. "I miss you like hell, buddy." Then he downed the tequila. He'd held off for a couple of hours, but today had been such a stinker that he finally gave in. All it did was burn on the way down, and didn't help his mood one iota.

He should have gone to the birthday party. But his darkness wouldn't have helped things there, and probably would have affected the kids. No. It was smarter that he stayed at work, although damn, he hoped Becky was all right.

"That was tequila," Sabrina said, knocking her shoulder against his. They were both pouring drinks while Tiffy and Viv tended the tables. Most of the customers were in town for a big golf tournament this weekend, along with the usual locals, but for a Saturday night, the place wasn't all that crowded.

"Yes. It was."

"You never drink when you're working."

"Yeah, well, things change. Who knows? I might end up a drunk, just for the hell of it."

She sputtered a laugh. "Yeah, right. As if we don't have enough of them in here. Your buddy Arnie is about to fall off his chair."

"Dammit. All right. Who's free to take him home?"

"You told Viv she could clock out early. She'll get him there."

"Good."

A very dressed-up couple came into the bar, already lit. They must have left the reunion party early. Or maybe, given their weaving, they'd been asked to leave. They laughed too loud and nearly knocked the table over.

Wyatt shouldn't even be here. Not when he was this morose. But going to his apartment without anything to occupy him would be worse. He was glad Becky had decided to cut back on going to the grandparents' celebrations. She'd still send the kids, who always had a good time, but it was time for her to move on with her life. Just thinking that made his gut ache. For her. For Adam. For everyone he'd lost.

"Champagne," Viv said, interrupting his dour thoughts as she leaned on the bar. "They want Cristal."

"Did you tell them—?"

"I did. They still insisted on Cristal. The guy

waved a hundred at me. I told him no liquor stores were open this late, but he just kept waving it."

"A hundred? Cheap bastard. Tell you what, take the hundred and the Bollinger but use the ice bucket and hide the label. They're wasted already, they won't notice."

Her eyes widened. "You're kidding, right?"

"Nope."

"That doesn't sound like you at all."

He shrugged.

"If he complains, you're dealing with him."

"Sure, why not." It was just the kind of thing he imagined Grant would do. With that suit and tie and leather satchel. Dismissing Wyatt with that curled lip of condescension. Put him in a dinghy in the middle of the Persian Gulf and see how far his silk tie would get him. At that moment, Cricket appeared at the entrance like a gift, wearing a sexy gold-and-white dress, her very high heels dangling from her left hand. He watched her brush the top of her right foot over her calf to shake off the sand. When he looked up again, she was staring at him.

Grant was nowhere in sight. That helped Wyatt's mood.

And then she smiled.

After slipping on her shoes, she walked over to an empty seat at the bar. He made sure he was right in front of her.

"Is that rain check still good?" She took a

quick glance over her shoulder at the crowd. "Or maybe later?"

Damn. Why did he tell Viv she could leave early? "Give me an hour?"

"Absolutely. Give me a drink?"

"Scotch?"

"Oh, yes."

Wyatt made sure she got the good stuff, and then went back to filling orders, because now, all of a sudden, everybody wanted a damn drink. It didn't let up, which was good and bad, but he didn't have a spare minute to let the bad win. Besides, every time he looked at her, she was looking at him.

If the staff noticed he was doing double duty, mixing drinks and serving, no one mentioned it. Finally, just before he was going to throw in the towel, Viv decided the tips were too good to leave yet.

"Hey." Sabrina sidled up next to him. "If you wanna go, we've got this."

He glanced at Cricket, and then noticed another couple entering the bar. "You might get hammered with reunion people."

"So what? That means more tips. Anyway, in two hours it's last call."

Damn, he was tempted. Tiffy would help Sabrina finish up. They'd both make a few bucks extra for it, so they'd be happy. Although he had the feeling they would have done it regardless, seeing that he was finally interested in someone. That part didn't thrill him. He didn't need them making a big deal out of nothing.

"Okay. Thanks." He picked up a clean rag and wiped his hands. "If you guys get slammed, call. I shouldn't be far." He caught Sabrina's little smile before she nodded. Everyone probably thought they were headed upstairs to his apartment. Nothing he could say would change that. And then again, it wasn't that bad an idea. "Ready?" he asked Cricket.

Her eyes widened. She glanced around. "You sure? Because I can wait."

"Nope. Let's get out of here." He refused her money with a snort, and offered his hand, although she was steady in those stilts of hers. Once they were on the deck, he refused to look back. "Where to?"

"The beach?"

"Of course," he said, leading her down the path. The night was perfect for a late stroll, especially with the almost full moon. Tomorrow night would be the real deal, but this would do fine.

At the edge of the sand, she stopped and slipped off her heels. After he'd tucked them under the last step, a secret he'd learned only recently, he stashed his boat shoes, as well. It had been a long time since he'd gone barefoot.

"Oh, this feels wonderful," she said, scrunching her toes. "I've missed this. I used to be a menace on this beach, running everywhere with nothing on my feet. It didn't matter if it was freezing outside."

"That doesn't seem wise," he said, waiting for her to pick their heading.

"I was fine. By the time I was ten, the bottoms of my feet felt like leather soles. I could handle the rocks, no sweat."

"And now?"

"Try me."

He laughed. "So north or south?"

To their left, several couples were strolling along the shoreline. A breeze coming up from the south brought the sound of laughter. Cricket looked out at the gentle waves churning out silvery foam. "Too many people out here," she said. "I know a place that's more private. But beware, we might run into pirates."

"This secret place—you're staring out at the water. Should I be worried?"

"What? You can't swim?" Her wide-eyed innocent look gave way to an infectious grin.

"Okay," he said, nodding. "I see how you roll. Lead on, Captain."

There were fewer beachgoers as they walked up the craggy incline toward Pirate's Cove that was nearly a mile away. It was nice and easy, and he liked that she didn't need to fill in the quiet spaces.

It was him, in fact, that broke the silence.

"You sure you want to be climbing around in that dress?"

"What do you want me to do? Take it off?"

Wyatt thought a moment. "I'm pleading the Fifth." Evidently, she thought that was pretty funny, and laughed until she got a chuckle out of him. "What happened to your friend?"

"Which one?" She stopped and frowned. "You mean, Ginny?"

"Grant."

Her eyes closed briefly. "Colleague," she corrected. "As a rule, friends don't stab friends in the back."

"Ouch."

"Yep," she said, nodding, then started walking again. "I work for a big law firm in Chicago. You've probably never heard of it, but it's old, prestigious, places in the top fifty firms in the country. And I was very lucky to be hired right out of law school. But I'm also good at my job."

"Which is?"

"Contract law. It's nice and neat. That's the area of law I chose and what I do. I am most definitely not a criminal attorney."

"Okay..." he said, waiting for the punch line.

"Grant, my so-called friend, and his precious, very important client, who shall remain nameless, are trying to blackmail me into joining the team defending Mr. Big's son against a rape charge. Why? I have no idea. The last person they'd want representing the damn sociopath is me. I've dealt with him. I wouldn't be at all surprised if he's guilty." She stopped and stared out at the waves. "But because Richie Rich's daddy asked, I'm supposed to drop my morals and say fine. Then play to the jury—oh, wait. That's right. A focus group determined that juries tend to like me. That's why they want me on the team, even though I'm unqualified."

"That doesn't sound kosher. Wouldn't the judge object?"

"Bingo. You're not even an attorney and yet you get it. I've only had a half dozen court appearances, and I knew I was in the right. Even if I hadn't been, I'd have fought for my client. But a rape case?" Cricket shuddered. "Then again, if they're wrong about the jury, and the degenerate is convicted, they might try to use my inexperience as grounds for an appeal. Stupid bastards."

"Wow. I had no idea lawyers could be so sneaky."

She turned to look at him, and in the moonlight her eyes seemed to glow. Not necessarily from amusement. He considered offering to let her slug him, but then she laughed. A really good laugh. The kind that shook her shoulders, and made her eyes crinkle.

They were already at the dune that would lead to the small inlet at the edge of the cove where the treasure was rumored to be hidden.

"I promise I'll shut up now." She smiled. "And

how was your day?" Her voice had gone high and far too peppy.

It made him grin. "Well, let's see, I missed out on a great date with a beautiful woman, then listened to tales of woe from sloshed customers, but what can I do? I'm a bartender and that's my job."

"And I'm a lawyer, and I can tell when someone's lying."

"Really?"

"No. I was there when your favorite customer busted you for trying to use that line. I believe he said something about you telling people to stick it, you're not a therapist?"

"Nah. That doesn't sound like me."

"Uh-huh."

Wyatt paused, lost in thought for a moment. The night was perfect, the temperature, the water, the moonlit sky. It didn't seem fair. "Today's my friend's birthday."

Cricket had hiked her dress up a few inches, but she'd need to lift it higher to step over the knee-high boulder. "Oh." She turned back to look at him. "Why aren't you celebrating with him?"

"Adam's dead."

"I'm so sorry."

Wyatt shrugged. "It's been almost three years. Hell, I don't even know why I said that."

"Probably because we're strangers and I just told you something personal. So it's kind of a quid pro quo."

"It's just not my style."

Cricket touched his arm and he jumped. "Look, if you want to talk about your friend, it's okay. I'd love to be your official listener."

He studied her face in the moonlight, the earnest brown eyes and lush lips. Her skin looked soft and smooth, and he could barely think of anything else besides touching her. "Thanks," he said finally. And held out his hand. "How about I help you over the rock?"

"Why, thank you." She slipped her hand in his as she stepped over to the other side.

Releasing her hand, he let his fingers trail her lower arm. Damn. He'd never felt softer skin. Not even on the kids. And he recalled vividly how amazed he'd been the first time he'd touched Rose when she was about three. It had scared the hell out of him, he'd been so sure he would bruise her.

"Same goes for you," he said as they continued walking. "Talk all you want. Those people you work with sound like real bastards. I know the type. Sometimes you need to just hash it out. Like getting the poison out of your system."

"The last thing I want is to bore you."

Wyatt smiled. "You couldn't. Trust me. Tell me about the blackmail…what did they threaten you with?"

"Losing my job and any chance of a good reference."

"Damn. That's hitting below the belt."

"As Shakespeare so eloquently stated, 'The first thing we do, let's kill all the lawyers.'"

"Not all of them I hope." He slowed their pace as they neared the bronze marker that announced the entrance to the inlet and told the supposed history of the pirates and their buried treasure.

"Hey… I should start a hit list. I bet that would make me feel better."

"Nah. Leaving any kind of paper trail is never a good idea."

Cricket's laugh was lifted by the wind, which made it even better.

"You sure are a mystery, you know that?"

"Me?" She lifted a shoulder. "Not really."

"Classy, like the other preppies, but you're not—" Hell, he didn't want to insult her.

"A privileged jerk with an inflated sense of entitlement?"

"Your summation, counselor, not mine. But yeah, let's go with that."

Grinning up at him, she leaned a little closer on the cooling sand, the wind ruffling her shining hair. He wanted to kiss her, and he'd gotten the vibe that she was up for it, although, he'd been out of touch in that department for too long.

Now it was his turn to move a little closer. "I like you."

"Yeah?" she said, a sly grin drawing his gaze to her moist lips.

"Yeah."

# CHAPTER NINE

CRICKET SIGHED WHEN Wyatt inched toward a kiss. The gesture was nice, but unnecessary. She wanted to kiss him, had since this afternoon before Grant had shown up. Wasting no time, she met him halfway, lifting her chin so his lips pressed against hers.

Wrapping her hand around his nape, she urged him closer, and he responded in kind, pulling her against him. His chest was solid in a way that made her shiver, and the muscle she gripped to steady herself felt like iron.

When his tongue touched her lips, they parted, and the taste of tequila and him made her moan.

They explored each other, and it reminded her of all the kisses she'd tried on this beach, all the clumsy boys and the clumsy men, and those very few who made an impression. But Wyatt, he was something else altogether. It wasn't strictly technique, which was impressive, it was his stubbled jaw that was rough against her chin, the fact that she knew so little about him, and yet she wanted very much to lose herself in this enigmatic man.

His hands had moved to hold her upper arms,

and it was a lucky thing because the dune shifted under her and they both would have fallen if he hadn't been prepared. She hadn't had a clue, and this was her beach. She knew every inch of it.

Had known. She wasn't that kid anymore.

"You okay?" he asked.

Standing as they were, his eyes were shadowed, while her face was bathed in moonlight. She wished it was the other way around. "I'm fine. I think I'm just a little more tipsy than I planned on being."

He let go of her arms. "We can go back."

"Not yet." Turning to the ocean, she let the waves calm her heart. "You think there are any sunken treasures out there?"

"It's a good story. And stranger things have happened."

"Huh."

"What do you think?"

"I doubt it. So many people have tried, and with really sophisticated equipment, too. But I still like the story. I used to dream about it when I was a kid. And of course, the fish people talked about it all the time. They'd say they found gold and doubloons or whatever, but everybody always said they'd put it away somewhere safe, where no one could find it." She turned to him again. "I think they were fibbing."

"You dreamed about treasure, huh?"

"All the time. Especially after I found out about

Anne Bonny, who was a pirate that ran rings around the king's ships."

"And yet you became a contract lawyer."

"Yep. Go figure."

He moved close to her again, and took hold of her hand. Somehow that made her pulse race faster than the kisses. It was sweet. Unexpected.

They walked, quietly, her wishing she'd brought water, and him, just silent. Hand warm, firm.

"What are you going to do?" he asked, as they reached the opening of the cave that cost three dollars to explore. It was closed now, but she already knew there was nothing but junk inside, planted by the city council.

"I don't know. Chicago is home to me now, so losing my job would be…inconvenient. My friends are there."

"Any of your school buddies?"

"No. And honestly, there aren't many. I used to consider Grant one of them until he threw me under the bus. It's just that I own a condo. I'd put down roots there. I even have a little veggie garden on my balcony."

"That's putting down roots, all right."

She giggled, although she'd really worked hard on those stupid pots.

"I thought Temptation Bay was your home."

"It is. Mostly. But after my folks got divorced, I spent summers following my mother and her many husbands all over Europe. It wasn't as fun as it sounds. Too many changes. Too many husbands. But I'd always come back to my dad's for school."

"So, you're a dreamer who craved structure?"

She looked up at him again. "What did you do before you owned Sam's? Were you a therapist?"

He laughed. "No. Definitely not."

"You're either very intuitive, or I'm being extremely transparent."

He turned them both around, heading south, still holding her hand. "Well, I do know something about human nature. Bartending will do that. And you're not being transparent, just honest. Which is an admirable trait."

"Honest. Admirable, yet not worth a lot in certain circles. What about you? What on earth made you come here?"

He shrugged. "I was kind of like you in a way. My family moved around a lot. But no place was home for me, not really. Too many schools. All that packing. But I've got people here I care about. And I like this beach. I like that it's untamed in the winter and kind in the summer."

She nodded, liking the interesting way he'd described the water. "Military brat?"

"Yeah," he said, giving her a half grin.

"And your last place of residence?"

"Was just like all the others. Virginia."

"Mom or dad?"

For a second he looked puzzled, and then nodded. "My dad. And he's still at it. Hasn't retired yet."

"Wow. Must've been some pressure for you to carry the torch?"

"Definitely." He kind of laughed, and stared out at the sea. "Someone has the right idea."

She followed his gaze and saw the faint flickering light. "I used to love moonlight sails."

"Not anymore?"

"Well, not in Chicago. Though Lake Michigan is nice. It's not the ocean but an acceptable substitute, I suppose."

He wasn't dodging her, exactly, but she could tell he was reluctant. Normally, that would be a red flag, but there was something else going on just under the surface that made her want to be patient. Besides, it wasn't as though this was headed anywhere. She'd be gone soon.

For the next few minutes they watched the vague outline of the sail as it glided north on the moonlit water, and enjoyed the pleasant breeze making the night nearly perfect. Even better, his thumb was making small circles on the back of her hand. She had no idea if he even realized it.

Finally, it was Wyatt who broke the silence. "What you mentioned earlier," he said. "I did a stint in the Navy. Not so much because of the pressure, though."

"You didn't like it?"

"I did. For a while. Until I didn't."

Cricket waited for him to say more, but she wouldn't push. Although his thumb had stilled. And then it occurred to her that she should warn him about her plans, in case it mattered. "I'm not leaving tomorrow," she said, hoping it didn't stop him from sharing more about himself.

"No?"

"My dad's not feeling well, even though he refuses to admit it. So I'm going to stick around and make sure he gets a thorough checkup. You wouldn't know it by his behavior but he's not a young man anymore. I think he forgets."

"So he still lives here."

She nodded. "You know him, in fact."

"I do?"

"Ronny?"

"Surfer Ronny?"

"Yep."

He let out a laugh she couldn't interpret. "You're not kidding. That's your father?"

"Oh, yeah, he's my dad, all right."

"Huh." Wyatt rubbed his jaw. "Things are starting to make sense."

"What do you mean?"

"Classy, but barefoot."

She laughed. "Classy, huh?"

"That's not the only reason I like you, though." They started walking again.

Oh, how she wanted him to say more. But no.

Patience. Now she might have a few more days to wait it out. Or much longer, if everything fell apart at work. God, she couldn't let her mind go there and ruin the rest of her night. "So, tell me more."

"More what?"

She shot him a look and was overcome by a terrible case of the giggles. It was his expression, and her shameless attempt to get him to flatter her.

And now Wyatt was laughing, which didn't help.

After a couple of missteps in the shifting sand, and a brief run of hiccups, she was beginning to regain control. It was still touch and go when she decided to give her voice a try. "I was fishing for compliments," she said, but he showed no sign of comprehension. "You said there were other reasons you liked me. So I said—"

"Okay. I get it." It was clear he was trying not to laugh again, but he sure got her to sober up when he put his hands on her waist, and then pulled her against him as he bent his head.

His kiss was warm and sweet, but insistent. He stroked his hands up her back, and she mirrored the movement, loving the feel of his body, of all the planes and muscles of his back and shoulders. His skin was hot, and so was his breath as he swept his tongue into her mouth. A moan caught in her throat. She shuddered, and his arms tightened around her. The faint sound of laughter carried on the breeze.

At first she thought it was her imagination, but Wyatt had tensed, so clearly it wasn't.

"I should get you back," he said, although he wasn't quick to release her. He took another light swipe at her lips, just as she was about to ask for more.

The laughter was getting closer.

They pulled apart, and started walking again.

She wrapped her arms around herself to keep from shivering. It wasn't cold. Her body just missed his. "Do you have to go back to work?"

"Not sure."

She didn't think he was being evasive. His expression told her that he really didn't know. "Don't tell me you never play hooky."

"Actually, I haven't," he said, laughing. "This is the first time in the two years I've owned the bar."

"Oh, right. Like you don't have customers hitting on you all the time."

"Well, not *all* the time."

Cricket grinned. "So, what do you usually do for entertainment?"

"I'm usually wiped out at the end of the night. Or some idiot wrangles me into a poker game."

"Ah, a gambling man."

"Not so you'd notice. It's actually me who's the idiot for playing. I tend to lose more than I win."

"I don't believe that for a minute." Not with that poker face of his.

"Why would you say that?" He bumped her shoulder, and she bumped back.

"You're very observant. I'd think you'd be able to suss out the other players immediately." Plus he knew just how to answer a question without giving too much away, but she kept that to herself.

"Those games are where I let my mind wander. I don't do that at work, because I need to be on top of things, and I don't have much time off, so…"

"I can understand that."

"The stakes aren't that high, and…" He sighed. "I don't know."

"I'm not judging. I wish I had a place to let go. My life has been all about work for the last seven years, and before that it was school and internships. I go home and collapse. I wasn't even going to come to this reunion, but I'm really glad I did. Not just because of Ronny, either. It's been too long since I've seen my friends. They're good for me."

"They seemed like a lot of fun."

"We were complete misfits at Prep. The only reason I got to stay with Ronny was that school. Which my grandparents paid for. Jade was a scholarship kid, one of the fish people, and she got a lot of harassment over that. Harlow and Ginny lived in the north, but didn't fit in, either. We all worked really hard, though. Got great grades, which certainly didn't make us more popular. They were my haven growing up. Until college at least, and then, well, we spread out all across the country. But we keep in touch on Facebook. I miss them. What about you?"

"With all the moving I didn't make a lot of friends. Not until college."

"What about Adam? Was he a college friend? Or military?"

Wyatt stiffened. Not only that, he distanced himself. Not a lot, but enough for her to know that she shouldn't have asked the question. "Military," he said. "But now I live the easy life. I watch the bar, take care of my friend's kids from time to time. I run every day, past Ronny's all the way to the fish market when I need food."

"You ever hang out with the fish people?"

"I like them more than some. You'd be surprised how many Waverly Hills people are regulars at the bar."

"No, I don't think I would."

They were almost back where they'd started. Before they went down the last dune he turned in front of her. "I've enjoyed tonight."

"Me, too."

"I'm also glad you're not leaving tomorrow. Maybe we could go crazy, go out for more than just a walk."

"You wild man. I'd like that. Give me your cell phone. I'll give you my number."

She did, and when she handed the phone back, he pulled her in for another kiss, and he took his time. Stopping only to adjust the angle and deepen the kiss.

She sank into his embrace, glad it was already a new day. And so very tempted to invite him back to her room. He'd relaxed a lot since she'd foolishly brought up Adam, and still, she debated saying one more thing. But he'd been kind to her tonight. Listened to all her whining and given her carte blanche to whine some more.

She broke the kiss and looked up into his eyes. This time it was Wyatt's face bathed in moonlight. "I just wanted to say again that I hope you know you can talk to me…about anything at all. I'm happy to listen."

His eyes narrowed. He squared his shoulders, and it was as if he had actual shutters he'd closed.

"Never mind," she said, giving him her most winning smile. "It's late, and I'm a little tipsy. But I'm all in for doing something tomorrow night, if you still want to."

"Of course I do," he said.

She didn't know whether to believe him or not, but she couldn't think about it now. Being betrayed by someone she'd thought she could trust wasn't easy to get past. The best thing she could do was go to the room and get a good night's sleep. Rising up on her toes, she kissed him lightly on the cheek.

She started walking back, not getting too close to him, but not too far, either. She hoped she hadn't blown it, but she'd find out in due course.

# CHAPTER TEN

BECKY ARRIVED AT the bar just as the last customer was leaving, and Sabrina was about to lock the door.

"Hey, you're out late," Sabrina said, waving her inside.

"Yeah, I had a party to go to." She glanced around, but didn't see Wyatt. "Where is he?"

Tiffy stopped wiping down tables and exchanged a look with Sabrina.

A very odd look that hurled Becky's heart to the pit of her stomach. After an emotional dinner with Adam's grandparents… "Is everything okay? Tell me he's all right."

"Oh, yeah. Way better than okay." Sabrina burst into a grin. "Well, I don't think I'd call it a date, exactly, but—"

"Wait. Hold on." Becky put up a hand, not sure she'd heard correctly. "We're talking about Wyatt."

Both women nodded.

Viv came around the bar slinging her massive purse over her shoulder. It did nothing to dim the shock of her side-shaved-turquoise-and-yellow hair. "Quit gossiping about the boss," she said on her way to the door. "He'll be pissed."

"The hell with that," Becky said, stepping aside to let her pass. "Tell me everything."

Viv was still laughing as she let herself out.

"Come have a drink while we close out," Sabrina said, motioning for her, then pointing at a barstool.

A drink sounded perfect about now. Her mind racing, Becky took a couple of steps before she remembered Rose and Josh. "Oh, God, I can't. The kids are asleep in the car."

"Where are you parked?" Tiffy asked.

"Right outside the door," she said, glancing back at the Highlander, parked illegally so she could keep an eye on it.

They were both dead to the world, and she expected to be carrying them to their beds once they got home, but how could she have forgotten about them for even two seconds? She'd been so excited about the possibility that Wyatt was finally dating.

"I'd planned on stopping for a minute and figured Wyatt could talk to me here where we can see them. What's this about a date?" After another look at the car, she positioned herself so that it was easy to see the kids, and still hear every bit of this new development.

"She's a customer," Tiffy said. "The high-class kind. Her heels alone must've set her back five hundred bucks. Worth every penny, though. Totally awesome. I think she's here for the reunion."

Now, that surprised Becky. As far as she knew, he'd never gone out with a customer before. Claimed it was too risky. And a high-end woman? That didn't seem like Wyatt at all. Huh.

"We shouldn't have called it a date," Sabrina added, studying Becky as if only realizing now that they shouldn't have said anything in front of her. "She came in kind of late and sat at the bar."

"Yeah, but tonight wasn't the first time they met. Wyatt already knew her—" Tiffy frowned mightily. "What?"

Becky caught Sabrina trying to give Tiffy the eye. "I'm not jealous, if that's what you're thinking. There's nothing going on between Wyatt and me. God, he's like a brother."

"That's what I thought," Tiffy said, her eyebrows still cocked at Sabrina.

"Well, yeah, you thought right. It's just—the woman you described usually isn't his type."

"Oh, but she's totally cool, not like most of the reunion crowd." Tiffy started wiping the next table, a grin tugging at her mouth. "So, what is his type?"

Becky laughed. She knew quite a few of the waitresses, current and former, had crushes on him, and she could certainly understand why. "Did he say where they were going?"

Tiffy shook her head. Sabrina thought for a

moment. "I assumed upstairs." The second the words left her mouth, she winced as if she'd sucked on a lemon.

Tiffy's fake cough was far more expressive.

Becky pressed her lips together.

"I didn't think that through," Sabrina said. "It's not like I picture him in that way..."

"Sabrina!" Tiffy had both hands on her hips. "Stop."

"Right. Yes. No idea, Becky. None."

It wasn't easy to not laugh, but she held herself in check. It would be a very good thing for him to start dating. Not just for his sake, although that was important to her. They both needed to expand their horizons. Now that she'd met Ned, a Realtor who was charming and nice-looking... she smiled as she remembered his introduction. Josh had run into him in a particularly painful and awkward way at the market, and while Ned had clearly been...uncomfortable, he'd been so nice to Josh and Rose that he'd captured her interest immediately. When he'd asked her if she'd like to have some coffee, she'd agreed on the spot, insisting that she pay for whatever he wanted.

The kids had had ice cream, and she'd liked the man enough that she planned on seeing him again. Although she wasn't at all sure how to tell Adam's grandparents. Or her kids. Or Wyatt. But if Wyatt was going out with someone, that would make things easier all around.

"Becky, can I get you a drink?" Sabrina asked.

"A piña colada if it's not too much trouble."

"You got it."

Becky moved closer to the door. "Better make it a virgin," she said, keeping tabs on the SUV, knowing the kids would be out cold after running around like heathens at Grandpa and Grandma's. They'd eaten their weight in spaghetti and cake, then played on the jungle gym in the backyard.

Her thoughts strayed back to her in-laws, and how much she cared for them. It would be difficult to tell them she wasn't going to attend all the holidays anymore. Some, yes, but not all. She'd have to have a talk with them, separate from letting them know she was going to start dating. Surely they'd understand that she would always love Adam. Nothing on earth would change that. But she hadn't felt truly alive in years. Not that it would happen right away, but it needed to begin, if not for her, then for Josh and Rose. They deserved a mother at her best. Not in constant mourning.

Wyatt deserved to feel the same. He'd been dedicating himself to her and the kids and Adam's family in a wonderful way, helping all of them get through such an awful time. But he needed his own life. His own family. In fact, she'd been thinking lately that his involvement with them had been a way for him to not think about himself. It wasn't healthy, him being so stuck in the past.

"Here you are," Sabrina said, putting her drink on the table closest to the door. "If you'd like, I can run out and check that the kids are still sleeping."

"No, that's okay. I'd be able to see if they sat up. Anyway, I don't plan on staying much longer."

"You're just waiting for Wyatt to get back," Tiffy said. "But what if he doesn't?"

"Then that's his business," Sabrina said.

Becky, after taking a sip of the drink, laughed. "I'm not waiting. I'm drinking. That's different. Besides, what makes you think he'll tell us anything?"

"Yeah, like he tells us so much about himself already." Tiffy sighed dramatically, flipping her gorgeous hair back as if it were a cape. "Once he told me that when he was fourteen, he'd run away and joined the circus."

Becky almost spit out her last sip.

Sabrina's laugh was more like a bark. "That's the worst one yet."

"And him being a mob boss was better?" Tiffy said. "Or a spy for the British government. He's about as British as I'm Hawaiian."

"My favorite was that he was a stand-in for John Travolta in *Saturday Night Fever*. He wasn't even born when that was made."

Becky smiled wryly at Sabrina. Of course the woman knew a little more about Wyatt than any of the other girls. She was his backup bartender and ran the bar in his absence, but more than that, she was in trouble, and that was Wyatt's specialty. Becky had hated to hear that the poor thing was being abused by her boyfriend, and hoped she'd end it with the bastard, but at least Wyatt was intent on teaching her a few self-defense maneuvers. He'd told Sabrina he'd been in the military, but that was all.

Becky just hoped whoever this mystery woman was, she wasn't someone to be added to his collection of the walking wounded. That also needed to stop. And it wouldn't hurt if he would just be honest about himself. Well, at least more forthright.

As soon as she finished her drink she'd leave. Carry the kids into the house, tuck them in. "So, this woman. Anyone know what she does? Where she lives?"

"Nope." Tiffy switched immediately to gossip mode. "But I saw her shut down Bobby Cappelli like a pro."

"She has expensive taste," Sabrina said. "Lagavulin. Although, she did say something about liking beer."

"That's an encouraging sign. What does she look like?"

Sabrina zipped up the bank pouch. "She's got beautiful shoulder-length brown hair. And brown eyes, I think. Great taste in clothes."

"Hmm."

"What?" Tiffy said. "Still, doesn't sound like his type?"

"No, nothing like that," Becky said, hoping she didn't sound as if she was judging. Though she kind of was, which was unsettling because she honestly did think of Wyatt as a brother. "You don't think she's like most of the prep school crowd?"

"I don't know," Tiffy said. "She's not afraid to go barefoot. I know that for sure."

"Really," Wyatt's voice came from just behind Becky, and it sounded pissed. "That's all you're sure of. Not her taste in clothes? Her drink of choice?"

"Wyatt," Sabrina stammered, her face turning red.

"The door wasn't locked," he said, standing just inside. "Anyone could have come in. You could have been robbed. Killed. You all know better than that. It's the first thing you learned when you came here. You, too, Becky."

Without realizing it she'd sat down. She stood up immediately.

But he ignored her and finished putting the last few chairs on top of the tables. He didn't look at any of them, or say another word. He'd gone straight to Silent Warrior mode. She recognized the version of him from the day they'd met. Stoic, silent, keeping every emotion locked tight inside. The girls scampered to get everything put into place.

Becky wasn't quite so intimidated. As soon as he finished his demonstration of strength and fortitude, she walked over to him, took his arm and pulled him out the door.

"THE KIDS ARE asleep in the car," Becky said. "I had planned to stop for just a few minutes."

Wyatt clicked back to reality. She had just come from the party. He had no business jumping down her throat. "Hey, how was it? How are you?"

She shrugged. "Not quite as bad as last year. But still difficult. They miss him so much. Yvette made all the kids' favorites, and spaghetti of course, the way Adam liked it. Peter played with them outside, until Yvette had to force him to come in. He was winded, and I got him to sit down and drink some water. I think he needs to go back to his cardiologist. I don't know. Getting them to slow down is rough. And of course, they told all the old stories about Adam. And about you."

Wyatt cringed. "I should have gone. It was a mistake to skip this one. It's only been—"

"Years, Wyatt. It wasn't a mistake at all. In fact, it helped me."

That made no sense. "How?"

"Look, I know it's not my business, but I'm

glad you went out with someone tonight. That's fantastic. You haven't done anything for yourself since you moved out here."

"It was nothing," he said, wishing like hell she hadn't brought it up. "She's only here for a little while. And dammit, Sabrina knows better than to leave the door unlocked."

"I'm pretty sure she did it for my sake," Becky said, quietly. "I kept checking on the munchkins."

He glanced at the car as something occurred to him. "You stayed late. What's up with that?"

"The kids were asleep and Yvette and I were still talking… Now quit avoiding me. I don't care if this woman's only here for one night. Tell me about her."

He didn't want to, but Becky's concerned look got to him. Besides, he owed her for not going to the party. He leaned his elbows on the railing. "She's nice. Smart. An attorney from Chicago. She's sophisticated, but she grew up here, on the south side with her father. But she also traveled a lot in Europe with her mom…" He was surprised he'd said so much. Although given how much he'd been thinking about her, maybe not so surprising.

"She sounds fascinating. And from what I gathered, quite the looker."

A smile slipped out before he caught it. "She's pretty. And I enjoyed our walk."

"Only a walk?"

"Yes. Only a walk. We went out to the pirate

thing. Looked at the ocean. She told me about her job, and I…beat around the bush."

"No." Becky faked a gasp. "You?"

His grunt made her smile.

"It's good for you to get out of your routine, even if it's for a couple of hours. To be with someone who interests you." She leaned on the rail beside him, staring out at the moonlit water. "I wanted to tell you something. You know I would never want the children to forget about Adam. That I'll always keep his memory alive no matter what. Right?"

"Yeah. Of course."

"He'll forever be in my heart. Which doesn't mean I'm not going to move on."

"What?"

"It's hard, all right? It's hard to even admit it to you. But I'm not being the mother I could be, the woman I should be. I've been locked inside a bubble I don't want to break. But I need to start living again." She drew in a deep breath. "I've actually met someone. He seems nice, and if he asks me, I'm going to go out with him."

Wyatt felt gut shot. How could she even…

He closed his eyes. She'd said herself it had been years. That was true. And her kids were growing up fast. He'd known Becky before. She'd been vibrant and alive and she'd made Adam happier than he'd ever been. He'd loved her so much.

Her and the kids. How dare Wyatt not want her to be that joyful again.

It felt impossible, but she deserved a full life. Adam's grandparents might not ever get over his loss, and in truth, neither would Becky. But things could change in time. That's what everyone told him. "Adam wanted everything for you," he said, although it felt as if the words tore his throat open. "Even someone else to love you, as long as he loved you well."

"He wanted that for you, too, Wyatt."

He reached out and touched her arm. Wanting her to believe him, no matter what he'd sounded like.

She put her hand over his. "You deserve to be content and purposeful and, dammit, in love. I mean it," she said softly. "And you deserve to stop feeling responsible for Adam's death."

# CHAPTER ELEVEN

CRICKET WALKED SLOWLY across the sand, shoes in hand, a wide-brimmed hat shading her eyes. Her smile hadn't left since brunch. Her friends were amazing. All of them. God, she'd missed them.

Harlow had made them all promise to show up at the Yacht Club mixer at four o'clock because she'd met the manager, a tall, handsome ex-football player, whom she'd liked enough to postpone her trip home until tomorrow morning.

Jade was going home tonight. And Ginny, who'd been a little subdued, had still promised to go to the mixer with Cricket.

It had all been wonderful. The mimosas, the eggs Benedict, telling her friends about Grant and her issues at work. Not that she'd shared all. No, she'd reserved that dubious honor for Wyatt last night. And gotten a great night's sleep because of it.

Despite not hearing the worst of Grant's traitorous behavior, Jade offered to find out what scents he was allergic to, and send him a large batch of cologne that would make him suffer. Cricket had been tempted, but the truth was, her determination had withered a little in the light of the new day. There was more than her pride at stake, and she had to carefully think through her next moves. The firm really could make her life a misery, and she was used to a certain lifestyle, which she thought didn't matter, but she wasn't a rash person, not ever, and she wouldn't start now.

But the gloomy subject of her career dropped the moment she'd mentioned her evening with Wyatt. Everyone had hoped it would turn into something more intimate, but Cricket kept quiet on that front, as well, although she was looking forward to the same thing.

As if her thoughts had summoned him, her cell rang with his number. She wished she wasn't on the crowded beach, but she was an old hand at blocking out noise. "Good afternoon," she said, plugging her open ear with her finger.

"Is it?" he asked, sounding a little grumpy.

"What's wrong?"

"Nothing."

"You sure? Remember, I'm a good listener and you sound…"

"Like a grouch. I know. One of my waitresses was MIA when we opened, so I had to fill in. Her excuse when she finally arrived was pitiful. To atone, she's staying late tonight."

"Oh?"

"Which means, if you're still up for it, we can go out anytime you want."

"I'm definitely up for it. Have anything specific in mind?"

His deep, raspy chuckle made her pulse flutter. No big mystery what he was thinking. Then he said, "Not yet."

"Good. I have an idea. How awful would it be if I sent you to pick up food and we ended up eating on the deck at the hotel?"

"Not awful at all. You don't like any of the local haunts?"

"No, I do. It's just that this is the last day of the reunion, and I promised a friend I'd go to the mixer at the Yacht Club. I'll be there until five. I thought we could eat at six because, well, I kind of made arrangements for a little surprise at seven thirty."

"For?"

"You. For us."

"Oh, really?" he said, his voice lowering.

She laughed. "Not that kind of surprise."

"Oh." He sounded disappointed.

"Not that I wouldn't be interested in that kind of... Oh, hell, you know what? I'm going to just walk away from that." Before she tripped over the sand. "So, does the timing work for you? If you'd rather, we can order food and still do the rest. Or something else entirely."

She heard that deep chuckle again. "Your plan is great. I'll see you on the deck at six, with dinner. And maybe, if you get there first, you can order me a drink."

"What kind?"

"You choose. I'm looking forward to whatever you have in store."

"Me, too. See you later."

She disconnected and grinned until her cheeks ached. She'd already picked out what she was wearing tonight, and while the resort didn't usually let people bring their own food on the deck, turned out she knew one of the assistant managers, who'd been happy to help her with her surprise. The best part would be what happened after, if Cricket had her way.

Of course she wasn't going to tell Ronny anything about Wyatt. Or her job. She was worried enough about him and his health to add stress to his already booked schedule. The summer was always like this for him, and she was glad she'd have a couple of hours before the mixer to meet with him. If he hadn't already told her about tonight's booking, she would never have accepted Wyatt's proposal to get together.

The thought made her butterflies stir, but she would put them to bed before she got to Ronny's. Who already had quite a contingent of surfers spread out in front of the shack.

She recognized Igor, Wendy and Jim, but not the others. One of whom looked a lot older than Ronny's usual crowd. Maybe closer to her age.

"Hey, Cricket," Igor said, before she'd even reached the side of the shack. "You coming in today? We've got a nice three-foot swell, which is rare for this late in the day."

"Nope. I'm just visiting Ronny, but you all have fun." Stepping over surfboards, mostly fish and longboards, she gave her shave-and-a-haircut knock, then walked in to find her father putting out the coffee makings, and also the blender and a tub of vanilla ice cream. "You're determined to fatten me up, aren't you?"

"If I can. But honestly, I just like making things you love."

"You don't have to, you silly man. I'm happy just to be here with you. I meant it when I told you I was staying on for a few more days."

"Can you make it a week?"

"I can try. I have the vacation time I'm owed, but I also have to—"

"Consider work. I know the drill."

"If I hadn't just finished brunch with my lunatic friends—who all say hi by the way—I'd be all over that shake. Maybe tomorrow?"

"What? I'm seeing you three days in a row?"

He looked so happy. Wearing his board shorts and his ancient Channel Islands surf T-shirt, there was no one in the world who seemed to love his life more than Ronny. And her, of course. He'd always adored her, no matter what. "You know I still call her Mom and not Victoria."

He looked startled, and why not, since it came out of nowhere. "Why?"

"She's just Mom. That's all. And you are always Ronny."

He put his hands on his narrow hips. "I'm going to take that as a compliment."

"Good." She walked to the cabinet where he'd put the second coffee maker, and started fixing a drinkable pot. "Did you make an appointment with Ira?"

"That's Dr. Zachi to you, young lady."

"So, that's a no. All right, if you won't do it, I will."

"The hell you will. It's the height of the season. I've got bookings up the wazoo and you want me to take hours out of my schedule for a checkup? I don't need it."

She finished counting out the scoops of coffee grinds, then turned to him, her own hands on her hips. "Yes, you do. Don't even try to talk me or yourself out of it. It's clear you've lost weight you can't afford, and I'm guessing you're having dizzy spells you neglected to tell me about. That means a full physical."

"No. I will not. I am not having dizzy spells. For God's sake, Baby Girl, I know when I'm healthy and when I'm not."

She laughed. Hard. "You were in a surfing competition when you had walking pneumonia. Once you had a broken wrist and still took a group of drunks deep sea fishing. You've pulled every muscle in your body, and I'm pretty sure you've broken almost every bone, and you always wait until it's so serious that you've almost died twice."

"Fine. I was more reckless when I was young. But I'm older now—"

"And just as reckless. I'm calling Ira first thing tomorrow."

He crossed to her and put his tanned hands on her shoulders. "Don't make me get mad. You hate it when I put my foot down."

"Very funny. I'll be the one getting mad if you make light of this. I'm going to take you to your appointment, and I'm going to be there when you're done, and I'm going to speak to Ira."

"Baby Girl, you're crazy if you think I'm getting a physical now. When the weather turns and business slacks off? You bet. I'll have Ira call you with the results." He crossed his heart.

"As if that's going to convince me."

"Gotta go get the boat ready. I have a sunset sail tonight and a fishing charter early tomorrow."

"It's only a quarter to three, and you told me you were free until four."

He dropped his hands and turned his back. "I lied."

She slid her arms around him, right over his arms, holding him tight. "You never lie. Not to me, and you aren't starting now."

"Let me go. I've got work to do."

"You've got to go, Dad. I mean it. Don't make me go back to Chicago and worry every single day that I'm going to get a phone call that something's happened to you. I can't bear the thought of that."

Ronny moaned. "Dad? You just said I was always Ronny."

"Unless you're making me terribly sad," she said, letting him loose.

"Blackmail. Below-the-belt blackmail."

"You're mixing up your metaphors."

"It's my shack, I'll mix up whatever I please."

"Do you want me to call Ira tomorrow?"

"No. I have to work things out. Find out how long this physical will take. It'll have to be on a day I don't have a charter booked. I can get Igor or Jim to step in for my surf lessons, so that part's no sweat."

"Fine, but you're to call me as soon as you've got the arrangements made. I mean tomorrow, Ronny. Not next Friday. I do have to return to work, so please try your best."

"How I let you manipulate me so easily is something I will never understand."

"Yeah, it's so hard when you're the biggest softy in the world."

"I'm not," he said, although it was a weak retort. Then he went to the fridge, put the ice cream back in the freezer and brought himself out a bottle of beer.

"I'll be right back," she said, heading toward the back of the house.

"Don't be long. We don't have much more time, and I want to talk about things that will cheer me up."

"Think good thoughts. I won't be a minute." She used the facilities, then when she passed her father's bedroom, something on his dresser stopped her before she reached the hallway door. It was a picture, one she knew wasn't there yesterday. Expecting to find one of herself, she was a little taken aback when it turned out to be an old photo of her mother. From when Cricket was a toddler. When they were still married. She knew Ronny had taken the shot, and that the look of love and contentment on her mother's face was from staring at her husband.

She picked up the frame and went back to the kitchen. "What's this?"

"Just what it looks like."

"She was gorgeous, wasn't she?"

Ronny smiled. "Yep. Still is, I imagine."

"Is she the reason you never married again?"

He stopped between one step and the next. For a split second, she thought he might be dizzy, but he slowly shook his head as he put his other foot down. "I never met the right woman."

"I worry about you being alone."

He pointed to the window, where it was blocked by surfboards that weren't his. "I never get the chance." He plucked the frame from her hands, and put it on the table, then pulled her into a hug. After a minute, he moved his head back so his mouth was about level with her ear, although she couldn't see him. "I'll always love your mother," he whispered. "And I knew, still know, that I'd never do better."

Cricket sighed. She believed him. It had been a bitter blow to him, when they'd separated and eventually divorced. All because of her strait-laced, disapproving grandparents, Connecticut blue bloods from way back, who couldn't see past their patrician noses. She doubted they'd given Ronny one single chance.

It was all so sad. Love was such a fickle thing. Not that she had any personal experience. She just wished that Ronny could've let go and moved on. And now Cricket had to wonder if that was also the reason her mother had married so often.

Wyatt hadn't planned on the food taking so long, but he managed to get to the Seaside on the Bluff five minutes early. He ended up letting the valet park his truck, which was ridiculous, but the food was hot and so was Cricket.

He wore chinos, a button-down tan shirt and a charcoal sports jacket, although he'd actually had to think about the choices. That hadn't happened since…in a long time. He hurried through the hotel lobby, and he found Cricket at an ideal table—great view, no one on their left, a table with a couple facing away from them on the right and a beer for each of them with the place settings. But the real treat was her.

She stood, reaching out for one of the bags, and he looked her over with great appreciation. Her top was kind of a bra-ish type thing with flowers on it, and below it was a strip of bare skin that bordered on an almost translucent flowing skirt covered by the same floral pattern. Gave him a tempting view of her great legs.

"My eyes are up here, sailor," she said.

"Pardon me, ma'am, but you look too good for a quick glance."

"You're forgiven."

He put his bag on the table, and while he wanted to pull her into a serious kiss, he held back. Not to say he didn't kiss her lips and let her know he was happy to see her, but it wouldn't cause a scandal.

It helped that she kissed him back just as eagerly.

When they parted, their eyes locked for several heartbeats. More than several. Her cheeks pinked and finally, she shifted her gaze to the bags. "I know these bags. These bags are from Iggy's. I love their food. What did you get?"

"Open it up."

Her eyes widened as she pulled out the lobster rolls, four stuffed quahogs and a large serving of cinnamon sugar doughboys. "This is everything I ever wanted."

"Really?" He grinned, but he was very pleased with her reaction. "More than, say, winning the lottery, or a place on the Supreme Court?"

She looked him straight in the eye, without a hint of joking. "Yes. I dream about this food. More than is healthy. I have to eat this lobster roll right this second. I hope you don't mind if I ignore you completely."

"Not at all."

She did exactly that. Sat down with her roll, bared it and took a large bite. Her lashes fluttered closed and her moan made him itchy for how he hoped the evening would end.

In the meantime, he pulled out the rest of their food, and got himself comfortable. She'd even ordered Town Beach Pale Ale, the local favorite made one town over. "I should probably work more on my accent," he said. "I'm a big fan of the cuisine."

She hummed a vague response, way more interested in the lobster than him. But he didn't mind. To be fair, the lobster rolls were one of the best things he'd ever eaten. It was also sexy as hell to watch her enjoying her food so much. He had an excellent window into what he could expect if they capped the night off between the sheets, and frankly, it was difficult not to get carried away.

"Aren't you going to eat?"

"Yes. I was going to have the second roll, but if you want another, I can move on to the quahog."

"No. God. Thanks, though." She took a healthy drink of beer. "I plan to eat two quahogs and at least two doughboys. I like the cinnamon sugar ones the best. Very good guessing on your part."

He bowed his head graciously. "I tried to figure out what a woman like you would want."

She almost choked. "And you came up with *this*?"

Wyatt frowned. "Okay, are we still talking about food?"

"If we aren't, I suppose we should be," she said, laughing and dabbing her mouth with a napkin. "So, back to these lobster rolls—"

"Hold on. Let's not be hasty…"

"Nope. Not going there. Yet." She started laughing again. Must've been the hopeful puppy dog eyes he was giving her. "Okay, so you just got your favorites, and by sheer chance they happened to be mine. Is that your story?"

"Not exactly."

"Then Ronny told you, although why, I can't imagine."

He had to grin at that. "He did. Before I knew you, in fact."

"What? Why were you talking about me?"

"I think he talks about you to everyone. He didn't go into details, or anything touchy. Not with me, at least."

"What I like to eat isn't details?"

"Well, I meant personal things like boyfriends or what you actually did, other than that in his opinion, you're the best and smartest lawyer in the country. Ruth Bader Ginsburg, be damned."

Cricket smiled. "I suppose it's only fair. I think he's the best surfer in the world. And a terrific dad. He really is. It's probably easy to assume he was too permissive when I was young, but he wasn't. He'd come down hard on me if I needed it, but he was always fair."

"It's nice that you two like each other."

"You don't like your parents?"

"I respect my father, and I care for my mother, but it's not a mutual admiration kind of thing."

"That's a shame. What about siblings?"

"One brother."

"Do you two get along?"

"Yeah, when we see each other. Which isn't very often."

"I would've liked to have siblings. I think." She took another bite and thought while she chewed. "Friends might be better, though. You get to choose them."

Wyatt smiled. "Good point." Naturally his thoughts went to Adam. He'd been both a friend and a brother. The best kind. Huh. Wyatt realized he was thinking of Adam and still smiling. Might be a first. "Well, you hit the jackpot with Ronny. Being a friend and a father can't be an easy thing to balance."

"True. And you're right. He is something special. So is my mother in her own way. I was too young to remember anything about their split, of course, but I know my grandparents and that she'd stood up to them at all, and married Ronny… Well, that says a lot."

Since Wyatt had started on his lobster roll, he had to take a moment before he could respond. "My father was very strict, very Navy. I rebelled all through high school, telling everyone I was going to be a race car driver, sure I'd hit it big. But I also joined ROTC. When it came time to pick my first choice for college, it was the Naval Academy. Not just to prove myself to him, but to myself, I think. And partly because Nelson—my brother—was in his junior year there."

"I bet your dad's proud as hell."

He took another bite, and nodded, which wasn't exactly a lie. Just close.

Cricket got out the stuffed quahog, the big shell filled with chopped clams, a bunch of spices, bread crumbs and hot sauce.

"This is so good," she said, digging in. "They sell clams in Chicago and call them quahogs, but they really aren't."

"I was gonna get you a chowda and a grinda, but I was runnin' late."

She giggled at his accent, so much that her cheeks and the tips of her ears were pink. "Fuggeddaboudit. Dees sangwidges and stuffies are a reglar paty."

"I can't even begin to compete with that. Did you ever have an accent?"

"No," she said, in her natural voice. "My grandparents would've slapped it out of me if I had—figuratively speaking of course. Now chow down, because we have to be somewhere at seven thirty on the dot."

"You won't tell me where?"

She just kept on eating, smiling and looking beautiful.

CRICKET HAD LEARNED about the resort's hidden gem a couple of years ago, though she'd never been. She hadn't known anyone who had, but it sounded so charming it was on her bucket list.

"I've never seen anything like this before," Wyatt said, his expression equal parts surprise and amusement as they walked slowly down the aisle of puzzles, each one handcrafted. "Handcut puzzles for two, made of cherrywood. They look complicated."

She nodded. "They're devilishly difficult because some pieces can fit in more than one space.

Oh, and they have a wine service with some pretty nice selections."

"So we'll be here all night?"

"No. We can leave whenever, and they'll save our puzzle for us to come back to later, if we want. Or we can try one of their Tidbits, which are only fifty pieces."

"I'll follow your lead," he said, taking her hand. "Since this is your surprise."

His warm firm grip had her rethinking the evening, but then she saw the host coming to take them to their table and she decided to stick with the plan. For the time being, anyway. He led them past some plush banquettes and family-sized tables to a separate alcove set aside for couples. There, he gestured to a love seat at the far table, nearly private, as all the tables to their right were empty.

The puzzle she'd reserved was already spread out on the beautiful teak table, the box showing the completed prize set on a frame next to it at the far edge.

"Treasure Trove," Wyatt said. "I'm sensing a theme here."

"We can select another one if you'd like."

"No, this is fine."

"May I send over the sommelier?" the host inquired.

"Yes, please," she said.

Once they were alone, Wyatt leaned in. "A sommelier just for the puzzles?"

"There's also one for the spa, and for the deck." Cricket picked up the list that had been left on the table for them.

She chose a glass of Chablis while Wyatt ordered a Merlot. They sat close to each other, their hips and shoulders touching. It was the easiest thing to lean on him, to kiss him when he found the right puzzle piece. Easier still was the way his hand rested on her knee as he searched the table, his thumb petting her with light, swift strokes.

When she successfully added to the Treasure Trove, he turned so his mouth was near her ear and then he talked like a pirate in a low, gravelly voice. "You'll never get my booty."

She laughed so loudly several people turned to look at them, as if she'd just slammed a book down in a library. That didn't stop her, though.

The hand on her knee went to the small of her back, and his lips pressed against her neck. She felt more than heard his laughter, and while she tried to call him out on his blatant cowardice, he stalled her silent with a lick and a nibble where neck met shoulder.

When he finally sat up again, she met his highly pleased gaze.

"Think that was slick, huh?"

"Aye," he said. "Matey."

"Is this going to continue all night?"

He blinked. "I know a very good way of shutting me up."

"Do you now? Matey."

He looked at the barely started puzzle. "How set are you on finishing this thing?"

"Not very. But we haven't even gotten our wine yet."

"I'll buy you a bottle."

"We'll see," she said, as she picked up half of a doubloon bit and connected it to its other half.

He immediately put his mouth to her ear. "Shiver me timbers. Please."

She did it again. Laughed too loud. Leaned too close. Closed her eyes when at the first touch of his lips on her neck.

At some point, he sat up and they stared at each other, grinning. His eyes were so full of mischief it was all she could do not to grab his hand and run for her room. Just as Wyatt squeezed her knee, the waiter showed up with their wine.

She thanked him, took a sip and forced herself to search for the next piece of the puzzle. She realized it wasn't working when she tried fitting the same sword into the same pirate's hand three times. In a row. She needed another distraction.

"So," she said, no longer whispering, "do you like fishing?"

Wyatt somehow did a completely still double take. "I'm not big on fishing, no. I tend to get my seafood at the dock."

"Good," she said, and while she meant to continue this lively discussion, Wyatt took her hand in his, then moved it to his thigh. High up on his thigh. She felt his heat through his chinos. "Yeah, I think the puzzle can wait."

"Amen to that." Wyatt pulled some bills from his pocket and laid them on the table.

"No, this is my—"

He caught her hand and pulled her to her feet. They abandoned the puzzle and their wine without so much as a backward glance as the two of them darted out from their love seat and hurried past the other tables.

As soon as they made it to the lobby Wyatt asked, "Where to?"

"Is that a joke?"

"Does it help that I have all my fingers crossed?"

"So, Ronny's it is, then."

The way his eyes widened in absolute horror made her laugh.

"Fine. If you're going to be that way, I suppose we could go to my suite," she said, and shivered as his expression changed. He was staring at her with so much longing her stolen breath got in the elevator way before she did.

## CHAPTER TWELVE

THE SUITE WAS exceptionally large. Done in tones of blue, white and polished wood, the living room had a fireplace, a roomy couch, a couple of wing chairs and a bank of windows that showcased the vast blue water of the Atlantic. "Pretty swanky," Wyatt said. "How many suites do they have?"

"No idea. Everything else was sold out. Now I'm just sorry that I didn't let the firm pay for the damn thing. Grant had offered. Maybe I'll turn it in as an expense anyway, since they're already planning to can me if I stand my ground. Quite possibly if I don't. You know, not being a team player and all."

He pulled her into his arms and looked into her gorgeous brown eyes. "The only time it makes sense to play for the team is when the team has earned your loyalty."

"I shouldn't have brought it up." She ran her hands up his back. "Let's not talk about unpleasant things when there are so many enticing discussions we could be having."

"For instance…?"

"Wine. I'm going to order a bottle. Anything you want to add to it?"

He kissed her lightly, briefly brushing his lips against hers. "I'd like to say for the record that I've been thinking about you since I woke up this morning. I would have been fine if we hadn't ended up here, but I'm glad we did."

"I would have been disappointed as all get-out if you hadn't joined me. I've been dying to see those abs the waitresses are always mooning over."

"That's it? You just want me for my abs?"

"Don't know. I haven't seen them yet."

Wyatt grinned and slid his hands lower down her back, stopping short of her nice round bottom. She felt good and smelled good, which was having a predictable effect on his body. "You mean to check out all the optional equipment before you let me return the favor?"

"I'm pretty sure what came standard is going to be fantastic."

"Quite the sweet-talker, aren't you?"

Cricket bubbled up with laughter. "Actually, no. I must've come up with that by accident."

Wyatt laughed with her. For so long he'd felt like an engine running on fumes, but not when he was with Cricket. A smile, a brief touch, a sassy quip, it didn't take much to fire up something inside him.

He probably should just get the ball rolling

since his erection was getting a little out of hand. "Now, wine. You have bottled water, right?"

"Yep."

"And other necessities? I brought a couple condoms, but if there's anything you'd care to add to the festivities, that would be A-okay with me."

"Wow, hadn't thought beyond the basics." She kissed him on the lips, but just as he was getting ready to take that to the next level, she broke away, and backed up straight into the bedroom.

Which was large. The centerpiece was a four-poster, king-size bed. On one side was another fireplace and sliding glass doors that led to a balcony. On the other side was what looked to be one hell of a bathroom. He caught a glimpse of a large tub, which he'd make sure to remember. Later. After he had her all to himself in that bed.

It took a moment to fold down the soft fancy sheets and turn on the overhead fan, which set the perfect breeze swirling around them. He removed his sports jacket as he listened to her order the wine, then unbuttoned his shirt. Belatedly, it occurred to him that they should've waited to call room service…later, in an hour or so. He sure as hell wasn't going to feel like getting out of bed to answer the door.

Although they could still delay the order. Before he could make the suggestion, she'd hung up the phone.

She watched him shrug out of his shirt. "Holy

mother-of-pearl, I'm totally keeping my clothes on. You'll just have to get creative and work around it."

"Like hell you will." He probably sounded like a caveman, but he hadn't wanted a woman this much in a while. "Come on, take off that bra-top thing."

"Bra-top thing?" Evidently Cricket thought that was funny.

"Now would be a good time."

"Is that right?" Her grin was a quarter shy and three-quarters wicked. It slackened when she noticed the ugly scar on his chest, but came right back.

"How else can I kiss every inch of you?"

Her gaze lifted and her mouth opened, but she didn't speak at first, then said, "Well, I guess there's no arguing with that."

"Nope." He moved closer to her. "Just in case I can be of assistance."

"Let's make sure you can get those chinos off without hurting yourself."

He looked down at the insistent bulge. "I'm pretty good with my hands. I think I'll manage."

After reaching behind her back, she did that thing women did that always drove him a little nuts. He could tell she was undoing the strap, but only by the movement of her elbows. It shouldn't have been hot at all. Then the top fluttered to the floor.

Meaning to unfasten his button, his hand stilled completely. "Aren't you a stunner," he said, his voice lowered as his libido rose.

Blushing, she motioned for him to hurry. "I was thinking," she said, slipping off her sandals, and swaying just enough to make him want to moan. "We should postpone the wine."

"I agree. I meant to say something."

"Why didn't you?"

"I was a little distracted."

"Oh. Then you're forgiven."

"Thanks." He slowed himself down as he unzipped his fly. "You need me to help you with that skirt?"

"Nope. Although, I wouldn't put up a fuss. Only after you've disrobed."

"I'm at your service, ma'am."

"I'm not old enough to be a ma'am."

"It's got nothing to do with age, all to do with respect."

Her face changed. It wasn't obvious like her grin or her sexy little pout. This was something new. A moment of clarity, he guessed. If he was wrong, he honestly didn't want to know. Some things were meant to be unspoken.

After dropping his chinos, he stepped out of them and folded them the way he'd been trained. His clothes had been set on a tufted bench at the base of the bed. Everything except for his boxer briefs.

"Daniel Craig just dropped two spots," Cricket said, giving him a leisurely once-over. Twice. "I'm used to guys with gym bodies. I'm not talking about weight lifters, either. I mean guys who take care of themselves and look good." She finally met his eyes. "Not that I've dated a wide range…"

Admittedly, Wyatt had started to wonder.

"But you, sir, are a damn fine-looking man."

"Yeah, yeah," Wyatt said, trying to hide his embarrassment. "Quit stalling."

She let out a soft laugh. "I'm not."

This time when her gaze drew to the scar, he said, "Afghanistan," and thankfully, she just nodded.

He stepped closer to her as he lowered his briefs, using his thumbs. There was an adjustment made, then things moved smoothly down and down. When his underwear hit his feet, he stepped out of them, and reached with both his hands underneath Cricket's skirt. Which he then proceeded to raise, little by little, letting his palms brush the silky skin that was slowly being revealed.

"Oh." Her voice caught on a gasp. "There went Matt Damon."

He'd reached the swell of her hips, and yet he managed through great determination to not rip the damn skirt off and throw her on the bed. He kept going, until he reached a pair of skimpy pink panties that matched her budded pink nipples. He could feel the heat from her body, smell the sweet scent of her skin. It was driving him crazy.

"I have a confession to make," he said, purposely moving his gaze to her eyes. And if he'd slowed down at her chest area, well, that couldn't be helped.

"What's that?"

"I have no idea what to do with this much skirt now that I've gotten it up here."

Her laughter was the perfect note. It set the tone, as if everything else hadn't, for an evening that he wanted to savor.

When she pushed down the whole thing, including those little panties, he thanked the stars that he'd somehow gotten his luck back. Now, if he could only hold on to it for the night, he'd be in heaven.

It had to be a dream, Cricket decided, even as she ran a hand across his muscled shoulders and down his broad, hard chest. Wyatt couldn't be for real. For God's sake the man actually listened. If she were to give him a quiz, she'd bet the farm that he'd be able to repeat everything she'd ever told him. Granted, she'd known him for only a few days, but that didn't matter. Most of the guys she knew back in Chicago would've used the time to talk about every little detail that made them God's gift to the universe.

Even the way he touched her was a revelation. Slow, gentle hands, purposeful and thrilling, the long, deep kisses, while paying close attention to what she liked, what she craved and what she wanted to do more than once—which was just about everything. Wyatt had very clever hands. Among other things.

This man was so different, and so…mysterious. She wanted to know much more than she did, and she wanted him to want to tell her.

Then again, maybe it would be a mistake to learn more about him. Because, God, he was perfect. And she would be leaving soon, so why risk tarnishing her impression?

No way was Cricket going to linger on that thought, not when he slid down, under the covers, leaving a damp trail between her breasts with his tongue.

Closing her eyes, she clutched at his hair.

Perhaps too hard.

"You okay?" he asked, lifting his head from about halfway down the mattress.

She nodded, unwilling to sit up until her heartbeat had eased away from the panic zone. No clue where that had come from. Was it the thought of leaving Temptation Bay? Of not having a job to return to?

"Good. There are miles to go before we sleep."

"Miles, huh?"

He gave her a crooked grin. "I sure hope so.

Fair warning, you've already taken me past my old record."

"Twice is…well, two and a half times is your record? I don't believe it."

"Fine. My record after I turned thirty. Happy now?"

"Wait. What was the record when you were in your twenties?"

He just smiled and went back to pleasuring her until she was a shivering mass of need.

SOMETHING WAS RINGING. Her phone? Or was it a dream? But that couldn't be because Cricket had nodded out for only about two minutes, five tops. Probably her phone. Thankfully, it stopped before she'd even opened her eyes.

"CRICKET?"

That was Wyatt's husky voice.

"Huh?"

"That's your phone," he murmured, his face buried against the side of her neck. He slowly moved the arm he'd thrown over her while they'd slept, but she caught it and held him firmly in place.

She snuggled closer and he lightly squeezed her bare ass. "It'll go away. Honest. Go back to sleep." She breathed out a yawn, and that was it.

"CRICKET?"

THIS TIME, SHE MANAGED to lift her head a little.

No way was she opening her eyes, but at least she'd made an effort. "Huh?"

"Your cell keeps going off. I think it might be important."

"Important?" Her head dropped again. Damn telemarketers. "It's the middle of the night."

"It's six forty-five."

"A.M.?" She opened one eye to a slit. Sunlight was sneaking in through the gap between the drapes.

"It's still ringing. If you tell me where it is, I'll go get it for you."

"You sure it isn't yours?"

"I'm sure."

"Dammit. If it's a telemarketer, I'll—" It dawned on her that it was probably Grant.

It would be like him to call early and wake her. The bastard. She would've preferred a telemarketer.

Wyatt was next to her, under the covers, his hair wild on the white pillow, his scruff darker. Their legs were tangled together, and neither made a move to break apart. "Want me to get it?" he asked, and started to pull away.

The room faced west, and was far too bright. Her cell was in the other room, by her purse because no one was supposed to call her. At least not at this ungodly hour.

"I'll take care of it," she said and kissed his chin. "But thanks."

He caught her arm as she was about to get up. "Come back to bed after, huh?"

"Oh, yeah."

Ironically, it was his sleepy smile that woke her up a bit. She segued by the bathroom and grabbed one of the robes, pulled it on, then found her purse just where she'd left it. The phone had stopped ringing, though.

The temptation to turn the stupid thing off and go right back to bed was quite inviting. But as she reached to shut it down, another ring came through. She picked it up, and read the caller's name. Temptation Bay Hospital.

That woke her up completely, and before the caller could say a word, she asked. "Is this about Ronny Shaw?"

Although she already knew it was.

## CHAPTER THIRTEEN

"YOU HONESTLY DON'T have to come in," Cricket said, walking as quickly as she could from the parking lot. According to the nurse, Ronny hadn't been seriously hurt. That was the main thing.

Wyatt didn't respond other than to keep pace with her.

"Thank God Skip was with him and called the paramedics," she muttered for what had to be the twentieth time. Wyatt was probably sick of hearing it.

"Doesn't Skip normally go with him on charters?"

"I don't know, but my dad was getting ready to take out a group, so maybe..." Cricket sighed. If Ronny had been feeling poorly but didn't want to admit it, he might've started taking Skip with him under the guise of wanting to *show Skip the ropes*. That would be just like Ronny.

"Look, I like Ronny. I stop by his place. I drink his horrible coffee. I want to see how he's doing."

She looked up at Wyatt, knowing full well he was mostly there for her. "Have you had the coffee in the hospital before?"

He opened the emergency entrance door. "Nope."

"It's on par with Ronny's, just a little more bitter."

"As soon as we have some info and you're settled, I'll make a run, okay? Now, come on, let's find your father." Wyatt took her hand, and headed toward Admittance.

She wasn't going to mention the hands. Or even that it wasn't helping with the rapid heartbeat. Instead, she told him what she'd learned about Ronny's health since she'd arrived.

"Damn." Wyatt shook his head. "Sometimes men can be real idiots."

"Are you telling me that you have regular checkups and do what your doctor recommends?"

"Back when I was in the military, I had no choice."

"And now?"

He just smiled.

"That's what I thought," she said, letting go of his hand and walking up to the woman standing near the unmanned admittance desk. "Ronny Shaw?"

The brunette looked up, her hazel eyes narrowing before she smiled. "Cricket? You probably don't remember me. I'm Kit. I used to work at the fish market while I was going to nursing school."

It took Cricket a moment. "Of course. Nice to see you," she said. Kit was a good ten years older so they'd had only a passing acquaintance. "Any chance you know what's going on with Ronny?"

"He's still waiting for Dr. Oakden. It's been a zoo around here this morning. A big car accident on the expressway before dawn, and then there've been a lot of the regular tourist crises. I honestly can't tell you much, except that Ronny has been bitching about not needing a doctor since he came through the door."

"That's encouraging, but I really do need to know more. The hospital notified me, so I must be his emergency contact. I'm also his only relative."

Kit seemed reluctant to say anything else.

"Skip, the guy who was with him and called the paramedics, said it might be a concussion?"

Kit pressed her lips together, and gave a slight nod.

"Did Ronny happen to mention that he's been feeling light-headed for a while now and that he's had a couple of accidents?"

Glancing back at the chart she held, Kit's expression spoke volumes. Ronny hadn't said a word, which wasn't surprising at all. There was concern in her eyes, something she may have felt for any patient, but it triggered a memory for Cricket. She was pretty sure Kit had been one of the many girls who'd had a crush on Ronny way back when.

"All I can tell you," Kit said, "is that he's lucid

enough to make his own decisions. But I'll let the doctor know that you're here, and that you have questions."

"I'd like to go in with him and wait for the doctor."

"That shouldn't be a problem. I'll tell Ronny you're here."

"Yeah, I'm sure he'll be thrilled." Cricket glanced at Wyatt and sighed. "Guess we'll be in the waiting room."

Kit smiled. "Hey, how are you doing, Wyatt?"

"Good, thanks," he said. "You and your rowdy friends haven't been to the bar in a while. It's getting too quiet."

"Careful what you wish for. The nursing staff is having a party there in about a week. You know how we get when we're finally let loose."

"I look forward to it," he said, then smiled at Cricket. "So, coffee?"

"I'd skip the machines, if I were you," Kit said right before she turned to answer a call.

Cricket actually managed a laugh. Now that she knew her father had been cogent enough to complain, she felt slightly better. Leading Wyatt through the two doors, past the water fountain and the terrible coffee station and vending machines, they found themselves in the crowded waiting room. That was par for the course during tourist season. Didn't matter what time, there was almost always someone who'd been hurt having too much fun.

Luckily, there were a couple of chairs separated by a small table covered with magazines. She sat down while Wyatt went back to the vending machines. She heard the clunk of a soft drink, and then he was in front of her. Only he was holding out a bottle of water. "I can tell your mouth is dry."

"You can…" She put her hand up to cover her mouth. "My breath is that bad?"

"No. Your speech is slightly altered. This will help. When people are anxious, they tend to get dry mouth and can have a hard time remembering things. Like what you want to ask the doctor. Drinking will activate the parasympathetic nervous system, which will help you relax and calm down."

She blinked at him. "Huh?"

"Trust me on this. Your brain will be able to discern that even though you're stressed, you're not in danger. And your prefrontal cortex will come back online."

"No, I meant—" Shaking her head, she took the bottle from him. "That was unexpected."

He shrugged. "It's just something I know. Water and deep breathing are what I turn to first when I'm in a tight spot."

She set her purse down and twisted open the cap, drinking mostly so she wouldn't give in and start grilling him. She'd bet his military training had something to do with how he'd come by the information. But just because she knew things about him that others didn't, it wouldn't be right to bring it up too often. Plus, she was touched he'd shared that with her. It had worked, too. She felt much more at ease.

He smiled and sat down on the other side of the table. "I didn't realize you spoke to Skip. When was that?"

"I didn't." She took another quick sip. "It was a bluff. At least I know they suspect a concussion."

Wyatt laughed, then took out his cell phone. After he swiped a bunch of screens, and typed a bit, he smiled at her before looking down at the ugly carpet. "Hey, Skip, it's Wyatt. Where are you?"

Cricket leaned forward, wishing Wyatt would put the call on speaker, but she didn't want to make a fuss with all these people around.

"What happened this morning?"

Wyatt was quiet, but he didn't look alarmed, and about a minute in, he said, "Hold on a sec," then lowered the phone. "Ronny slipped on the deck. Hit his head. Was out for a short time. That's why Skip called 911."

Cricket was grateful for the information, but wished she could speak to Skip herself. Maybe she'd call after—

"What about the charter?" Wyatt asked. "Alone?"

Another brief pause.

"No, Jim's a good guy. I'm sure he'll be a big help. So, I'm assuming you've checked to see if the boat needs fuel?" Wyatt pulled out his wallet, and while he settled the cell phone between shoulder and chin, he did a quick check. "Okay. Good. What about the supplies for the guests?" Wyatt listened and nodded. "Sure. That's smart."

He smiled again at Cricket, who was still marveling at his thoughtfulness. She hadn't considered the bookings or the money or any of it.

"Fine. Call if you need anything. If for some reason Jim can't make it, I'll jump in. Just make sure the boat goes out on time. I don't want Ronny having an excuse to get back to the dock right away." Wyatt chuckled. "Good. You sound like you have everything under control, and I'm sure the guests will really like your music selections… I'll tell him. And her. Go get 'em, kid. You'll do great."

"Okay, what rank were you in the military? I'm guessing colonel? General?"

He looked a little abashed, or maybe just hesitant, but her cell phone rang, and she wasn't about to let it go to voice mail, not after almost missing the call this morning. She didn't even check the name before she said, "Hello."

"Jessica," Grant said, sounding as if he hadn't expected her to answer. "Tell me you're here in Chicago."

Her first instinct was to tell him to stick it but

this was no time to make a snap decision. Not when she was this scattered. She glanced at the time. It was barely after 6:00 a.m. in Chicago. Grant must be panicked if he'd call her this early. "I told you. I'm taking care of my father. He's ill."

"Look, I'm sure your father needs some help, but you do realize what's going on here, right? If you think they're going to budge on this because of a sick family member, you're wrong. You're putting everything you've worked for at serious risk here, Jess. I mean it. Ulrich is really pissed, not to mention the hell being wrought by Burbidge. If you have any sense of self-preservation, you'll get off your moral high horse and get on a plane today."

As she was about to tell him that it wasn't a ploy, the hospital intercom went off calling for a Dr. Hyland to go to the nurse's station.

Obviously it was loud enough for Grant to hear. "What was that?"

"I'm at the hospital, Grant. Waiting in the ER for my dad to be checked out. I'm not playing games. And if you think I'm going to hop on a plane today, you're mistaken. If the partners need a doctor's note, I'm sure I can get my father's cardio surgeon to write one."

Grant exhaled. "Fine. Call me later."

He was gone, without a single word of concern or compassion. The stupid bastard hadn't even acknowledged her sarcasm.

When she met Wyatt's gaze, she felt her cheeks heat. She'd been so determined to walk away, to tell the firm to shove it, when they'd talked on the beach. Unfortunately, it wasn't that simple. It was horrible that it occurred to her that being in the hospital was convenient, when the last thing in the world she wanted was for Ronny to be ill.

"I'm glad that happened," Wyatt said.

"What?"

"I couldn't help overhearing…at least he knows you weren't lying. Personally, I can't believe the SOB had the nerve to accuse you of using your dad as an excuse."

"To be fair, I did lie about the cardio surgeon. At least I hope it was a lie."

"After what he did to you? That's the least he deserves."

She smiled her thanks, looking for judgment in his eyes and finding none.

Kit came around the corner and walked directly over to Cricket. "Look, if you want to see your dad, I'll take you in, but I decided it was best not to tell him that you were here."

"Great call. Thanks." Cricket got to her feet, along with Wyatt. It had occurred to her that if Ronny refused to see her, it would be game over. She wouldn't be able to put in her two cents with the doctor. As they followed Kit down the corridor, Wyatt found her hand and gave it a light squeeze.

Considering this was just a brief fling, he was

being remarkably considerate. Attentive and comforting. Partly because of Ronny, she knew that. And maybe this was her fear of going home speaking, but she wouldn't mind taking a legit vacation to get to know him better. A lot better.

They entered the area where a number of patients occupied a row of beds, each of them separated by a wraparound curtain, while they waited to be seen by the doctor. Wyatt let her hand go, and she looked at him. "You don't have to come in," she said. "I know you probably have a lot to do, and Ronny's going to be a big baby about all of this."

"Hey, I'm your backup plan. Besides, I promised you coffee, which I'll get once we know all is well."

Kit led them past the only two empty beds, and Ronny's voice came through from behind the next curtain. "There's nothing wrong with my head. People slip and fall all the damn time. I'm fine."

"Mr. Shaw." The young nurse, who was standing guard, as Ronny, wearing a hospital gown, tried to get around her, put her hands on her hips. "I'm sorry, but you can't leave yet."

"Wanna bet? I know all about AMAs. Not to mention I've got a real smart daughter who's a lawyer. She won't put up with you keeping me here."

Cricket folded her arms. "Wanna bet?"

At seeing her, Ronny broke out into a wide

smile, but that changed to a scowl a second later. "What the hell are you doing here? This is your vacation. Who called you?"

"AMAs," Cricket muttered under her breath. "You're not leaving against medical advice. Under any circumstances. Now get back in bed, or I'll have Wyatt put you there."

Grudgingly, he sat on the edge of the bed. "What are you doing here, Wyatt?"

"I gave your daughter a ride."

"Traitor," Ronny mumbled, and then something caught his attention behind Cricket. "And *now* he shows up. Great."

"Good morning. I'm Dr. Oakden." Fortyish, wearing green scrubs, he looked up from the chart. "I see you had a fall."

Ronny sighed, pushing a hand through his long unruly hair.

Kit mouthed "Good luck" to Cricket and slipped away.

"Hello, Doctor. I'm his daughter, Jessica Shaw," Cricket said, pointedly ignoring her father's groan and shaking the doctor's hand. "I imagine he hasn't told anyone about his dizzy spells, or his vertigo. Or his accidents."

"Dammit, Cricket—"

The doctor frowned at the chart. "No, he hasn't. How long has all this been going on?"

"I think it's been a couple of years. But I only heard about it secondhand."

"I'm sitting right here. In person."

Cricket threw a glare Ronny's way. "As if I trust you to tell him anything. Right now, consider me your power of attorney."

"I'm not senile," Ronny said, clearly hurt.

"No. You're not. But stubborn can be just as dangerous." She looked back at Dr. Oakden. "I'm sorry, Doctor. I know you're busy."

"That's okay." He moved closer to Ronny. "Does your regular physician know about any of this?"

"Sure, Ira knows everything."

He was lying. Cricket could see that as plain as day. She suspected the doctor wasn't fooled either, but she kept her mouth shut. For now.

"Ah, you're Dr. Zachi's patient," the doc said, and Ronny winced a little. "You're in good hands."

"Exactly." Ronny darted a smug glance at Cricket.

"I'll give him a call." Dr. Oakden pulled a flashlight out of his pocket, ignoring Ronny's sudden worried expression. "Now, let's have a look at your eyes."

She'd known Ira Zachi since she was a kid. He'd been her doctor. He was the one she needed to speak to about getting her dad a complete physical. She backed up to give them room and realized that Wyatt had stepped out to the corridor. Cricket hoped he didn't think she was the most awful person ever. The last thing she wanted to do was bully her own father, but she knew Ronny. He'd have to be half-dead before she'd get him to see a doctor again.

No, Wyatt was merely being polite. The doctor was asking Ronny questions about his health and the fall. His answers were probably all lies, but Wyatt wouldn't want to intrude.

After Dr. Oakden had finished and explained that he was ordering some tests, he went on to the next patient, and Cricket motioned for Wyatt.

"I'm not hanging around here," Ronny said. "Ira can give me those tests. Where are my damn clothes?"

"Please don't make this any harder than it has to be, okay? As much as I'd like to stay here indefinitely so I could keep an eye on you, I—"

"You have a job. An important one. I know." He sighed as if all the joy had left him in one breath. "But truth is, I've got a job, too. And this is my busiest time of year."

She went to the bed and took his gnarled, tanned hand. "Dad, I know. What I also know is that there isn't anyone on this island who wouldn't help you. Right now, your morning charter is on schedule and halfway to the best fishing spot in the bay."

"How?"

"Skip and Jim have it all under control. Wyatt made sure they had plenty of fuel and the supplies were in order." She smiled at him as he came to stand beside her. "And you know full well one word would get you a dozen more volunteers."

Another thing she knew better than anyone was that her father was a complete sap, so it was no surprise that his eyes had gotten a bit glassy. She stood her ground until he could get it together, which he did pretty quickly.

"Maybe, if you're still here, you can come skipper with me. It's been a long time since you've done a run. We can all go out to the old lighthouse." Ronny looked at Wyatt. "You asked about that trip a while ago, and I owe you double now."

"You don't owe me anything, buddy. But you might want to take it easy on your daughter. She really is worried about you."

After a discreet sniff, Cricket kissed Ronny's cheek and said, "I'd love to go. The minute you're well enough."

"Oh, for Christ's sake…" Ronny stood up again, but he had to balance himself with one hand on the bed.

Cricket didn't have to say a word. She just wished he didn't look quite so sad as he sat back down. "Look, full disclosure… I'm going to speak to Ira about getting you a complete physical, top to toe. Okay?"

"You can't do that without my say-so."

"Actually, I can say whatever I want to Ira. He's

the one who's bound by patient confidentiality. At least I'm not going behind your back."

Wyatt laughed. Probably at Ronny's annoyed expression.

She and her dad both looked at him, and he shook his head.

"Wait till you have kids," Ronny said. "Better hope none of them turns out to be a lawyer."

"Right," Wyatt said. "Look, I don't know Cricket that well, but I'm thinking you're better off getting all this over with."

"Hmm. I'm not sure how to take that," she said, glancing back at some noise in the hall. "Do you remember Kit?" Cricket lowered her voice. "She used to work at the fish market and had a crush on you."

"When?"

"About fifteen years back. I think she might be interested. And she's still hot as a firecracker. You probably shouldn't be in such a rush to leave here."

Ronny snorted. But then his brows went down in thought. When he looked up, it was at Wyatt. "You get that vibe, too?"

Wyatt paused a second, then nodded slowly. "I think you should go for it."

Ronny smiled, just as Kit herself walked into the room.

"It's showtime," she said. "You ready?"

"I guess if you're going to be my escort, it can't be all bad."

Wyatt and Cricket got out of the way, and she could tell he was holding back a grin. "I'll see you later," she told her father before she got to the door, then she stopped, pointed at him and said, "Behave."

Her dad looked at her as if she was his whole world. His smile, when it came, was all Ronny—big and so full of love it hurt. "Why would I start now?"

As they watched Kit roll his wheelchair down the hall to radiology, Wyatt said, "That went well. How about I get that coffee, and meet you in the waiting room?"

"That sounds amazing, but don't you have to work or something?"

"The bar's not open yet. Now, give me your drink order, and if you want something to eat, I can do that, too."

She debated for a minute. "I'd like the biggest hottest caramel latte they have with two extra shots of espresso. I also want a bagel and a schmear, or a cinnamon bun, whichever is more convenient."

"Got it. If you think of anything else, just call me."

She raised up on her toes, and he met her in a kiss that really did make things better. Then he backed away, almost running into a gurney that was left in the hall.

"I'll be quick as I can."

"Good," she said. "You're not what I expected."

"You'll have to explain that when I get back. Now go call one of your friends and try to relax."

Cricket watched him walk swiftly down the corridor until he turned out of sight. Missing him already was probably more about the situation than the man. Although the man was pretty incredible.

# CHAPTER FOURTEEN

THE WAITING ROOM wasn't as crowded as it had been earlier, which was a relief. She found a comfortable chair against the farthest wall, making sure to put her purse on the seat next to her for Wyatt.

First thing she did was get Dr. Zachi's number. Unfortunately, he was out of town for the weekend, but due back later today. She did talk to his nurse, however, whom she vaguely remembered, and was assured the doctor would get back to her promptly.

Despite her worry about Ronny, she found it difficult not to think about work. About Wyatt. About the plants in her apartment. She used her time to call her assistant. Felicity would be worried about her anyway. She had a key to Cricket's apartment, and once she told her about her father, Felicity was happy to help. She also asked about the case, and Grant, but when Cricket said she'd like to wait until she knew more about what was happening with Ronny to talk, Felicity understood, no problem.

By the time she'd spoken to her neighbor, who

agreed to pick up mail or any packages that would collect at the door, then tried Ginny and left a message, Wyatt returned, coffee in a cardboard drink holder, and food in a familiar bag.

She took her caramel latte—not anything she chose on a regular basis—and the first sip was all she'd hoped for and more. The bagel was still warm, and it was nice to see that not only did Wyatt have a big coffee, he'd gotten himself a bagel, as well.

"No news, huh?"

"Nope. But I didn't expect anything this soon. Also, I tried calling his doctor, who just so happened to be away. His nurse promised to give him my message when he called in. I really don't want Ronny leaving here without having every test he needs, even if it means admitting him overnight. It won't be easy getting him to come back."

Wyatt nodded. "So, you're going to hang out here I'm guessing."

"Afraid so. Sorry."

"No, I think you're right. It would be tricky to get him admitted, though, unless they have extra beds and his doctor orders it."

"He's supposed to be back this afternoon, but I know he'll call." She touched his arm. "I'm not asking you to stay, I'm sure you have a busy day. And you've been so great. Thank you. In case I haven't said it. And even if I have."

Wyatt smiled. "I made a couple of phone calls

while I got the coffee. I'll need to go open the bar at two, but tonight everything's taken care of. I'll swing by the dock when Skip's supposed to be back. Check on supplies and gas, find out if we need to get someone else to take out the next charter."

"I can do all those things, except take out the boat. Ronny won't be happy about it, but tough."

"Wait, do you want to? I don't mind sticking around here if that would ease his and your mind."

"Oh, no. I'd be a nervous wreck out there. Not that I couldn't handle the guests, but worrying about my father? I know he'll chase me out, but I'll feel better sticking close, just in case."

"Yeah, that makes sense. Anyway, we should have a plan in place, though let's not jump the gun. It might be something as simple as an ear infection and he'll be good to go in a few days."

"I hope so." Cricket sipped her latte. She appreciated his moral support but she didn't share his optimism. They would've known by now if it was an infection.

"Look, I know this is too obvious, but has his doctor ruled out swimmer's ear? Or in Ronny's case, surfer's ear?"

She nodded. "I asked Ronny the other morning."

"Okay." Wyatt took a really large bite, and they lapsed into silence while he was busy chewing, which gave her the opportunity to stare at his strong jaw, shadowed by a couple of days of stubble. He looked damn good.

"You sure you didn't promise your friend Becky you'd watch her kids?"

After he swallowed, Wyatt smiled. "No, but I did call her so she wouldn't worry that I'm MIA."

Cricket focused on her breakfast, taking a pretty big bite herself. She hadn't realized she was this hungry until she'd started eating. By the time she'd polished off the bagel, she noticed there was something else in the bag. "What's that?"

"A cinnamon bun."

"Oh, you got both." She searched for a delicate way to ask. Oh, the hell with it. "For me?"

Grinning, he passed her the bag.

"We can share," she said, but he shook his head.

She'd only reached the second swirl when her cell rang, and it was such a surprise to hear that tone. She put the bun on a napkin, and answered. "Mom. Hi. Is everything all right?"

"Yes, of course. Why wouldn't it be?"

"So, you're not calling about Ronny?"

There was a pause, but the connection from Paris was excellent, which wasn't always the case. "No. I wanted to hear about the reunion. What did he do now?"

She filled her mom in on all that had been happening. About Ronny, not her job, not Wyatt, not even much about her old friends.

"Is that why you're not in Chicago?"

"Well, yes. I'm at the hospital right now. You know him. He wouldn't get a physical on his own. I'll be staying until we find out what's been causing his balance problems. Besides, I have weeks of vacation time accrued."

Her mother's silence was filled with unsaid advice, but Cricket knew exactly what it was. That she shouldn't be using her vacation this way, and that Ronny should be old enough to take care of himself.

"I'm very happy that you're with him," Victoria said finally, completely surprising Cricket. "He needs someone there. Someone who can look after him, and not just a wild bunch of young surfers."

"He knows everyone and they all keep an eye on him, but I'll spread the word at the fish market that he could use some extra TLC. Anyway, I'm not going to leave without feeling sure that he's fine."

"That's actually a relief." Her mom sighed. "However, that means you don't know when you'll be returning to Chicago."

"Why? Were you planning to visit?"

"Not anytime soon, but—well, you never know. Anyway, I hope you were able to attend some of the reunion festivities and see your friends."

"I did." Cricket glanced at Wyatt. "It's been great," she said, unable to hold back a smile. "You know, I don't even remember mentioning the reunion to you."

"It's been a while, but yes. Anyway, I should let you go. I'll expect to hear from you in the next day or two?"

"Absolutely. Say hi to the judge."

"I will. And tell your father I'm thinking about him."

WYATT PROBABLY SHOULD have left the waiting room while Cricket spoke to her mother, but since he'd ended up holding both coffees and the bag, he stuck around. As a bonus, it gave him another small window into Cricket Shaw, who was turning out to be someone he'd like to get to know better. She'd woken him up to parts of himself that had been dormant for years.

He'd come to care about Adam's family and his bar crew—which he'd done his best to avoid. Unfortunately, over time, he'd let his guard down. After what happened in Afghanistan, he'd gone into lockdown and had lost the key somewhere between the Helmand Province and Little Creek, Virginia. Caring had caused him more pain and guilt than he ever could have dreamed, but his traitorous mind had worked against him.

Now Cricket had lit a fire that had grown with each encounter. If she'd been a local, he'd have pulled back by now. She was safe and dangerous at the same time, and it would be wise to remember that. All he'd wanted by moving here and buying the bar was to do his duty for the friend and brother who'd died, and nothing else. No other responsibilities, no one who would count on him.

It wasn't as easy as he'd imagined.

Thinking about them last night in her room, while Cricket was talking about her ill father to her mother bordered on sleazy, but the feel of her body lingered like a potent perfume. Before, his trysts had been brief and physical and not to be repeated. Yet the want for another night with Cricket was stronger than his good sense.

When she put her cell phone down, he handed her coffee to her.

"Thanks," she said.

The way she smiled at him brought an unexpected tightness in his chest. All he wanted to do was keep looking into her eyes, the amber more vivid in the sunlight coming in through the window. It was easy to picture himself kissing her, right there, in front of everyone, making up for all the kisses they'd missed by being ripped out of bed.

"I wonder what's taking so long," she whispered, her coffee-sugar breath wafting over his lips.

They were leaning in so close to each other, he could—

Cricket jerked at the sound of her phone. Smiling as she read a text, she typed a brief reply before meeting Wyatt's gaze. "That was smart. Dr. Zachi kept things kosher by calling Oakden to get the information. Not that Ronny would cause any trouble but he'd probably use the opportunity to bitch about his *confidentiality.* I feel better just knowing Ira's in the loop. He won't put up with Ronny's crap for a minute."

"Poor guy." Holding on to a grin, Wyatt shook his head. "Ronny doesn't stand a chance."

"Poor guy, my foot," Cricket muttered, her lips beginning to curve.

"Cricket Shaw. I knew it. This was meant to be."

The woman's voice was louder than the clomping of the wooden crutches under her arms. Wyatt hadn't met her but he'd seen her at the fish market. The guy with the hangdog look beside her was Nate, a frequent customer at the bar.

"Mrs. Upton. What happened?"

"You're a lawyer," the woman said to Cricket. "I want to hire you."

"I don't—"

"I heard you were in town, but now I don't have to chase you down. How come you haven't been to see us? You don't visit old friends anymore?"

"I've been busy with the reunion."

"You think that's busy? You try running a fish stall in tourist season. And now I got to do it all with a broken leg. That's why I want to hire you. I'm gonna sue this old goat."

She bumped into Nate with more than just her shoulder. Queenie wasn't a small woman. "For six months, he's been promising to fix the loose floorboard in the kitchen. Six months! And I told him, Nathan, you fix that board or one of these days…well, now it happened. Should have been him on his ass covered in Raisin Bran, but it wasn't, and now I need a good lawyer to sue the pants off him."

Cricket let out a laugh. "It doesn't work that way, but for what it's worth, I'm pretty sure he's going to be fixing every last thing on his honey-do list starting today."

Nate frowned, but he also wasn't standing near enough to Queenie for her to knock him over.

"How much do you charge?" Queenie asked. "Is it by the hour?"

Looking exhausted, Cricket slumped back in her chair.

Wyatt decided to rescue her. "I can help," he said.

"You? You're the enabler that keeps your liquor prices too low. He's either at your bar, or too drunk to do a damn thing around the house, except rub me the wrong way."

"That's what I was referring to. How about he gets banned from the bar until he's finished with his to-do list?"

"What?" Nate's nasally voice shot up a few decibels. "You can't do that. That's gotta be illegal," he grumbled, looking at Cricket for help.

"It's a deal," Queenie said, ignoring her husband.

"It's actually not, Mr. Upton. It's his bar. Wyatt can ban whoever he chooses."

"Well, I'll just go somewhere else, that's all. I hate those damn cooking shows Queenie watches on TV, and she won't let me turn the channel. How's a man supposed to live like that?"

Wyatt noticed Kit standing at the door of the waiting room, and he got Cricket's attention. They both stood up. "I'll wait for you to give me the go-ahead, Mrs. Upton. And I'll let the bar staff know they shouldn't serve him till you say so. Within reason, of course."

"You heard that?" The glare she gave Nate turned into a smile for Wyatt.

"Thank you. You're a good boy."

Wyatt couldn't help laughing. "I try."

"And maybe I don't have to watch cooking shows every night," Queenie said with a sideways look at Nate, who eyed her back.

"You take care of yourself, Queenie. And make sure you keep all your doctor appointments," Cricket said, turning to go.

"What are you doing here, anyway?"

"Ronny fell on the deck this morning."

"That man is getting clumsy in his old age."

Nate snorted. "He's at least ten years younger than you."

Wyatt took Cricket's arm. "We've got to get going. Good luck, both of you." He didn't wait for a reply, just kept moving toward the hallway. Halfway there, he bumped her shoulder. "You ought to think about moving back and hanging a shingle here. You'd have all kinds of business."

She stopped so fast she startled him. The glare she was giving him was scorching. "That's not funny."

He tugged her forward. "It was pretty funny," he said.

Cricket just sighed.

# CHAPTER FIFTEEN

WYATT HATED LEAVING Cricket at the hospital, but it was necessary. Sabrina had closed for him two nights in a row, and she deserved her day off. Luckily, she'd been showing Tiffy the ropes. She was a responsible kid and would end up being valuable down the road, but Wyatt wasn't sure she was ready to handle things by herself. Sabrina thought she could, but he'd have to give it more thought. She wasn't scheduled until four.

It was just two o'clock when he opened the bar, and it didn't surprise him at all that no customers were waiting. Monday was notoriously slow, and now that the reunion and the golf tournament were over, he doubted things would pick up until later in the evening.

After making sure his cell phone had enough juice in case Skip or Cricket called, he took the chairs off the tables, his thoughts staying on her and Ronny. Vertigo could be a messy problem. He'd known good men that had washed out of the service because of it.

"Hey, boss." Viv and Lila walked in together, both of them with energy drinks in hand, but it was Lila who'd spoken. "You been enjoying your time off?"

"Yep," he said with a brief nod. "I want to get as much set up as we can before customers start rolling in, and I don't want to skip the inventory of the bottles that are out. I know some are low and need replacing."

"Sure thing," Viv said. "We'll just go stash our purses and get to it. I brought an extra Red Bull with me, if you need one."

"I'm good, thanks."

He finished with the last few tables, took a quick look around to make sure no one had put anything in the potted plants. There was always somebody who stashed a glass or a condom or an empty bottle of beer. Sure enough, there was a martini glass, empty but for a toothpick, behind the fern. Maybe he ought to just buy a bunch of cactus plants.

The girls started putting away the glasses that had been washed the night before. He left them to it to go in the back and check over the stores he'd marked for reorder. He wouldn't place the call until they were finished up front, but he already knew the order would be sizeable.

Something hard tripped up his left foot. A nail that had come up. Easy enough to hammer it down again, but it made him think about Ronny and his double slip at the dock. As soon as possible, he'd go down there with his toolbox, make sure there were no obvious hazards. Technically, the harbormaster was responsible for upkeep and repairs on the actual dock. Ronny only had his slip to worry about. But the dock was already wet and slick by the time the first boats went out, and a mess at the end of the evening. No need to add to the risks.

By the time he'd gone back up front, Viv was filling the beer tubs with ice, and taking notes as Lila checked bottles. There was room enough for him back there to begin cutting the limes and lemons. It was soothing, hearing the quiet talk, Lila for once not trying to get his attention. Guess some of the others had told her she needed to knock that off. Especially after the gossip-fest about his love life.

Time slipped past him as he finished enough limes, lemons and pineapple wedges to get them through the night, then put them in containers that would keep them fresh. When he pulled out the cherries, Sabrina walked in.

"What are you doing here?" he asked. "It's your night…" Her arm had a vivid bruise right above where her sleeve ended. She looked like she might have been crying again, or just hadn't gotten enough sleep.

He left the cherries and followed her into the back room. It was three thirty, and still no customers had come in. Sabrina stood at the filing cabinet where the women kept their purses, her body still and hunched.

"You're not on the schedule tonight."

"I know," she said without looking at him. "Is it a problem if I work anyway? I don't want to make everyone mad over tips."

"Look, a day off could do you some good, but if you want to stay, you can pour drinks so tips won't be an issue. In fact, you can run the place."

She looked back at him. "You sure?"

He nodded. "Go ahead, sign in. Then tell me what happened. I'm assuming that was your boyfriend's handiwork?"

"He didn't hit me. Just grabbed me too hard, that's all."

"That's all," Wyatt murmured, although he was sure she heard him. "If I ask you to come with me upstairs, would that be all right?"

"I came here to work, Wyatt. I don't need another lecture."

"I don't recall ever lecturing you," he said calmly. "If I did, I apologize."

She signed the time sheet, then put her purse in the bottom drawer. Finally she met his gaze. "You didn't. I'm sorry."

"So? Upstairs? It won't take long." He waited. "You trust me?"

"Of course I do."

"Good. Come on."

They went back out to the bar and he asked

Viv to take over for about an hour. "Text me if you need me."

She nodded. No one questioned it when he led Sabrina outside to the stairs.

Once he got his door open, Sabrina stepped inside. The place was its usual mess. He remembered the last time the kids had been there, and the havoc they'd wrought, and how he'd had to leave before he could make them pick up. "Sorry."

"I think you're fighting a losing battle with this stuff. The kids like playing here more than your office, or I'm guessing, their own house."

"I have no idea why," he said, tossing Matchstick cars and loose Legos into the toy chest.

"Probably because it makes you go a little nuts."

"That sounds about right. If you wouldn't mind, I'd like us to get the floor clear so I can teach you a few self-defense moves."

"Wyatt. I don't need—"

"Every woman needs to know what I'm going to teach you. In fact, I'm going to make a point of showing every woman who works here how to defend herself. It's smart, and nothing too difficult. In this day and age, especially working in a bar? I can't believe I haven't done this before."

Her hesitation was brief, then she got busy picking up Rose's things—the dolls, and the tea set that he'd been forced to participate with more times than he cared to remember. When he got to Josh's Lego in progress, he lifted the whole cardboard platform Wyatt had made for the project, and carefully walked it to the kitchen counter. "Josh has been working on this for a couple weeks. Evidently, this Lego set is for ages five and up, but Josh has been building it all by himself."

Sabrina laughed. "Sounds as if you might have heard that once or twice."

"Every time he's here. And sometimes he even calls, just to remind me."

"You're so good with him and Rose."

"I'm patient. Have to be."

"I guess you want to have your own someday, huh?"

"What? Me?" He hadn't thought about it. Not since he'd joined up. "Why would I when I already have two rug rats driving me insane."

"I don't believe that for a second. Not only are you a natural, you're a total softy."

He grunted, unwilling to acknowledge any of it. At all. "Okay, you ready?"

She wrung her hands together. "I'm not sure."

He waved her over. "Stand right here in front of me. This is lesson number one, and it's straightforward, but the key is to run it over and over in your head. A lot. Like every time you walk out a door. Every time, okay?"

"Uh, sure?"

"Now I'm not going to hurt you, so don't worry

about it. This is a simple straight punch. If some-one's in front of you and you can tell they're a threat, or think they're a threat, especially if you've told them to back off or leave you alone, but they're still in your face? Push from the ball of your dominant foot and thrust your hip and fist forward at the same time."

He demonstrated, and it didn't surprise him that when he faked the punch she jerked back. Not that he was trying to trick her, but now he knew the degree of fear that asshole had condi-tioned in her. "That'll maximize your strength. Now stand next to me, and imagine there's a guy making an unwanted move. Get ready to use your dominant hand. Don't put your thumb underneath your other fingers. Just make a fist, take a deep breath, then really drive from the ground and don't let your elbow flip up. Go on, give it a try."

Sabrina seemed nervous, which was normal. She moved her leg and her arm at the same time, anyway. "Good start. Great job. Now, remember to lean your whole body in to follow up with that fist. You're aiming with your pointer and middle finger knuckles to hit whatever you can reach easily. That can be his chest, his face, whatever will give you the most bang for your buck. Now try it again."

She did, and this time she brought some heat.

He moved to stand in front of her, and pre-pared himself. "Okay, you're going to hit me now. At your height, you can punch me square in the chest."

"I'm not doing that."

"Don't worry, it'll be fine. I do this kind of stuff at the gym."

"Don't they use gloves or something?"

"You don't have to use all your might if you're worried about hurting me. You need to feel what it's like to strike someone with your fist. I'm assuming you've never done that before."

She lowered her gaze and shook her head.

"Okay, trust me. Please. And go for it."

If she'd realized how often he'd been smashed in the chest, she wouldn't have hesitated. When she finally got up the nerve to strike, she did a pretty good job. It hurt, but didn't cause anything close to real pain. "Excellent. What was it like?"

"Scary, but also kind of exhilarating?"

"It's a hell of a feeling, knowing you can handle yourself. That you're not at someone's mercy. Give me five more, as hard as you can."

"Wyatt, no."

"No, I meant shadowbox. Show me the moves."

She started slow. But steady.

"The more vulnerable the target, the better. Eyes," he said, walking around her as she practiced. "Also the nose and throat are the most effective and it'll give you plenty of time to get out of Dodge."

After five more, she was huffing, but she looked more alive than she had in a while. "What's next?"

He grinned. "This one, you're not going to try on me, but I'll let you hit something that won't be crippled, okay? This is how you do a knee to the groin. We'll follow that with a kick to the groin. Both have their merits."

"Well yeah, I get to kick some douchebag in the nuts."

"That's right. Now, here's how you want it to look when you're in a tight spot." He showed her both the knee and the kick, then went back to the knee, and by the time they were finished, she was sweating, and she looked like she could do some damage.

"This is really awesome, Wyatt," she said. "You're right. Every woman should know this."

"You need to take a rest before we go to the next move?" he asked.

"Nope. What do I get to hurt this time?"

In the middle of trying out the choke defense, he got a text from Skip, letting him know the boat was in dock and everything was going great. He also offered to take tomorrow's charter out, only this time with Wendy. Wyatt texted back that he'd check with Cricket, and that for now, he should just clean up the boat.

By the end of the hour and a half he'd spent with Sabrina, they sat down with a couple of cold waters from his fridge. She was breathing deeply, sweaty but not very concerned about that.

Finally, after downing most of the water, she looked at him without that small smile she'd worn since her first successful hit. "I've been planning to leave him, you know. It's not easy, though. He's got a big family, and I don't have anyone out here, not since my uncle died."

"You've got me. And everyone who cares about you. You're family at the bar, got it? And we work with a lot of tigers down there, and real soon each one of them is going to know more about self-defense than Tyson's whole family put together. If we need to get a restraining order, we will. In fact, you can count on it."

Sabrina touched his arm with her chilled fingers. "Thank you for this. It was the push I needed."

"Good. Now, you still have the night off if you want it."

She frowned. "No, I'd rather work. I feel safer here than anywhere else, and I can use the money."

"You want to stay here tonight? I have somewhere I can go, so you don't have to worry about that."

She stood up. "Thanks, but I'll ask Tiffy if I can stay at her place. There's a cop that lives next door to her, so it's real safe there. And working will keep my mind off the asshole."

"Your call." He rose, and held the door for her and she led the way down the stairs, complaining about how sticky she felt.

They were two steps to the landing when a squeal of tires made them both stop. A second later, Sabrina's jerk boyfriend threw open the door of his souped-up truck and started screaming before his feet hit the pavement. "What the hell are you doing? You don't work today. You haven't answered any of my calls and texts, but I guess you wouldn't while you were fucking your boss."

"Tyson, I didn't! I wasn't!"

"Yeah, I'm really gonna believe that when I know you're always running to him and crying on his shoulder." He was racing up the lower steps, his Metallica T-shirt a size too small, his steroid-enhanced muscles almost bursting out of the sleeves.

Wyatt stepped in front of Sabrina.

Tyson got right up in his face, trying to intimidate Wyatt with his bulk. He wasn't worried, but before he did anything, he leaned his head to the side, keeping his eyes on Popeye. "You want me to call the cops?"

"No. No, don't. I'll get him to leave."

His face an ugly red and spittle coming out of his foul mouth, Tyson's glare moved past Wyatt. "I'm not buying the innocent act. You were always a slut, and now you're a cheating slut."

"I suggest you get back into that truck of yours," Wyatt said, "and get the hell out of here." He held his temper in check for Sabrina's sake. It wasn't easy, though. He wanted to squash the idiot like a cockroach, and he knew just how to do it. But he also knew that Viv, Tiffy and Lila had opened the bar door and were watching them.

"What, you think I don't know you screw every one of the girls who works for you? Isn't that why you opened the bar in the first place? You old pervert, you just like 'em young and once you're giving them a check, they can't say no." Tyson took a step forward.

With a tap of the side of his hand, Wyatt hit the bastard's vagus nerve, and he started to go down like a dead tree, howling in pain. Wyatt caught him by the back of his shirt so he wouldn't go over the railing, ripping a sleeve in the process. That made Wyatt feel a little better, but not enough.

Tyson recovered quickly, and backed away, so pissed he was trembling.

"Go on. Get the hell out of here before I really hurt you."

Like the true coward he was, Tyson scuttled back to his truck, but the idiot had to make one last comment. Unfortunately for him, it was to Sabrina.

"You'll pay for this, bitch. You just wait until I get you home."

Without a second thought, Wyatt vaulted over the second-story railing, and was at the truck before Tyson knew what happened. Grabbing him by the ear in one of the most painful maneuvers Wyatt knew, he had the jerk on his knees, Wyatt's arm at his throat and his mouth close to the ear he could so easily have torn off. "If I see one more mark on Sabrina, or even think I do, I will end you. I don't give a damn if it's you that put it there or not. If I find out that you've picked another victim, I'll make sure it's the last choice you ever make. And trust me, asshole…they'll never find your body."

Wyatt eventually let him go, but only after tears glistened off the big man's face. He stumbled into the truck and put it in gear, trying to scare Wyatt by aiming the truck at him, but he held his ground in that loser's game of chicken, and sure enough, Tyson sped off.

When Wyatt finally looked up, he saw the girls standing on the deck outside the bar. They were staring at him as if he'd grown a third arm.

He wanted to leave that minute, but he couldn't. He had to make sure Sabrina was all right, and that she could go to Tiffy's tonight where Tyson couldn't get to her.

It was a long walk up the few steps with adrenaline coursing through his body like an electrical shock. It had been a while since he'd engaged in physical combat, and never before with a civilian. But goddamn it, he wanted that scumbag to remember that Sabrina—or any woman—wasn't his property.

As he reached the bar level, he realized Sabrina was surrounded by the other three and two long-time customers, both of them from the fishing community. Damn, he wished they hadn't seen him behaving like a gorilla.

"What the hell was that?" Tiffy asked. "You were like Superman out there."

He scowled at the lot of them. "Don't you all have work to do? Did you leave any customers inside? With the cash register?"

"Don't worry, boss," Lila said. "No one's in there. We all came out when we heard the tires squealing. Viv thought it was an accident."

"Well, get back to it. Do I need to finish stocking the shelves?" He paused at the entrance and looked back to make sure Tyson wasn't lurking anywhere. No sign of him, but Wyatt could swear he saw Becky's car leaving the lot. Damn. He hoped she hadn't seen any of the altercation, or worse, that the kids hadn't gotten an eyeful.

"You need to have a drink and chill," Sabrina said. "Since I'm taking over for you tonight, I'll make you one. How about a Kamikaze?"

He couldn't help acknowledging the humor, glad Sabrina was standing tall. "I don't need to chill."

"I think you should go find your girlfriend,"

Viv said, following him inside. "I bet she'd be hella impressed."

He shook his head. "Look, that wasn't something for me to be proud of. Yes, I'm glad I have the skills to defend someone I care about. But ideally, I hope I never have to use them again. I did what had to be done to protect Sabrina. The end."

Tiff nodded, then threw her arms around his neck and gave him a hug. "Thanks for all you do for us," she said, her voice low and sincere. "We all appreciate you."

He patted her back, and got out of the hug as quickly as possible. "Yeah, yeah. Now let's get cracking and give these two a drink on the house," he said, nodding at the customers.

The men were happy to accept, but had already turned their interest to the TV over the bar.

"What's that?"

"Hurricane heading this way soon," the older of the two fishermen said. "Rare in June, but I still remember Hurricane Agnes. It wasn't no Perfect Storm or Sandy, but it hit plenty hard back in '72. A lot of folks lost their boats, and three people drowned."

"Don't get excited," the other customer said. "It's losing steam. By the time it hits us it'll be downgraded to a tropical storm."

"How soon?" Wyatt asked, concerned that he hadn't known a thing about it. Usually, he was on top of everything weather related, no matter what the season. But he'd been so wrapped up in Cricket his routine had gone sideways.

"If it keeps coming up north, a day or two. But it'll probably hit land lower down the coast and turn into a tropical storm."

"Let's hope so," Wyatt said, then waited for Sabrina to finish pouring the drinks, then took her to the back room, gave her a new T-shirt and offered her his shower. "You sure you want the bar tonight?"

"Yes. Now go find your friend. I'm fine here. Better than fine. I'm surrounded by tigers."

"Okay. Then yeah, I'm gonna go, but if anything happens, you dial 911 first, then call me. I'll be within running distance, you got that?"

"Yeah, I do. Now scoot."

"Scoot?"

Sabrina laughed as she left his office, and although he still felt like punching a wall, it was a damn fine sound.

# CHAPTER SIXTEEN

GRABBING THE TOOLBOX he kept in his office, he hurried upstairs to change. Sabrina wasn't the only one who needed fresh clothes. A quick shower did wonders, and by the time he was dressed, it was just after four thirty.

Luckily, he didn't have to drive at all, just take a quick jog down past Ronny's to the dock. The run helped dissipate some excess energy, so by the time he arrived, he'd calmed considerably. Determined to find the loose board Ronny had tripped on, he started with the dock adjacent to his slip, and did a thorough search, plank by plank.

A few minutes later, someone touched the back of his arm and he swung around, nearly hitting Cricket with his toolbox.

"Whoa. I'm sorry," she said. "I didn't mean to scare you."

"I should be the one apologizing. Are you all right?"

"Yeah, it didn't get me. What are you doing out here?"

He shrugged. "Trying to take care of anything that might trip Ronny or anyone else."

She smiled. "That's why I'm here, too. That and checking out the boat before I let Skip and Jim take it out again."

"It's Skip and Wendy, last I heard. How's your dad?"

"Okay, except they've tacked on more tests, plus a CT scan, though the machine won't be available until much later. If that doesn't show anything, he'll have an MRI tomorrow. The good news is, I talked to Dr. Zachi and he had Ronny admitted overnight. Which, as you can imagine, really pissed Ronny off. Claims everyone's lying about the CT scan being unavailable just to keep him there. They're going to put him through all the hoops. So I figured I could sneak in some repairs while he's otherwise occupied."

"Great minds," Wyatt said, wanting to touch her, but not sure about doing so in such a public place.

"Oh, I meant on the shack."

"So did I." The way she looked at him was a little confusing. Mostly because she seemed so surprised. He didn't know why but he didn't ask. "You look great," he said.

"Me? Oh, for heaven's…these are Ronny's cargo shorts, and this T-shirt is older than I am."

"Your point?" he asked.

"I bet you'd love seeing me in my ratty old house slippers and patchwork robe."

"I bet I'd prefer seeing you out of them."

"Okay," she said, laughing. "No fair."

"What?"

"That kind of talk when we can't do anything about it."

"Who says we can't?"

"On Ronny's boat?"

"Certainly doable."

Cricket shook her head, still laughing. "You're so bad."

"That's not what you implied last night." He smiled at her light blush, then glanced over at the *Baby Girl*. "The boat looks good. Skip and Jim did a nice job cleaning it up."

"Yeah, my dad said he can really depend on Skip. Clearly his first preference was that I spring him, but he seemed relieved that Skip is handling the charters. That you're his backup helps, too." She gave him a sweet smile. "Have I told you how terrific you are?"

A rogue gust of wind whipped past them, strong enough to force Cricket back half a step. Another followed, then things went back to the gentle breeze that had been blowing throughout the day.

"I assume you know about the storm warnings," Wyatt said.

"Oh, yeah. It was on a loop on the hospital TV. It's weird for June, but not unprecedented."

"So I heard. What happens in a case like this? Would Ronny cancel tomorrow's charter or play it by ear?"

"Good question. I know what I would do, though the harbormaster might take the decision out of both our hands." Her brows drawing together, she turned to look out at the sea. "I heard conflicting reports as to when the storm is supposed to hit. What about you? Did you hear anything solid?"

"Nope. No one seems to be scrambling to drydock their boats." Two couples, who definitely weren't locals, strolled by them, chatting and laughing. "Even the tourists don't seem concerned."

"Probably summer people," she said, glancing at the group. "Temptation Bay has been fairly lucky over the years. That said, we should seriously consider canceling tomorrow's charter."

"You want to run it by Ronny?"

"I'll wait till he asks."

Wyatt smiled. "Look, how about I get to work here. You can go back to the house and I'll meet you there when I'm done."

"No, I'll help here." She grabbed a handful of her hair when it blew into her face. "Dammit. I should've worn a ponytail."

"I kind of prefer you wearing nothing."

She choked out a laugh. "Um, ditto."

HE STEPPED CLOSER, his gaze locked on hers, and she held her breath, not sure what he had in mind, and wanting nothing more than to feel his arms around her. But they didn't dare. "We'll have to put that thought on hold." She looked around and didn't recognize anyone. There were surfers at the shoreline and in the water, even though the swell was small this late in the day. The fishing boats weren't all in, although she saw quite a few.

When she looked back at Wyatt, amusement glinted in his gray eyes. "Think this'll help?" he asked, holding out a bandana. "It's clean."

"Oh." Cricket laughed. "Thanks."

"How about we see to this dock and check on the boat? Then we can figure out what comes next."

"Okay. But I vote we cook some dinner. I'm sure Ronny's got beer in the fridge, and since he's always feeding his band of surf bums, he's probably well stocked."

"Great. After we're finished here we can check out the fish market. See if they've got anything decent left."

"Sounds like a plan." Cricket had felt Wyatt's pull since she'd spotted him from up the beach. Missing him at the hospital had seemed silly. Now that he was in kissing distance she realized how much she wanted his touch, his lips pressed to hers. It was foolish, and far too soon to feel this strongly. Not smart at all. Not when she had such important decisions to make, and barring a catastrophe, she had to return to Chicago soon.

She went to scour the left side of Ronny's slip, and Wyatt went right, but they both kept sneaking peeks at each other, grinning like kids. Which was how he tripped and almost landed on his face.

Rushing over, she could see quickly that he was all right, just pissed. The way he was staring at the board that had caught his shoe, he meant business. He got out a hammer, then crouched in his board shorts and T-shirt, which showed off all the muscles she'd run her hands over last night. It wasn't polite to be staring, but damn, his body was like a Lamborghini, built with care and an engine that could go all night.

That got her to look away. Although her shame wasn't deep enough to keep her eyes averted for more than a few seconds. Besides, she wanted to be at the ready if he hit his finger or something.

Naturally, he handled the problem like a pro, even taking out his level to make sure his work was perfect.

With a confident nod, he stood. "You find any big problems on your side?"

"No, in fact, it looks fairly well maintained." She sighed. "So you know what that means."

Wyatt took her hand and gave it a gentle squeeze. "At least he's getting the works. Whatever's wrong they'll find it."

His touch worked its way up her arm and filled her with a warmth that competed with the sun. "The rational part of me understands that, but it's that pesky emotional side that keeps sneaking up on me."

"Well, we'll just have to keep you occupied."

She arched her brows at him, and he laughed.

"That's not what I meant. Not that it doesn't have merit. Sabrina needed some extra hours tonight, so she's got the bar. I'd still like to go check in at least once."

Nodding, she slipped her hand out of his and drifted toward the other end of the slip. "I'm going back to the hospital at around seven thirty, take him his book and some toiletries. He wants me to bring clothes, but I'm afraid he'll do a runner, so oops, I'll forget that part."

"Smart, but he'll see right through you," Wyatt said, before crouching to continue his inspection.

"I know. He will. I honestly don't understand why it seems to be some kind of masculine badge not to want appropriate medical help. It's not as if getting a checkup means anything but being smart about your own body."

"There's a lot of craziness that gets drummed into guys from day one. You think it's bad with men in general, you should see what happens in the military."

She stopped and looked at him, but his head was down. He'd already shown he didn't have a lot of hypermasculine traits, like not listening or being dismissive of a woman's opinion. Maybe she'd gotten too used to the Grants in her world. There were certainly men in her acquaintance that had admirable characteristics, but they tended to be in the support fields, and not front and center making the big bucks. Then again, she knew just as many high-powered women sharks.

Guess it had to do more with nurture than nature, but what did she know? She'd been brought up by one of the most generous and kindest men in the world, and though her mother was of a different ilk, her main goal was that Cricket find happiness. Of course Victoria's idea of happiness involved a very large bank account.

"Hey." Wyatt wasn't where he'd been a minute ago. In fact, he was on Ronny's boat. "You find something?"

"Nope. You?"

"Everything looks good. I guess we're done here."

Cricket managed a smile, even though it was now quite clear the problem lay with Ronny.

THE WALK TO the fish market was different, not just because Wyatt had gone there only in the mornings, but because he had Cricket with him. She'd let him know it was all right to show some signs of their connection, and he didn't hesitate to take advantage of it, which was something he'd have to think through later.

He'd never been much of a hand-holder. He knew a lot of guys who had no problem with public displays, but that hadn't been in his repertoire. Maybe it had something to do with the strict training he'd received since birth, although he liked to think he made decisions for himself, and not out of concern over how others might see him. But that was probably wishful thinking. He'd been in the military for most of his life and he represented a long line of officers who'd done nothing to bring their honor into question. Until him.

A gust came off the water, spraying a mix of sea and sand. Wyatt tried to block it with his body but all Cricket did was lift her face to the spray, a faint smile curving her lips. Man, it was hard to imagine her living in Chicago. Or any city. She belonged here every bit as much as Ronny.

"It looks like most of the stalls are already packed up," Wyatt said. "Think we'll get lucky?"

"I do. With the bluefish running, I know several stands put some aside. At Willy's they even fillet the fish for you. Which is nice because I want to try a recipe that needs to marinate."

"Do we need to pick up anything else for dinner?"

"Nope. We'll be good."

"And what about this hand-holding thing at

the market. You know everyone's going to make a deal out of it."

Cricket smiled. "I'll go with whatever makes you comfortable. As for me, I'm too old and cranky to care what anyone thinks."

"Good, because I can tell they're already staring at us."

"That's my fish people for you. Living on seafood and gossip."

"Don't forget liquor. That seems to play a large part."

She laughed, and bumped against him as they walked, slowing down just a little. "Have you been here for any major storms?"

"Only one that did any real damage. We lost a small section of the beach. The wind toppled a few trees, broke some windows, a couple of shacks were flooded."

"Not Ronny's?"

"Nah, I think he had some minor roof damage." Wyatt shook his head. "I swear he has a spell on that old shack of his. It seems to be impervious to weather."

"It's far from that. When the Perfect Storm hit in '91, the whole front of the shack was destroyed. He saved some of the more important, sentimental things, but he had to replace everything else."

"You must've been only five or six. Were you here for that?"

"I was with my mom and her family and dis-

234 THE NAVY SEAL'S RESCUE

appointed that I missed all the action," she said, grinning. "But in 2006 I was home from college when Tropical Storm Beryl made landfall on Nantucket and we had ten-foot waves. The shack was fine, but Ronny broke his leg while surfing, the dope. Then of course, there was Sandy. We lucked out in the Bay, but the winds were strong and power was out for over twenty-four hours. He had to do some repairs after that, and there's still a lot to be done."

"The weather is so unpredictable these days. A June hurricane this far north isn't all that strange anymore."

"It's not truly a hurricane," Cricket said, and he nodded, having been corrected by the locals a couple of times already. "You have everything you need to get through it?"

"Yep. From water to enough boards to cover all our windows, we're set, and we have drills throughout hurricane season so everything runs smoothly."

"Wow, maybe you should mention that to Ronny. He's such an overgrown kid at times. I swear, he does rain dances for big waves," she said, just as they hit the market.

"Well, if that isn't Cricket Shaw then I don't know what."

Cricket grinned as Hetty, the woman who did a clambake for the locals every year, stood with her hands on her hips, her wide-brimmed hat bobbing in the wind.

"Hey, Hetty. How come you look like you just turned thirty? I need your beauty secrets."

Wyatt kept himself in check. He knew for a fact Hetty had spent most of her life on this beach, and she looked it. But the smile she was beaming at Cricket told him far more about the woman.

As soon as they stepped onto the boardwalk leading through the rows of stalls, Cricket got swarmed by three other women. There weren't any tourists or customers that he could identify, but he sure recognized the folks that made their living on the ocean. Every one of them hugged her as if she were family. And directly after each hug, he was stared at, with raised eyebrows and shifty-eyed looks that bounced between him and Cricket. It was as if they had landed in a puppet show with lazy puppeteers.

"Yes," Cricket said, moving closer to him. "We're dating. It's nothing serious. I'll be going back to Chicago soon. Does that cover it?"

"I heard you were going to help Queenie sue that lazy old man of hers," one of the women said. "How can I get in on that?"

"I'm not helping, and she's not suing. Anyway, do any of you have any bluefish we could buy? If it's filleted, I'll pay extra."

"I don't care about the lawsuit. I heard he can't

go to Sam's Sugar Shack until Queenie gives the go-ahead." She looked directly at Wyatt.

He didn't know all their names, but they obviously knew him. "That's true," he said, wishing he'd kept his big mouth shut. "Always glad to be of help." That got a lot of raised eyebrows, as well.

Not Cricket. Laughing, she looked at him as if he was insane.

"I've got some fish in the fridge," a woman said, then turned to Wyatt. "I'm Rita Mae, Willy's daughter, and you're the guy who goes running most mornings." Not waiting for a response, she gave Cricket and Wyatt one more inquisitive look before she walked away, heading to one of the bigger stands, with Cricket following.

"So, you two seeing each other, huh?" the only guy on the boardwalk asked. "You know, Cricket's one of our own. Ronny's kid. Victoria, that's her mother, she don't live here no more, but Cricket, she'll always have a home here."

Wyatt just nodded.

"I heard Ronny was up to the hospital. What's he got, cancer? I know too many folks around here got the cancer."

"We're not sure what's wrong," Cricket called from one stall away. "I'll tell you about it in a minute, Vern. And don't you go giving Wyatt the third degree or telling stories. He already knows Ronny, so stop it."

"All right already," Vern yelled back. All the ships at sea probably heard the man, but when he faced Wyatt again, he was smiling. The guy was old. Really old, but his lungs sure worked fine.

Before he got another word out, Cricket whistled. Also very loudly. Maybe that was a thing about Rhodies he didn't know? "Wyatt, I need you, please."

"Excuse me, Vern. The lady calls."

Vern nodded, then got busy settling into a canvas chair.

Of course, Wyatt was given a thorough head-to-toe examination as he joined Cricket. Lila could learn a thing or two from these women about discomfiting a man. He felt as though he was being graded like tuna. Only not as highly. The fact that the three women decided to walk with him didn't surprise him at all.

"She's got four fillets all ready for the grill," Cricket said. "But she's also got some bass, if you prefer it."

"No, I want to try out that recipe you mentioned."

Rita Mae nodded. "In other words, he wants you to do the work."

"Don't you fret," Cricket said. "He'll have plenty to do tonight. Count on it."

All four of them laughed. He wasn't quite sure how to take that. Good thing he was used to rowdy women.

Another gust, this one stronger, made all the tarps in the market flap like crazy, and blew several signs off the tables. The only thing that didn't get swept up seemed to be Hetty's hat.

"Is that why hardly anyone's here?" Cricket asked. "Is everybody getting stocked up for the storm?"

"I've still got to go," the only woman Wyatt didn't recognize said. "But before you leave, I need to talk to you about something of a legal nature."

The woman looked as if she'd lived a tough life, too, weathered and strong as the women sailors he'd worked with, but older. Not Vern old, but Wyatt would guess in her late sixties.

"What's on your mind, Penny? You know I can't practice in Rhode Island. I only have a license in Illinois."

"Well, I wish you'd hurry up and get one here." She glanced around at the others, scrambling to pick up things scattered by the wind. "This isn't the time or place, but I'll tell you this much—the resort is trying to buy up beachfront land, and the way they're after the older folks has me worried. I'm not sure these elderly fishmongers know what they're reading, or worse, signing."

"Oh, no. I'm not sure how long I'll be here, but I'll give you a call after Ronny's home and the storm passes. We'll talk, and if you can get your hands on any paperwork or contracts they're pushing, that would help."

"That'd be great, honey. We'd all appreciate it. The lawyers in town want an arm and a leg just to look at a piece of paper."

Cricket patted the woman's tanned arm. "Don't worry about it, Penny. And you say hey to your family for me."

"I will."

Wyatt had paid Rita Mae for the fish and was about to move on when Penny gave him a curious look. "You're the Wyatt that goes out to help the coast guard, aren't you?"

"That's right," he said, not unaware of Cricket's obvious curiosity.

"You found Tom and his son back in November," Hetty said.

He nodded, holding the fish in one hand, his toolbox in the other. "Hate to rush you," he said to Cricket, "but we've got a lot to do."

Thank God she got the hint. "Oh, my lord, how did it get this late?" She started backing up. "Great to see you all. I'll be able to chat more the next time I'm here. And thanks for the fish, Rita Mae."

By the time their feet hit sand, she'd taken the fish from him so they could hold hands again. Wyatt grinned all the way back to Ronny's.

# CHAPTER SEVENTEEN

WHILE THE SUN was still above the horizon, Wyatt had gone out to do a full inspection of all the repairs that needed to be done on the shack. Cricket, meanwhile, had put the fish in the citrus and white wine marinade, set up the coals in the outside barbecue and found enough veggies to make a tantalizing salad.

The door swung open and Wyatt came in, his hair making it look as if he'd jumped out of a blender. "Is it that windy outside?"

"I may have crawled under the shack."

"When will you know for sure?"

His nose scrunched up adorably. "Fine. I was looking for storm supplies."

"You could have asked me. I would have told you."

"But would you have known how low on water he is?"

"No, but I would have told you that he's also got a closet by his bedroom where he's got most of the water stored, plus batteries, flashlights, a portable stove, even a large bag of wet wipes and toilet paper, and some excellent rum."

"Rum?"

"He finds that's the best beverage for hurricanes and tropical storms. Personally, I can't argue with that."

"Huh." Wyatt studied her as if she were a code he hadn't cracked. "You're a lot like that Treasure Trove."

She laughed but it took her a second to realize he meant that teaser puzzle they'd started last night. The compliment was actually nicer than she'd first thought. "Well, thank you."

"I meant impossible to put together when there's anyone else around."

"And when we're alone?"

"Ah, that's when I want to make you come apart."

She inhaled deeply and pulled him into a searing kiss. Whatever he'd been holding fell to the floor with a whoosh and a clunk, and then his hands were all over her back, and the heat around them rose at least five degrees. When he groaned, a deep guttural sound that made all the right parts clench, she ran a hand underneath his T-shirt across his smooth, slick back.

Then the timer went off.

Wyatt leaned back just enough to speak. "Is that critical?"

"Only if we want to eat before leaving."

He gave her one last, far too chaste kiss and stepped away.

"I'm not even hungry, though," she said, wincing at how whiny she sounded.

"You need to eat and so do I. Didn't you tell me you wanted help with your bedroom?"

Sighing as she walked back to the kitchen to turn off the annoying timer, she had to say yes. "I'd planned to get to it today, but we can wait till morning."

"I don't know, there's been some chatter about the storm coming earlier than predicted, I wouldn't advise putting off anything important."

"My room isn't important."

"Getting your father home is. And besides, I have to go check on the bar after we eat, while you go take your dad his things."

"Okay, but then I'll meet you at the bar, and if you can get away, which you don't have to, we'll come back here. It won't take very long. I just need to get into the closet. Since I have no clue how long I'll be here, with the exception of one sundress, I've only got fancy clothes with me. And I can't keep borrowing his cargo shorts. These are the only ones that fit me."

"Why don't we get the chores completely out of the way, then discuss what we'll do later."

"Are you suggesting the meal I've slaved over is going to be a chore to eat?"

He smiled. "You're not going to trick me into another kiss, you know."

She lowered her head. "Bet you I could."

He closed his eyes. "Fine. You could. But now ask yourself. Should you?"

Instead of going to the fridge, she jumped on him. Luckily, he caught her just fine, his big hands cupping her bottom as she attacked him with kisses. "I'm a grown-up," she said, between smooches. "I can do what I want."

"Uh-huh," he said, although it was mostly two grunts, as he started walking to the back of the house.

Unfortunately, he opened the wrong door. It was Ronny's bedroom, and that skeeved her out a little. She held his face between her hands as she stared into his gorgeous gray eyes. "Okay. Put me down. I'll put the fish on the grill, and you can make the salad dressing."

"Me?" He let her slide down his body.

She realized that was probably to make a point…seemed she'd stirred him up more than was nice. "It's not possible you don't know how to make salad dressing."

"What kind?"

"Whatever. I'm not picky."

"All right, but if you don't like it, don't blame me."

"Oh, don't even try to pull that guy crap. I know you better than that."

"Hey, that's not—"

"Don't make me call the girls."

"Hell, I'm outnumbered. I'm going to wash

up. Then I'll make the best damn salad dressing you've ever had."

She watched him walk to the bathroom, his butt a thing of wonder. Then she got busy with the grill.

THEY HAD JUST finished eating, with many compliments to his salad dressing, and to her exceptional fish, and he was tackling the dishes as Cricket went over the list of repairs. The list was long, and some of them she could handle, but some were way past her skill set. It was great that Wyatt had offered to help, but he had his own business to take care of. He might like Ronny, but he wasn't indebted to him, or for that matter, to her.

The water turned off and Wyatt grabbed a dish towel, while staring at her. "Everything okay?"

She nodded. "Have you heard anything about the resort owners trying to buy up beach property?"

"Yeah. They tried to buy the bar from Sam, but he didn't like them and refused to sell. That didn't stop him from using the leverage to raise the price on me, however. Not that I could blame him."

"They didn't try to pursue you?"

"Oh, yeah. But when I told them no, they backed off."

"Of course they did." The thought of a bunch of suits trying to strong-arm him made her smile, if only for a second. "What I'm worried about is them pressuring the older folks. I hate to think they're being taken advantage of. Not all of them had a lot of schooling."

"I couldn't help hearing your conversation with Penny. Can't say it surprises me." He studied her a moment, then hung the towel. "Is that really what's bothering you?"

"Mostly," she said. "I just have a lot on my mind."

He joined her at the table. "I may not have answers, but as you mentioned, I'm hella good at listening."

"Hella good, huh?"

He put his hand on hers. "For what it's worth I don't think you have to worry about Ronny. He's a tough old dude."

"I know."

"But...?"

She looked at their hands, liking the way he'd threaded his fingers through hers. "It's all jumbled together. I'd be surprised if he has good health insurance."

"Don't you think he's saved some money? His charter business is one of the busiest in the area."

"I don't know. He doesn't like to worry me, so of course, *that* worries me. I mean, obviously I'm going to make sure he has everything he needs regardless of his coverage. I'm lucky that I earn a good salary."

*For now at least.*

She kept the thought to herself, refusing to sound like she was complaining, or worse, making excuses for why she might need to swallow her pride and do what the partners wanted. God, it made her seem so weak and pathetic. She cleared her throat, as if that could keep the sudden nausea at bay.

"Look," Wyatt said, "bad enough you're faced with a life-changing decision, but now you feel cornered and helpless because your future depends on people who don't share the same values as you. It's a damn tough place to be. I understand because I've been there."

She swallowed around the lump in her throat. Maybe he really did get it. She wondered if it had anything to do with his decision to leave the military. Her thoughts bounced back to his purchase of the bar. It couldn't have been cheap. The land alone was worth a small fortune. Plus Sam had gotten an even higher price out of him. "Do you ever regret leaving the service?"

"Not for a second."

"What did Penny mean about you helping the coast guard?"

"I can fly a helicopter." He shrugged. "I've gone up to look for boats that lose communication, or when the sea turns rough and guys are late. That's all."

"That's all?" Cricket smiled. "Wait. Rough seas? Does that mean you go up during storms?"

"I have," he said slowly. "But only when it was safe to do so."

She let silence lapse, sensing his reluctance to talk about it. She couldn't help wondering if that had anything to do with him missing his old life.

Wyatt inhaled. Leaned back without pulling his grip away from hers. "Like I said, no regrets. And believe me, the decision wasn't an easy one. My whole family has been military. Great grandfather, grandfather, father, brother, uncles, all career military. I went to Annapolis, not just because it was expected of me, but because I wanted to. I wanted that life. Navy all the way. After a while, I got recruited into special ops, which was something else I'd wanted. I was doing what I was good at, and I didn't see an end in sight."

Cricket didn't have to say a word. She just watched his face as he mentally deliberated what to tell her next.

"After fifteen years of being part of a close extended family, which is what it is when you're in that kind of work, things changed for me. The job no longer fit. I couldn't do it anymore. Even when I knew without reservation that I needed to leave the service, it was the most difficult thing I've ever faced. My family still doesn't understand."

*Adam.*

It was the first thing that popped into her mind. If she didn't think it would hurt Wyatt, she'd have asked if his friend had anything to do with his decision. "Was it anything in particular that happened?"

His prolonged hesitation made her wish she hadn't asked the question.

"It doesn't matter," she said. "Not really."

"A mission went south, Cricket. Lives were lost. I know it happens. It's war. I've seen a lot of hard things. But this one hit different and there wasn't any other choice but to get out."

She squeezed his hand. "Thank you for telling me," she said, holding his gaze for several seconds, but unable to read him. Stricken by the awful feeling he might be reliving that horrible part of his past, she picked up the list. "Are there any urgent repairs that should be tackled sooner rather than later?"

"A couple, but watch the time. Didn't you say visiting hours are over at eight thirty?"

She nodded. "By the way, thanks for the list, but you're not on the hook for anything. I've got it all covered, although helping me out with my room tonight would be great."

"Okay. But what if I insist on helping after that?"

"It depends."

"On?"

"If I get to watch."

He flexed his back as if shrugging off a weight, and she was relieved to see the humor return to his eyes. When she stood up, so did he. Only he didn't pick up a hammer. Instead, he pulled her into a kiss that made her toes curl.

She kissed him back, but when he switched to nibbling on her neck, she wanted to drag him straight to her bedroom. They'd gone through this already, and if she didn't stop things right now, the whole plan would go to pot.

"Maybe," she whispered, "we could save some less critical chores for when Ronny's out with a charter. That would free up a little of our evening."

"Now you're talking. I have a whole list of things we could do."

"I've seen it."

He pulled away from her neck, and she wanted him back, right where he'd left off. "I wasn't talking about repairs—"

She laughed. She couldn't help it. "I really hate that I like you so much."

"We're even then. I hate that I like you, too." As he reached for her, his cell phone went off. "Speak of the devil…" He frowned at the screen. "My dad never calls," he muttered, as he put the phone up to his ear. "Good evening, Admiral, what can I do for you?"

"ARE YOU STILL in Rhode Island?"

Clearly the old man hadn't changed in the months since they'd last spoken. "Yep. Still own the bar, too." He could just imagine his father's twinge at that.

"I've heard there's a storm headed your way. A pretty bad one, according to the weather forecasts."

That stopped Wyatt cold. It wasn't like his father to worry about the weather. Either he was getting soft, or he was up to something. Or else... "How's Mom? Is she okay?"

"She's fine. Sends her best. She'll call you soon. I assume you've got things under control?"

"I do. Thanks for asking."

The admiral hesitated.

A weird feeling sent a chill down Wyatt's spine. "Everything all right with you?" Was it his brother? "Is Nelson okay?"

"I believe so. At least, I haven't heard otherwise. Everyone's fine."

"Good."

"Well, I won't keep you."

His father hung up, just like always. No goodbye, no sentiment at all, which was why Wyatt was confused.

"Your father's an admiral?"

He turned to Cricket. "Yep."

"Wow."

"To make things even worse, he's with the Pentagon."

"Huh," she said, obviously impressed, but she

also looked thoughtful. "So, in other words, he's
a pencil pusher."

Wyatt's laugh burst out of him like a shot.

"Was he special ops, too?"

"The admiral? No."

She put a hand on his hip. "What about the rest
of your family?"

"No, just me."

She gazed up at him without a trace of guile
in her eyes. "Well, then they really don't understand, do they?"

Wyatt's heart lightened. He pulled her close,
and all he could think was how much he really
liked this woman.

# CHAPTER EIGHTEEN

CRICKET WALKED INTO the bar, happy that for once she wasn't wearing high heels, but that was all she was happy about.

"Whoa, did something happen to Ronny?"

She slipped onto the barstool directly in front of Wyatt, who was mixing a G&T. "Did Sabrina have to leave?"

"She's covering tables for Shelly, who's on a break."

"Oh. Good."

He didn't bother asking about Ronny again—his right eyebrow did the job.

"I'm furious with my father."

"Why? What happened? Did he make a break for it?"

"No," Cricket said, thinking about stealing the gin and tonic before he could give it to a customer. And she didn't even like gin. "He lied to me."

"About?"

"He never got checked for surfer's ear. He told me he had, straight to my face. The doctor is almost positive that's what the problem is. It's not even that he could've had an unnecessary MRI, which would have cost a fortune. Just… Ronny's always been honest with me." She swallowed past the lump in her throat. "Or maybe he lied all the time, who knows?"

Leaning straight over the bar, she grabbed the drink now that the lime slice was on it. "He's having a CT scan tomorrow morning. Then he'll need to see an audiologist. There's a possibility that he'll need surgery. Though that won't stop him from being discharged tomorrow, so we'll need to get his stupid shack ready first thing in the morning. The doctor's going to call when they have his results." After taking a pretty big drink, she winced hard.

"Gin not your thing?"

"It's really not. But I'll finish it, don't worry."

He reached over and took the glass. "How about a beer?"

"That would be great. Thank you." She'd never been with a man who was so considerate before. Not about her drink, although that was sweet. There were lots of little things. And she knew without a doubt he'd keep an eye on Ronny after she left. Which was both comforting and upsetting. It was going to be hard enough to leave…

Why couldn't she have met him in Chicago? Of course, if he had lived there, she never would've met him anyway, because all she did was work. And hang out with other lawyers. How depressing.

As he bent over to get a bottle from the cooler, Cricket looked away out of self-preservation. She'd just noticed Leonard and Marvin at the end of the bar when she had a tiny epiphany.

When Wyatt set down her beer, she crooked her finger and got as close to him as possible so she wouldn't be overheard. "Special ops, father's an admiral, so...ex-SEAL?"

He gave her a crooked smile that melted her. "Yeah."

"So, when you mentioned that it might be swimmer's ear, you knew what you were talking about."

"I never had it, but some guys in BUD/S training did, and that was enough to disqualify them. It can be serious, if not taken care of. I know it can lead to hearing loss and infections, along with the vertigo."

"Oddly, Dr. Oakden doesn't think he's had it very long, or he wouldn't have been able to hide it at all. By all rights I should leave him in there for a week, but I know they'll need the beds if the storm is worse than they expect."

Sabrina walked up to the bar and smiled at Cricket, giving her a quick hello before facing Wyatt. "I need a pitcher of margaritas, please. Some guys from the offshore wind turbine crew had to evacuate and plan to spend the night here."

"Did you tell them we close at one and not a minute later?"

"I did. And they're calling motels as we speak."

"You let me know if there's any trouble, okay? I don't want them getting too hammered."

"I'll manage it, boss. No one ever guesses when I water down the punch."

He smiled, then got to work on the pitcher.

Cricket took a moment to look around as she washed the taste of gin out of her mouth. There weren't all that many customers, no surprise there, and most of them were locals. She'd known Leonard and Marvin from when she was a kid, and she guessed that they made a habit of coming here in the evenings. Naturally, they were watching the news about the storm. That was all anyone had talked about at the hospital. They'd been getting prepared, even though the last she'd heard, it had been downgraded again, and wasn't expected to make landfall this far north. Still, while she'd been yelling at Ronny, the hospital had run tests on their backup generators.

Someone she didn't know well, although she recognized her, was sitting next to Leonard. "Shut up, everyone. Shut up."

It was breaking news from WPRI. The storm was picking up speed as it turned west just past Virginia.

"That ought to slow it down even more," Leonard said. "It won't be anything except some wind by the time it gets this far."

"We don't know how long it'll be in Virginia,

though," the woman said. "Could just go right back out to sea at that new speed."

"Nah," Leonard said, after he'd drained his beer. "Landfall that far down the coast is always a good sign. Mark my words."

"I know this kind of storm," Marvin said, frowning at his buddy. "It'll hit hard. Not as hard as some, but on the beachfront? We'll see some heavy damage. I've already boarded our windows, and tomorrow me and the missus are going to her sister's inland."

"Are you nuts?" Leonard said, as if the man had insulted him personally. "It's June. Nothing's gonna hit the Bay hard in June. You're drunk, old man."

"I'm right about this. I feel it in my bones."

"And you're the only one who knows. Better than the guys who study weather for a living. Better than the coast guard and the mayor, whose only advice is to watch out for the windows near the beach, and be prepared for a possible power outage."

"Remember Sandy?" Marvin said, making a sour face. "We got slammed."

"Yeah, and we knew it was coming. Everybody knew it was a massive hurricane. This'll be nothing but a mosquito bite."

"Could Marvin be right?" Cricket asked, looking at Wyatt. "Are we being too cavalier about this?"

"If I hear this argument one more time, I'll be

the one causing some serious damage," Wyatt said, shaking his head. "We've got nothing to worry about. I've been tracking this storm since it hit the Bahamas, and we'll be fine. I even called an old friend of mine to make sure. Someone who'd know."

That made her relax. Whoever he'd called would have a lot more information than some guy in a bar. "I believe you, but if you need to stay here, I completely understand." She stood, beer in hand. "I'll just go back and get my room straightened out. In fact, I might as well check out of the hotel. Whether or not he needs surgery, I should be there in case he falls again. Who knows, I might even find out if he's hiding something else from me."

"Hold on a minute. I'm coming with you. It's slow, and Sabrina doesn't need me hanging around making her feel as if I'm doing her a favor by letting her run things. Anyway, the old-timers are driving me nuts. I can't take it."

"Oops." Cricket grinned. "Then I come in here bitching about Ronny."

"I don't care about that." He grabbed a towel and wiped his hands. "When, exactly, are you planning to check out of the hotel?"

She knew why he was asking. She'd thought about that herself. Sure would be a shame to let that amazing bed and tub go to waste. "I haven't really thought about it. Probably late tonight or early tomorrow morning. They're going to charge me for a full day, so it doesn't matter either way."

"Like hell it doesn't," he said a bit too loudly.

Cricket laughed, knowing he'd take the bait.

THE SUITE WAS COOL, plush and so welcoming after such a difficult day that Cricket felt like stripping down right that second and dragging Wyatt into the tub with her. But, he was on his cell, talking to Sabrina, then Becky, who was waiting out the storm inland with her late husband's grandparents. After that he wanted to call his friend Roy in DC who had up-to-the-minute weather information. So the tub would have to wait until the phone calls were done, and they'd gotten something to eat. Besides, she wanted to shower off the grunge from working in her old bedroom before she stepped into her oil-infused bath.

"You sure?" he asked, while opening the minibar. After another moment of silence, he said, "Okay. Call if you need me. I'll see you tomorrow."

"You hungry, too?" Cricket joined him, running her hand across his back. It was a great minibar, with high-end snacks and beverages. They could have themselves a nice picnic after the bath.

Wyatt closed the fridge and looked at her, a quarter smile making him look even sexier than normal. "Yeah, but food can wait," he said. "Let me help you get out of those uncomfortable clothes."

"Don't you have another call to make?"

"Roy isn't going anywhere."

Grinning, Cricket took his hand and pulled him closer to the big bathroom. "Your assignment, should you decide to accept it, is to make me forget about Ronny, the storm and my job. Think you can do that?"

As he closed the door behind him, he pulled off his T-shirt and kicked off his shoes. Then he lifted her sundress up and off, and relieved her of her bra and panties.

He kissed her forehead, her lips, the tip of her chin, then breathed warm air over her already budding nipples before standing up again. That just left his pants, which he stripped down along with his boxer briefs.

Her tummy fluttered like crazy and she almost gave up on her plan, but no. She could wait. "Let's shower off first, okay?"

"I thought this was all about the tub?"

"Trust me, it is." The fluttering got out of control as she watched him turn on the shower and adjust each one of the multiple showerheads. So she got busy, starting the taps on the big double tub, then she poured in her favorite body oil that would soothe their muscles and make them smell like cucumber and melon.

The moment she turned around, the sight of

the water flowing over his stunning chest stole her breath. Sparse dark hair swirled around his muscles, tapering down to a treasure trail that earned the moniker.

She stepped inside the glass shower, and he pulled her into his arms. The first kiss was soft and sweet, a mere brush of lips, but then his hands moved down her back, and as they rubbed against each other, the wet slick making every move smooth as silk, he took her mouth.

When she finally looked up, his dark hungry gaze met hers.

"We done in here?"

She shook her head and grabbed the fresh scrubby that had been left by housekeeping. It was her own body wash that she used, however, making a rich, lemon-scented lather.

He plucked the scrub right out of her hands and proceeded to wash her from neck to toe, taking great care not to miss any spots. It was better than any spa day she'd ever had. It didn't even tickle when he got to her feet, but she couldn't stop trembling.

Then it was her turn, and the pleasure was just as profound in giving as receiving. His body was a work of art, from his chiseled jaw all the way down to his muscled calves, and everything in between. He was so hard, Cricket's thighs clenched together involuntarily. That did nothing for the ache, though.

"I think it's time for our bath," he said, his voice low, eyes closed.

"Go ahead and rinse off," she said, handing him the scrub. "I have to get something." She left the shower, a little chilled at the temperature difference, but that only made her more anxious to get into the tub. It was almost full and since there would be two of them, she turned off the taps. It smelled gorgeous, and she knew the oil would make everything feel like heaven. The last thing she did was take out her jar of coconut oil and put it within reach.

It didn't take but a couple of minutes for Wyatt to join her in the tub. It was so large, that her lower body had floated until he was settled, and she could brace herself against him. His erection had eased up, but wasn't gone, and it was hard not to just watch it bobbing in the water.

She giggled, then saw that he was watching her boobs bob, too. "We're so easily amused. What does that say about us? I mean, we're in our thirties. This shouldn't be a novelty at all."

"It's you," he said. "Of course it's novel." He turned to his side, and put his arm behind her back, while his free hand cupped her jaw. "You were beautiful the first time I laid eyes on you, and you've gotten prettier by the day. How's that possible?"

"Huh, so it's not just me, then?"

"What, you also think you've gotten prettier?"

She nudged him with her elbow and watched the outside corners of his eyes crinkle. "You know what I meant. You've become so much more than I was expecting."

"In bed, or in general?"

"Both, as it happens. You've been incredibly thoughtful. Not just to me, either. I love the way you watch out for your staff, although…"

"What?"

"How come there aren't any guys serving drinks?"

"I serve drinks."

"Besides you."

"There have been in the past, and I'm sure there will be again. But I admit, I'm very careful with hiring. It's important that everyone feels safe, especially when I'm not there."

"Okay, I understand. But I don't know, wouldn't it be safer for the women if there were a couple of men there, too? I bet your female customers would appreciate it."

"Huh," he said. "And here I thought I was enough eye candy to satisfy everyone."

She kissed him. "You're more than enough, Mr. Ego."

"Kidding. You make a good point, but I'm also going to be giving all the staff self-defense lessons. I should have done that from the start, but now, I'll make sure they can all take care of themselves, no matter what."

"Great idea. Wish I was staying long enough to learn with them. Chicago can be scary."

In an instant his eyes turned a stormy gray. "Let's not talk about you leaving."

Cricket blinked. No, she didn't want to even think about it, either.

"I don't want to lose my cucumber scent high," he said, his mouth lifting in a faint smile, clearly trying to lighten the mood again. "It's weird. You know, bathing in vegetables."

She smiled back, playing along, unwilling to remain stuck on his unexpected reaction. "And fruit."

"Can't forget the fruit."

"But it's nice, isn't it?" she asked, teasing his lower lip with her finger. "It's soothing in all the right ways."

His hand moved down her body, until he was soothing her in a completely different way. "Now, this is better than nice," he whispered, watching her eyes until she couldn't keep them open another second.

By ELEVEN THIRTY the next morning, the wind was coming in at twenty miles per hour. Wyatt had made sure Ronny's shack was boarded up tight, and that Skip had gathered his gang to get the *Baby Girl* battened down.

Wyatt wished he could have gone to spring Ronny instead of Cricket, but in truth, she'd be fine and he needed to help secure the bar. Turned out the girls hadn't waited for him. "Man, you guys did an ace job."

"It was no problem," Tiffy said. "Viv was here for a while, but she had to go get her mom's house ready. The wind farm guys helped, though. They did all the heavy lifting."

"Okay, remind me, I owe them a few rounds on the house," he said, and caught Tiffy's little smile before she slid a look at Sabrina.

"Oh, they're totally fine." She shrugged. "But maybe we'll give them one round."

He wasn't even going to ask. "Well, thank you. Seriously. You ladies did great," he said, noticing how they'd secured the liquor to withstand anything short of the whole place caving in. He doubted it would, and even if there was a strong storm surge, it probably wouldn't do any damage. But there would definitely be something extra in their next paycheck. "Did you guys get any sleep?"

"Sleep is for sissies," Sabrina said, looking as if she would conk out in a second if she dared sit down.

"Why don't you two get out of here? Go home and get some rest."

"Nah, I'm staying," Sabrina said, and Tiffy added, "We both are."

"Well, you can go upstairs if you want. I appreciate you taking care of the hurricane shutters up there, and it shouldn't be so windy you'll be in any danger. Aside from Lego toys—"

"And your bed. When's the last time you changed your sheets?" Tiffy had her hands on her hips and was clearly bent on making mischief.

"Okay, *you* can catch a nap in the office. While Sabrina sleeps happily on my freshly laundered sheets. Also, there's a sleeping bag and extra pillows in the closet. But if the power goes out, it'll get warm up there."

Sabrina moaned. "At least we bagged up a ton of ice and filled the coolers to the brim. You have any food up there that's going to spoil if we're caught for long?"

"You might as well finish off the kids' ice cream. There's not a lot in the fridge but feel free to have at it." He felt for his phone, but didn't pull it out. "You guys know you can get me if there's an emergency. If necessary, you can come on down to Ronny's shack, but only if it's safer than staying here. I have it on good authority that the winds shouldn't go over sixty miles an hour, and we've weathered worse than that, right?"

"Way worse," Tiffy agreed. "Bet it's coming early, just like Marvin said…"

"Yep." Wyatt checked his watch. "And we'll be hearing about it for a year."

"Think we'll open today?" The bruise on Sabrina's arm had lightened some, which was good to see, but Cricket had been right. Regardless of the training, he should have a guy or two to balance out the team.

"How about I leave it up to you two?"

They exchanged startled looks.

"Okay," Sabrina said, standing a little taller. "We'll let you know what we decide."

Wyatt nodded. "Take care, sit tight and thanks again. I don't know what I'd do without the two of you. And I mean that. Now, stay safe."

"You watch out yourself," Tiffy said. "That shack isn't all that sturdy."

He smiled. "It is now."

"PLEASE, RONNY. JUST please stay here. Look, you can help get the food all cooked. You know you're going to have a whole tribe of people showing up before and after the storm. You can start putting ice in the coolers, okay? You'll be needing that sooner rather than later."

"Dammit, Baby Girl. My livelihood depends on that boat."

"And Skip has all the help he needs to get it ready. I'm still going to double-check everything is shipshape, and Wyatt's coming with me. So don't worry. And above all, don't worry me more than I already have been. I mean it. I love you, and I've got to go. You help Wendy and Ted now, and then you get some rest. If you feel dizzy, sit down right away. Remember that the air pressure might be harder on your ears than you're used to. So chew gum, don't get drunk and be safe. Okay?"

Ronny nodded, then pulled her into a fierce hug. "Don't you be out there too long. I won't give a damn about a boat if anything happens to you."

"I'll be fine. See you soon." She looked over at the two kids cooking up pretty much everything in the fridge. "Watch out for him, okay?"

"Sure thing, Cricket." Wendy waved the spatula. At least the girl was wearing an apron over her bikini. Ted was cooking shirtless. What could go wrong?

She left, hoping everything was all right at the bar and at the boat. It was windy, but nothing major yet. Even if the guys hadn't done much more than fix the anchors they would still have enough time to get the rest under control.

As expected the dock was a madhouse. Those idiot fishermen had been advised not to go out as of late last night, but did they listen? Of course not. She understood that they couldn't afford to miss a day's catch, but still. She hoped everyone had made accommodations for a speedy mooring.

Wyatt was already on the boat, fitting Ronny's old collection of retired fire hoses on the multiple lines that had been set by Skip and friends. As for Skip himself, he was fastening down everything that could possibly blow away, including antennas, cushions and all the fishing gear. Jim wasn't there, or maybe he was working on the other side, checking out the bumpers.

She climbed aboard, and though she wanted to go straight to Wyatt, she turned to Skip instead. "What can I do?"

He pointed to the helm. "Tape and cover."

She nodded, focusing on the pitch of the boat, but it was smooth enough in this chop that she knew the anchors were set well. She'd noticed the lines had been crossed to minimize shifting or breakage during the storm surge. It would get rockier, but she knew what kind of care Ronny gave the *Baby Girl*. It would hold.

Wyatt looked up as she crossed over to the cabin stairs. "Ronny okay?"

"Fine." She had to say it loud, considering all the activity on the dock. "I told him I'd kill him if he dared take a step out of the shack."

"You got your assignment?"

"Skip's the captain right now, so yep."

Wyatt got back to it, and she applied herself to the task of making sure anything electronic that couldn't be taken to the shack was sealed watertight. After that, she'd check to make sure all openings on the boat were secured.

It was hot as hell with brutal humidity. But the more she accomplished, the better she felt. Her mood brightened considerably when she saw how many of Ronny's friends and mentees had come out to assist. She'd do a walk-around before she went back to the shack, which she figured would be within the next half hour.

A horn from aft sounded from the harbormaster's boat, alerting everyone that Eddie was checking out the dock. She left the cockpit to join Wyatt and Skip.

"What's going on?" She had to yell at this point, because a lot of folks were trying to get Eddie's attention.

Wyatt pulled her close, his body blocking some of the wind. "Two boats are still out."

A minute later the *Sea Flyer* came rushing in, the guys on deck working frantically to stow all the gear. As it passed the harbormaster's boat, the captain bellowed, "Is Tony back?"

Eddie shook his head.

"He went pretty far out there, the old fool. Keep an eye out. The chop is pretty bad where he was headed."

Eddie waved him on, then took out his radio, probably trying to get in touch with Tony. He looked frustrated, and as he continued trying to signal, Stella, Tony's wife, ran past Ronny's slip, yelling and flapping her arms in an attempt to get Eddie's attention. The harbormaster was facing the open sea, and the wind wasn't her ally.

Stella gave up and hurried toward the *Baby Girl*. "Tony's radio is down. I can't reach him," she said, looking tearfully at Wyatt. "So is his GPS. He was supposed to replace it, and now he's not showing up at all." She paused, briefly closing her eyes. "Dear God, I hate to ask…"

"It's okay, Stella," Wyatt said.

Cricket didn't realize she was clinging to him until he pried her arms away.

# CHAPTER NINETEEN

WYATT KNEW THE wind was about twenty-five knots at this point, but Marty's helicopter was built for this kind of mess, even though he mostly used it to take tourists up. But if Wyatt was going up, he needed to go soon. Too much chance of crosswinds as the storm got closer.

"I'll call Marty, then head out to the heliport. You have any idea where Tony was headed?"

Wringing her hands together, Stella shook her head, then turned to look out at the choppy sea.

He pulled out his cell, but Cricket's hand on his arm stopped him. "You're going to fly in this?"

"It's safe. It's a great helicopter, built for rescues."

"What about the coast guard? Aren't they supposed to be the ones to go out there?"

"I'm sure they're already out searching for boats. But with Tony's radio and GPS down, they're going to need all the help they can get before the storm hits us."

"I hate this," she said, her voice low and soft as she glanced toward Stella, who was still turned away.

"Look, I won't be doing anything risky. If I spot Tony first, I'll be able to give the coast guard his coordinates. They'll take it from there. Seriously, if it was too dangerous, I wouldn't go up. Marty wouldn't let me. But that chopper has faced double this wind before. In fact, it used to belong to the coast guard."

"I'll go with you. Two pairs of eyes will be better."

"No, you're not. You've got enough to do right here."

"Skip's got this. Did you see how many people are helping out?"

"What about Ronny?"

"Wendy and Ted are with him. I trust them. And I'm going."

He admired the hell out of her, but no way was she going up with him. "Look, I'm sorry, but I don't need the distraction of worrying about you."

"You said it wasn't dangerous."

"Fine. Go check on Ronny, let him know what's what. I'm going to get in touch with Marty now, and head out to the heliport. You meet me there."

"You won't leave without me?"

"No. Now go," he said and started walking as he hit speed dial.

SHE ASKED SKIP to have someone else finish in the helm. It was time to do a walk-around, but she worried Wyatt would find a reason to leave without her.

"It's all right, Cricket," Skip said. "I've helped Ronny through two other tropical storms. I won't let you down."

"I know. Just be careful, and go to the shack before it gets bad."

He nodded, and she made her way through the crowd on the main dock. No one had time to stop her or make idle chatter. When she set foot on the sand, she jogged the rest of the way to the shack.

It smelled like a hotel kitchen, and Dr. Dre blared so loudly the windows were likely to end up imploding. Ronny sat at the table with three kids she hadn't seen before. Two girls, one a tall, willowy blonde, the other looked younger than Wendy. The boy sat at the edge of his seat, drinking soda and listening to Ronny as if he had the wisdom of the ages. When it came to surfing and boats, Cricket supposed the kid had a point.

"How's everything at the dock?" Ronny asked, causing everyone to stop what they were doing and stare at her.

"Skip's doing a great job. I'm here to make sure you're being good."

"Hey, Baby Girl, the last thing I want to do is worry you. Besides, nobody will let me lift a finger."

"Excellent. I'll be gone for a bit, giving Wyatt a hand. Okay if I take the Jeep?"

"'Course it is. Everything okay? I mean, if we still have power, it can't be that bad."

"No, Tony's boat might have gotten into a little trouble coming back in to dock."

"He's going up in the helicopter, I bet," Wendy said. "He found a friend of mine once. Well, the whole boat, but my friend was on it."

Cricket sighed. So, did Wyatt have this deep-seated need to rescue everyone? "Well, listen, I've got to run."

"You're not thinking of flying with him," Ronny said, "are you?"

"Don't worry. I'm just going to the heliport."

"Okay, I'm counting on you being here when the storm finally rolls in."

"I'll be back as soon as possible."

She quickly went to the table, kissed her father on the cheek, smiled at his entourage and ran to the Jeep. She got behind the wheel, and took some side roads and a couple of detours since the main drag was packed with folks on their way to higher ground. Finally, though, she turned down the road to the heliport. It had been built several years ago, after the hospital had added the new wing.

She stopped the car with too heavy a foot and jerked forward.

Wyatt's truck was there. The helicopter wasn't. *That bastard.*

She was so angry she was shaking. He'd promised not to leave without her. The Jeep shivered in a gust of wind, making her think about stupid Wyatt up in a stupid helicopter trying to be a stupid hero.

Yes, he undoubtedly was a hero, in a very real sense, but this? Had he ditched her on purpose? Known it was dangerous all along, but didn't want to tell her? Even Ronny had looked worried about her going up. *Ronny.* The thought made her even more furious.

She jammed the Jeep into Drive and sped the ten minutes it took to get to the bar. She figured he'd stop there first to make sure everything was okay.

After she parked she noticed she had a text. It was from Wyatt. Claiming that since the wind had picked up he couldn't wait any longer. She didn't believe that for a second.

The temptation to text him back was strong, but she wouldn't. Not while he was flying in all that wind. He needed to come back. Safely.

So she could tear him a new one.

First, though, she had to calm down before she went into the bar. The windows had already been boarded up, but the outdoor tables hadn't been moved. Someone had to be there because the door was propped open. She just couldn't see inside from where she was parked.

She hoped that they'd had word about Wyatt, or that someone knew who to call to find out his status. Feeling powerless, her anger surged inside her like the tide. Every minute, the wind was gaining momentum. He could be caught in a crosswind. Would he keep searching for the boat until it was too late? Would he even realize it could be too late?

Running their last conversation over in her head, she smacked her palm against the steering wheel. Hard. Dammit. He'd known from the second she'd said she would go with him that he wasn't going to let her. All he wanted was for her to leave so he could get to the heliport, go up without having to argue with her. Another lie, right to her face. How dare he pull this crap, especially when he knew she was still worried about Ronny. Wondering if she'd been a fool to bring him home. The shack might have been boarded up and fortified, but this was a tropical storm. Anything could happen. And now she was terrified for Wyatt, too.

Forcing a deep breath, she leaned back against the headrest and noticed Tiffy and Sabrina dragging one of the outside tables to the side of the bar, then turning it over. It was unwieldy in the wind even now. The umbrellas were down already, but the girls needed help, and Cricket needed to work off some of her anxiety.

Sabrina was just getting a grip on the second table when Cricket moved to the middle position closer to Tiffy. Both girls grinned at her, then at the count of three, they lifted the heavy table, walked it over to the side and flipped it over so it wouldn't blow away.

"Have you heard anything from Wyatt?"

Sabrina nodded. "One of our regulars who works at the coast guard office said they found Tony. He's fine, his boat not so much. It's being towed into the bay. And she thinks she heard that Wyatt's on his way back. He might've landed already."

Relief spread through Cricket, barely inching out her still simmering anger. Even the questioning look from Tiffy didn't loosen Cricket's clenched jaw and pressed lips as they finally got the other table down. The chairs still needed to be stacked, even though they were inside the bar already.

Doing the work helped, but not by much.

"You want a drink?" Sabrina asked.

It was tempting, but she wanted to be clear-headed when she talked to Wyatt. "No, thanks."

The next ten minutes felt more like an hour. Sneaking peeks between the parking lot and her cell phone. In fact, he had texted her again, indicating only that he was back. But it just made her angrier—she hadn't noticed it until after the fact because she'd been too pissed off to hear the beep.

It was Tiffy who spotted his truck. "He's here," she said, nodding to the parking lot.

Cricket walked outside to the railing, letting

the wind toss her hair and plaster her clothes to her body. It was unbelievably humid, the air full of ozone, the scent of the sea multiplied by a hundred, and oddly, petrichor, the smell of dry earth after a rain shower.

Wyatt parked, then stepped out of his truck and looked straight at her. An SUV pulled into the lot and parked on the other side of him, but he kept walking without even a glance at it. It could've been Becky, but Cricket was too busy practicing everything she was going to say to him the minute they came face to face.

They met on the last step.

"Cricket—"

She poked him right in the chest. "Don't you dare do anything like that to me again. You tell me to meet you there, promise me you'd wait, and then you take off without me? I'm not putting up with that macho bullshit. I'm not. I thought you were different, dammit." She took a quick breath, without breaking eye contact. "You don't ever lie to me again. You don't treat me like a child and you sure as hell don't treat me like some poor clueless woman who needs a man to make her decisions."

He opened his mouth, but she stepped in closer and jabbed him in the chest again. "Are? We? Clear?"

Wyatt looked stricken. Kind of. Too calm, though. Maybe she hadn't fully made her point.

"Are you going to let me talk?" he said, a hard edge to his voice.

"Why? So you can lie to me again?"

His mouth tightened. "Look, I'm sorry. But I did send you a text."

"And that's supposed to make everything all right? Well, it didn't. It was bullshit, just like Ronny's crap about his ears, and I've had enough of that slung at me in the last forty-eight hours."

"Hey, wait a minute." He put his hands on her upper arms, and while it was tempting to shake him off, she didn't, despite being pissed that it felt comforting. Because he was here in the flesh and she knew he was safe. "The wind speed had changed, and every second counted. I wasn't going to risk my life, but I had a small window of time to make that decision, and I made the call to go up. You can believe whatever you want, but that's the truth, and I'm not sorry for it."

The shaking hadn't stopped inside, but the ringing in her ears had let up so she actually heard him. "Can you honestly tell me that was the only reason you left me behind?"

"The truth? At first, I didn't want you to go with me. But that had more to do with me than you."

"Explain."

He didn't answer her. Instead, he looked past her into the bar, then turned his head and that's when Cricket saw that Becky had stepped out of her car.

"We'll talk about it later, okay? Not out here where we have an audience."

Still trembling, she couldn't seem to respond. It was as if a splash of ice water had woken her up. She'd been so... "All right. Look, I'm sorry, but I've never been more terrified in my—" She looked away.

His grip on her tightened and she looked back at him. He stared straight into her eyes. "Later. At Ronny's. Okay?"

She nodded, anxious to get away from the bar and their spectators. As soon as he let her go, Cricket gave Becky—who was hovering by the bottom step—the quickest smile ever, then dashed to Ronny's Jeep, got in and hit the gas.

WYATT'S EYES NARROWED as Becky stepped onto the deck, her ponytail whipping across her face. "What the hell are you smiling about?"

Her grin widened. "I do believe, Lieutenant Covack, that you've finally met your match."

Wyatt gave her the stare of death, but then he looked back toward the bar. The girls didn't even move from their front row seats at the railing. "What, no popcorn?"

Sabrina and Tiffy exchanged glances, then turned and went back inside.

He breathed in deep and slow. "Are the kids in the car?"

"They're with their grandparents. I don't think this will be anything to worry about, but Peter and Yvette feel better when they have their eyes on us."

He nodded. Closed his eyes for a second, then just asked the question that had been bothering him a lot. "Was that you I saw the other day?"

"When you scared the shit out of that guy? Yes."

He winced. "The kids?"

"They didn't see anything but *Aladdin* on the back seat DVD."

Relief flowed through him. "That was Sabrina's boyfriend."

"I figured," she said, although the humor that had been in her eyes had gone, replaced by worry. "All these years and I've never seen that side of you."

Wyatt thought about telling her it was an aberration, something he'd never do again, but he had no idea if that was true. He didn't want to scare her, and he sure as hell hadn't wanted to frighten the kids, but in that moment, he'd felt more like himself than he had in a long time.

"I'm not saying that was necessarily a bad thing. That jerk deserved a lot worse. It was just…" She shrugged. "Anyway, I came by to see if you needed any help before I went inland, and also I wanted to ask you something."

"What's that?"

She looked a little pink in the cheeks. "I was wondering, when everything settles down, and things are more normal, if you and Cricket would like to have dinner with me and Ned? Kind of like a double date?"

A double date? What the hell had happened to his world? Things had been going along fine for a long time, and now, he'd somehow ended up here. With Becky going out with a guy named Ned.

"I know the timing's rotten. I'd intended to ask you when I stopped by the other day. Anyway, think about it, okay? Maybe talk to Cricket. I really like her a lot. And I want you to meet Ned."

"Huh," he said, sure in a second he'd respond appropriately. But somehow, Becky was already getting into her car, and he still had nothin'.

# CHAPTER TWENTY

THE SKY HAD darkened with the pounding rain and Cricket felt as if she was caught in time, an endless spiral of noise and heat. Wyatt's quiet presence next to her on her bed probably spiked the temperature, but she didn't want him to move, unless he wanted to come closer.

The music and chatter coming from Ronny's gang melded with the cacophony outside, yet all she could think about was how utterly terrified she'd been with Wyatt up in that helicopter. She'd never felt that kind of rage before, not even when she'd been stabbed in the back by Grant. Or when she'd been cheated on by her college boyfriend. Nothing had hit her quite that intensely—all driven by pure fear.

That revelation had come when the storm had hit in earnest and they'd taken refuge in Ronny's shack. Probably because she was still angry at her father. Because he'd scared her. But how could she feel this way about a man she'd known for such a short time? She'd never been impetuous before, at least not when it came to relationships.

As for Grant, she hadn't ever considered him a love interest.

"Cricket? Would it be better if I went back to the bar? Left you alone for a while?"

"What?" Her exhaustion was as draining as the noise, and even shaking her head felt like it was beyond her ability.

"I'm sorry for leaving without you," Wyatt said. "I did wait as long as I could, but the barometer was rising by the minute and so was the wind speed."

It was a perfectly logical explanation, but she wasn't completely buying it. Now that she understood that he'd done this kind of thing before. That he'd helped the coast guard—who routinely went into crazy dangerous situations—told her a lot. To ask him the question might not be fair, but she needed to know. "Do you miss the action? The adrenaline rushes?"

Wyatt had moved closer, now sharing her pillow as he looked straight into her eyes. She'd seen him like this before—laser-focused, his brow furrowed.

"Yeah, I do miss it sometimes. And I do like to feel I can make a difference, but that's mostly because the military has been such a huge part of my life. Not just being a SEAL, but all of it. Serving my country was all I knew for most of my life. Hell, I was raised in the culture."

She nodded, impressed yet again by his honesty.

"I imagine it's how you must miss the ocean and the slower pace of Temptation Bay."

"Hmm," she said, giving him a brief nod, which probably wasn't the admission he hoped for, but she didn't want the focus to be on her.

He didn't push for more. Instead, he brushed the damp hair off her forehead. "When all is said and done, special ops got to be too much for me. I've made the right decision. Buying the bar, being here to help out with Becky and the kids. I'm happy where I am."

She cuddled against him, draping her arm across his chest. His muscles eased as he put his arm around her back.

The radio kept them up-to-date, the ongoing ruckus in the next room nearly drowning out the rain and wind, although they still hadn't reached fifty knots. "I'll put twenty bucks on the power going out at fifty-three knots," she said, running her hand under his T-shirt, finding his sweat arousing, which was a first. "Duration, five hours, margin of error plus or minus thirty minutes."

His upper body moved to his laughter. "Okay, twenty bucks on fifty-eight knots, duration twelve hours, margin of error plus or minus eleven hours."

She lifted her head, full of indignation. Only to find him grinning at her with the big, easy smile she wanted to gift wrap and send to herself in Chicago. "Try again, buddy."

"Spoilsport." He shifted her a bit, his hands cupping her bottom so she pressed against him more firmly. "Margin of error plus or minus thirty minutes."

"Deal," she said, but he kissed her before she'd finished the word. When he pulled back she started giggling. "SEALed with a kiss. Get it? SEALed?"

"That's not even a thing," he said, but despite his serious expression, she had proof he was laughing on the inside.

"You think it's funny," she said. "Come on…"

He kissed her again, and she forgot about the storm and the kids in the living room…basically anything that wasn't Wyatt. Until some idiot turned the music to eleven.

Wyatt winced. "God, I'd be okay with the power going out now just so that noise would stop."

"My father doesn't have surfer's ear. His eardrums have been blown out listening to this crap."

"Hey, you want me to brave the living room while we still have power? Get us another beverage or two, maybe top off the ice in the cooler?"

"Good idea, but I'll go," she said, pushing up on her elbows. "I want to make sure everyone's behaving, especially you-know-who. What can I get you?"

"Beer would be good at this point, I think. Sure you don't need me to hoist and carry?"

"I can manage. You keep listening to the weather, and I'll be back before you lose all your hearing."

AFTER CRICKET HAD left the room, Wyatt stripped the bed of everything but the bottom sheet and the pillows. He tried to call his friend about any weather updates, but the lines were overloaded.

The music suddenly went down. Way down. He couldn't hear what Cricket was saying, and he was sorry to miss it. She could keep up with any drill sergeant. Hell, she could go toe to toe with the SEAL trainers. Although she didn't cuss as much.

He sat, putting his elbows on his knees, and stared at the weird pale pink carpet. What was he thinking getting so involved with a woman who was going to leave any day now? Or maybe her leaving was what made it all right for him to get involved?

The last thing he wanted to do was overthink things. Instead, he tried his phone again, this time to contact the bar. Sabrina had let him know they'd opened, at least as long as the power held out. He got through, and according to Tiffy, all was well. The laughter in the background confirmed it.

Cricket returned with the small cooler, refilled with ice and four beers. He smiled, glad she was back.

"Nice," she said, nodding her approval at his redecorating. After putting the cooler down, and handing him a beer, she climbed on next to him.

Before he could say a word, a huge gust of wind shook the whole shack, followed by an enormous crack, like wood snapping.

"Oh, God, I hope that wasn't our green ash."

"I doubt it. That sounded like it was at least three hundred meters from here. That tree is much closer."

"I love that tree," she said, handing him his beer. "I used it to measure my height every year. Bet the trunk still has the marks."

"You'll have to show me."

"Maybe tomorrow morning, when we sweep the beach for damage. If the tree is still there."

HER PHONE RANG. Grant's ringtone. "Damn," she said, picking up her cell from the nightstand, but not answering it. She'd had a lot of time to consider what she was going to do, and although the thought of it made her ill, she'd come up with a plan that could work. The cell rang again, but she just put it on silent before setting it down.

"Grant?"

She nodded. "I'm not ready to deal with him. Not right now."

"If it's any consolation, I think the storm is already losing a little steam."

One second later, the power went out, making them both laugh. "Did you get the last measurement when I was in the other room?"

It was very dark, and would get much more humid without the overhead fan. "Fifty-one knots. And why is that music still playing?"

"Battery packs," she said.

"Ronny uses them to run the music?"

"No. Those are from his minions."

"He couldn't persuade them to power an air conditioner?"

She put her cold hand on his chest, and he jerked so hard he shook the bed. The flashlight was right next to her cell phone, but she didn't reach for it as she giggled, wondering if she dared touch him somewhere even hotter.

Then a shock of ice hit her bare thigh, and the shriek that came out of her was louder than the wind. The icy beer bottle was removed quickly, but that didn't lessen her thirst for blood. "Okay, buddy. You wanted war, you'll get war."

"Wait a minute. You started this whole thing."

She made her most affronted face, even though he couldn't see her. "It was just my hand, which I thought would cool you off. It wasn't my fault you decided to throw down the red flag."

"You did not touch my chest so I'd cool down. You did it to make me jump."

"I would never."

"Oh, I know your wicked ways, Cricket Shaw. You're wily. Too smart for your own good." His warm hand was on her thigh, moving upward at a steady pace.

Still in the eerie darkness, she found his arm, then the hand holding the beer. She snatched that away, putting it quickly on her nightstand, and moved over his upper body like a blanket.

"Trying to smother me now? Should I be worried about your intentions?"

"Absolutely," she whispered, right before she reached down to his waistband and slid her still chilly hand underneath.

His shriek was even louder.

HE'D DUMPED HER, nicely, on the mattress next to him, glad she couldn't see his expression as she laughed like a little girl. It was a great sound. One he'd like to hear more often, as long as she didn't use him as her giggle-factory.

"You almost finished?" he asked.

She didn't speak, just kept laughing, although she must have been shaking her head because a lock of her hair hit him on the cheek.

"When you are, could you give me back my beer?"

"What makes you think you deserve it?"

The room was pitch-black, but that was right in his wheelhouse. He moved as stealthily as possible until he was hovering over her, and lifted her shirt. Pressing his lips against her warm skin, he gave her a raspberry she'd never forget.

Cricket laughed harder as she shoved him away.

Finally, as the world around them banged and rattled, she grew quiet, her laughter easing until all that remained was a tiny hiccup.

"Truce?" he asked.

"Truce." Then the mattress wobbled, and there was his beer. He helped her sit up so her back was against the headboard, right next to him. Then he finally took a long draw, sighing as the chilled beer slid down his throat.

The music had gone from irritating to excruciating in the time Cricket had been back. "Hell," Wyatt muttered. "Don't they have homes?"

"They better, because as soon as this storm passes, I'm kicking them all out."

Ronny's voice, more strident than Wyatt had expected, yelled at the heathens to dial it down or go home.

"What about me?" Wyatt brushed his lips over her ear. "Do I get to stay?"

"I might make an exception."

He reached under her shirt again.

"Oh, no. Not with Ronny and the kids here."

Sighing, he leaned back. "I know you haven't had much time, but have you done any thinking about what you're going to do about work?"

She exhaled heavily. "I'll have to tell them something, but I'm not leaving until Ronny sees the audiologist. If he has surgery, of course I'm staying as long as I need to. I just hope by the time we're done getting him better, I'm not completely broke."

He winced. "So, you know for sure he has no insurance?"

"No, he does, I'm just not clear what his policy covers. But, going back to your question about work, I've thought of another option that I'm seriously considering."

"Yeah?" He'd found her hand and rubbed her baby soft skin with his thumb.

"I go back to work, do my best to hide my utter disgust with the case and the firm. Meanwhile, I'll update my résumé and start looking for another job. The fact that I'm still working at Burrell, Scoffield and Schultz, on what will likely be a high-profile case, will be all the recommendation I need."

"That sounds reasonable," he said, not liking the plan much, but in her circumstances, it was a clever move. "Where would you start looking? Someplace closer to Temptation Bay?"

She didn't answer, which gave him time to wonder what that would mean for the two of them. He'd like to explore the crazy connection they'd had from day one, but that was a scary proposition. What if it all fizzled out? Or it didn't, which would mean he could end up exactly where he swore he'd never be again. Caring too much. Setting himself up for disaster.

Since she still hadn't responded, Wyatt said, "I figured you'd want to stay close to Ronny. Or did you want to stay in Chicago?"

"I don't know yet," she said, her voice more subdued. "I have my condo there, which would make staying simpler, but I can also sell it fairly quickly since it's in a prime location. Actually, I might end up making some money off it."

"That would be a good thing."

"Yeah, but… I don't really want to stay in Chicago. In the end, though, it'll be the reactions to my résumé that will make the decision for me. Barring the West Coast—won't move there. And I'd prefer not to work in New York, but I can't afford to eliminate that, either. Boston's a possibility, and that's only an hour and a half away."

"Oh, hell, you'll have all kinds of interest. Probably have your pick of firms."

Her soft laugh bordered on derisive.

"I'm not just blowing smoke here. Your reasoning is solid as a rock. You've been levelheaded and methodical. And we both know you're articulate. You must interview well."

"Nope. Still not going to get laid."

He laughed, but he was pretty sure she knew he was being serious.

She didn't keep poking, and he didn't either.

But then, after what passed for silence in this maelstrom, she asked, "Would that be a problem?"

He frowned. "What do you mean?"

"You know, if I moved a lot closer."

Now, it was his turn to lapse into silence. It felt too soon to talk about his reservations about the two of them, or to admit he'd like to test the waters. Polishing off his beer granted him a temporary reprieve, and then the lights came back on, causing the kids to start yelling their heads off.

"That's okay" she said, moving closer to him, now that they could see each other. "I don't know, either."

He found her mouth with no problem, and their kiss helped him relax in the brighter room. It was late, and it was also quieter outside, now that someone had finally turned off the music.

The relaxation turned into something more urgent as they returned to sharing a pillow, and he knew he was in trouble. Unless... "Is it too soon to kick everyone out?"

"A little bit," she said with a husky laugh, as a gust shook the house. "Ronny loves having them all here so much. I think all his faithful followers and the surfing keeps him young. I just wish it didn't make him childish."

"Have you told him what's going on with your job?"

"Nope. I won't until I get some feedback on

those résumés. If I'm lucky enough to have a choice of firms, it'll be a difficult decision. Ronny would never intentionally want to influence me, but it is harder to stay away now that I see he's not a spring chicken."

"I agree," he said, meeting her gaze again with a different motive. "He just wants you to be happy. He's so damn proud of you. He'd never want you to accept second best just to be nearer. You deserve your dream job."

She studied his face, and although he could be exceptionally stoic, she was clever enough to know he wasn't just talking about Ronny anymore.

Cricket gave him a smile that made his chest tighten. "A new job will mean lots and lots of hours. It won't be easy to take weekends off, or to get away for any length of time. I do have to take that into consideration."

He would have liked to weigh in on the side of her moving closer, but he had no business saying a word. He didn't even know what the hell he wanted yet, and she'd admitted the same thing. The thought of her leaving was painful, though. He'd never expected anyone like her popping into his life—the simple life he'd imagined, owning a small bar on the beach.

But in all honesty, his life had already gotten more complicated the minute he'd made Becky and the kids his responsibility. Jesus, what was wrong with him?

"You know what I'm looking forward to?" she said.

"What?"

"Tomorrow morning. Scrounging on the beach. It's not like a hurricane where everything is dead and it stinks for ages. This kind of storm? We'd all race out to be first at the shoreline. It's a little like that Tom Hanks movie, *Cast Away*. Once hundreds of coffee containers and ramen noodles came ashore. Everyone was fighting over them, like they were real treasure. Seriously, there were fistfights. But I've found beautiful things, too."

"What was your favorite?"

"A puppy, who'd somehow made it through that wicked storm. He looked like a drowned rat, but he was a good dog. Ronny tried to teach him how to surf, but I made him promise not to ever do it again."

"How come?"

"Because Jessie didn't have a vote." Her big grin turned into an enormous yawn, which got him going, too. It was almost 1:00 a.m., and now that they had some airflow, it wasn't all that unpleasant. Not even when she curled up next to him, leaning her head on his chest.

As everything got quieter, and the kids settled down, he watched her sleep. It seemed impossible to already know how much he'd miss her, and how quickly life could flip upside down.

Or in Adam's case, end in a moment.

## CHAPTER TWENTY-ONE

THE BOAT HAD gotten through the storm like a champ. Ronny and Skip were busy going over the checklist, putting her back to rights with the electronics and assorted things they'd taken off her. But Ronny was in excellent spirits, which was a good thing considering it was just after dawn.

"Remember to take it easy," Cricket said, staring at her father with the full measure of her *I'm-not-kidding* look. "I don't want to hear that you've done anything that will get your ears wet. And you're not to lift anything heavy. Understand?"

Ronny sighed. "I hadn't planned on it. Jeez, Baby Girl. Enough."

"Think again. If you get dizzy, you immediately let Skip know, and he'll call me. If you fall, I swear to God…"

"All right, already. I'm not twelve."

"No, you just act like it." She turned to Skip. "I'm counting on you. He'll want to help everyone else on the dock, but he's not going to. Am I making myself clear?"

"Don't worry. I take my job seriously."

"Good. Where's everyone else?"

"Some are on their way. The others are lazy asses who'll pay for it. Trust me."

Cricket smiled. She liked Skip. "Call if you need me."

"Yes, ma'am," he said, saluting her.

When she turned to Wyatt, he was trying not to laugh. Not successfully, but she didn't mind. He'd made her coffee this morning, and he'd already gotten in touch with Sabrina. Except for a downed railing, she'd given the bar a clean bill of health, which meant Cricket was free to steal Wyatt away for her traditional treasure hunt. She hoped there were more tiaras than ramen noodles.

"Come on, you." Wyatt grabbed her hand and tugged her along past Ronny's slip. "There are already people at the shoreline. We can't let them win."

She squeezed his hand. He'd not only gotten her up in time, he'd reminded her that she needed to get in touch with Grant, and although he raised his eyebrows at her purposely vague and deliberately exaggerated update on both Ronny's condition and the storm damage, Wyatt didn't comment. Which was good, because in truth, she wasn't like that. Her anger at Grant's duplicity hadn't made the morning's decision a hard one, but he'd still end up getting what he wanted in the end. She was going to follow her latest plan. She just needed a little more time with Ronny. And...other things.

By the time she and Wyatt were at the shore, there were quite a few beachcombers, mostly the artsy crowd who were picking through the driftwood and interesting flotsam and jetsam. So far, Cricket had seen the traditional seaweed bloom, which would be dealt with as quickly as possible before the rising heat would make it too stinky for the tourists. Kids and teens were playing in the water, which wasn't the smartest idea, but she'd done the same when she was their age.

"You're awfully quiet," Wyatt said. "Is that part of the ritual?"

"I never thought about it, but yeah, I mostly did this solo. I had a very active imagination, and I used to be certain I'd find a mermaid, or a pirate, or a tiara."

"Well, that seems about right for a kid."

She turned to him, dead serious. "I was in my twenties."

He cupped her nape and pulled her into his arms. "You're nuts. Which is great, by the way."

"I thought you said I was levelheaded and rational."

"Sometimes. You know," he said, rocking her gently, "I'm sorry Rose and Josh aren't here. They'd have enjoyed the adventure."

"Oh, do you think we can call and maybe get them?"

"It's probably better to let them sleep in a little longer. Next tropical storm, I'll be sure and remember this." He pulled back, with a mildly worried expression. "Uh, I forgot to tell you. Becky wants us to go to dinner with her and the guy she's started seeing. Ned."

"The way you said his name, is that a clue that you're not fond of him?"

"I don't know. I haven't met him."

"Well, don't be so negative. Becky's a bright woman. She's not going to pick some deadbeat to date. How long have they been seeing each other?"

"I'm not sure. All I know is he's a Realtor, and she's seen him at least once."

"Wait, are you upset that she's dating? Wyatt, hasn't it been almost three years since her husband died?"

He shut down like a storm shutter, cloaking himself off to her both emotionally and physically. It was startling, because she'd thought they'd broken a lot of ground together, but she guessed Adam's death was off-limits.

Without his touch, she continued down the beach, noticing that aside from the debris strewed across the sand, several shacks had broken windows, and a few were missing shingles from their roofs.

Wyatt caught up to her and grabbed her hand once more, pulling her to a stop. "Sorry. It's okay for you to talk about Adam. It is. I'm just not prepared for Becky to be dating. I know she has every right, and I do want her to be happy, but…"

"You're worried about her?"

He nodded. "And the kids, although I know they deserve to have a father figure in their lives. I get that it's not easy for Becky to be a single mom. But it seems too soon, even though I know it's not. Three years is a long time to grieve, and I honestly don't want her to be miserable… It's my issue, not hers."

Cricket took his other hand in hers. "Do you feel as if you might be replaced?"

As always, he took his time before answering. Such an admirable trait. Maybe she could learn how to do that herself.

"I'm not sure, but I don't think that's it. At least not all of it. I'm sure I'll always be a part of their lives. And I'm happy to be the favorite uncle. That actually suits me better than anything else."

"But you have to be the favorite, right?"

He grinned in answer, and she felt free to laugh. Somehow the bond between them just kept getting stronger. She needed a different name for what they were. It couldn't be a relationship, not this quickly, and she didn't believe in soul mates, but she'd also never felt like this with anyone. Not her best friends and certainly not any of her boyfriends.

He'd as much as told her he wouldn't mind her moving closer. Truthfully, she'd like that, too. It wasn't a probable outcome, though. Besides, she wasn't sure this magic between them could stand the test of time. An exciting idea, absolutely, but it also made her nervous. She'd never made her love life a priority. Her focus had been on her career.

"I think it's time we headed back to Ronny's. I'd like to take one more look around the place, even though the storm surge only came up to the steps, I want to check underneath now that it'll be easier to scope out."

Wyatt nodded. "Good idea. Besides, I could use another cup of coffee."

By the time they could see the blue shack, Ronny was standing outside, giving it a thorough once-over. He called them over, but even several feet away, he started yelling out to them. "Tony's boat got all beat up, and he's going to pay up the wazoo to have his engine rebuilt."

They finally got close enough that he didn't need to shout.

"Penny's house lost a window when a big piece of driftwood crashed right through. Lucky she wasn't hurt."

"Well, lucky us, then," Cricket said, glad that there wasn't a houseful of surfers, which meant half of them were still getting the *Baby Girl* back into shape.

"Damn straight." Ronny looked a little smug as he eyed the porch and the exterior front of the shack. "The old girl has really held up all these years. Except for the Perfect Storm, but then only the front of the place got torn up. And half the roof. Didn't lose a single shingle or board last night."

Cricket's smile was genuine, although not for a very nice reason. "Yeah, that's right. It weathered the storm amazingly well. All thanks to Wyatt." Feeling a bit smug herself, she took a step closer to her dad. "Do you know how many reinforcements and repairs he made yesterday before you got out of the hospital?"

Ronny's glee diminished, not by much, but at least he was taking a closer look at the porch steps, the side of the house that had been woefully neglected, and even the newer looking shingles that now graced the roof. "Well, damn, son, that's nice work," he said, turning to Wyatt. "You have my blessing."

"What?" Cricket asked, the same time Wyatt said, "Pardon me?"

Ronny grinned like the kid he was. "You can marry my daughter."

Wyatt laughed, but Cricket blushed hotter than a sunburn. "Oh, for God's sake, Ronny..." Although her censure didn't seem to strike home. In fact, he was already looking past her with wide eyes and dropped jaw. "Holy shit, what is she doing here?"

Cricket turned around, spotting the taxi at the

break wall. A woman stood by the open trunk. "Holy shit," she echoed. "Mom?"

MOM WAS A very attractive woman who looked as if she'd had Cricket at an early age. It was clear where her daughter got that smile, but Cricket's eyes were Ronny's, just much prettier.

Cricket had pulled him along as she and Ronny walked to the brick wall that separated the beach from the parking area, past the trees—the green ash fully intact—to the cab, where Wyatt kept a short distance as Ronny and Cricket moved in.

"What are you doing here, Vic?" Ronny asked.

"We spoke yesterday," Cricket said. "Why didn't you say you were coming? We would have picked you up at the airport."

She looked from Cricket to Ronny, then up at the sky before she shook her head, then pointed to the phone she was on. "I'll have to call you later, Pilar, I'm being hammered with questions." She disconnected and hugged Cricket, then gave Ronny a European double-cheek kiss. "Why don't we get out of this terrible sun into the shack, assuming there's a roof still on it."

While Ronny kept right on talking to his ex, Wyatt got a look at the luggage in the cab's trunk. He immediately picked up the two biggest suitcases. Cricket got two herself, and handed Ronny the overnight bag. The cabbie closed the trunk and got behind the wheel, just as Vic started walking, the rest of them following like a family of ducks. Until Ronny rushed ahead to open the door, and everyone filed in. Cricket put down the luggage in the living room, and Wyatt and Ronny followed suit.

"You look great, Mom," Cricket said. "Seriously, but is something wrong?"

"Only with your father, as far as I know," she said, looking at Ronny. "I'm here to see how you're doing."

"Oh, gosh, I'm sorry. Mom, this is Wyatt Covack," Cricket said, pulled him forward. "My mom, Victoria Danes."

"Very pleased to meet you, Wyatt Covack."

"The pleasure is all mine," he said, and she smiled, then turned to Cricket.

There was another hug, the kind his family tended to avoid, then Victoria brushed the back of her hand over her daughter's cheek. "You look well, darling. I can't wait to catch up."

Victoria was very smartly dressed in a light linen skirt and silk blouse, with her golden hair worn up. Although he couldn't see her eyes behind her large dark glasses, she seemed polished and elegant, much like his own mother.

"What's all this?" Ronny said, standing by the five different pieces of luggage. "Haven't you learned anything in all these years? Two bikinis, two pairs of shorts, two T-shirts, that's all you ever need."

"Ronny, you irrepressible idiot, that's all the clothes I brought." Her grin was wicked when she ran a hand down his back. "The rest is lingerie."

"Hell, you know I always hated you wearing underwear."

Cricket winced. "Stop," she said, covering her ears. "You aren't allowed to say things like that in front of me. Ever."

Her mom laughed. "All right, sweetheart," Victoria said, removing her sunglasses. "We'll save it for when you're away with your beau." She gave him a once-over that reminded him a little too much of Lila. "Very nice, Jessica. Very…healthy."

"Oh, God." Ronny shook his head. "You've turned into a cougar."

"You," she said, turning to her ex, "have no room to talk. Lying to your daughter about Ira saying you didn't have surfer's ear when you knew perfectly well he did no such thing."

"I didn't lie. Not technically. I was just using lawyer talk, like Cricket."

"Hey!" Cricket sounded outraged, which Ronny must have expected. "That wasn't lawyer speak, it was a damn lie."

"No it wasn't. Think about it," Ronny said, looking very sure of himself.

Glaring like only Cricket could, she opened her mouth, but quickly shut it again. "You were deliberately evasive. And I mean deliberately."

Wyatt, turned away, although he didn't quite muffle the slight clearing of his throat. Cricket looked at him, and he felt guilty as hell when she blushed. It wasn't his place, and he had no right to embarrass her in front of her parents, no matter what.

"If I had known you hadn't had it checked," she said, in a much calmer tone, "it would have saved us all a lot of worry. As it was, you nearly had an unnecessary MRI, and that wouldn't have even eliminated the need for the CT scan."

"I know, Baby Girl. I'm sorry. I should have been more open." He then turned to Vic again.

"I'm parched," she said, taking Ronny's hand and pulling him into the kitchen. "Tell me you have some chilled wine in that fridge of yours."

"Beer. Gatorade. Coffee."

"Well, I guess we'll have to fix that straightaway." She opened the fridge door, and clicked her tongue as she shook her head. "I have to call and order some edible foods. What's with all this kombucha and yogurt? Have you become vegan or something?"

"Vegans don't eat dairy. It's what healthy people eat instead of pâté de frog wa and truffle muffins."

Wyatt and Cricket both laughed, but Vic didn't look so charmed. "I can see we're going to get on just fine."

"So what are you really doing here?" Ronny asked.

"I'm going to take care of you, that's what. Be

your babysitter, because we all know you staying out of the water is going to be a struggle. But rest assured, I'm going to watch you like a hawk."

"Why?" he asked, looking appalled, although Wyatt could tell it was about his surfing, not the company.

"So Cricket can go back to work, of course."

Wyatt and Cricket looked at each other, both of them with a bit too much alarm, which they quashed immediately, which wasn't easy, at least on his part. Now that he knew she had no more reason to stay, the thought of her leaving felt like a vicious kick to the head, one he wasn't prepared for.

His only hope was that Cricket would find a way to delay her departure. Although, with her new plan to look for a job while still earning her salary, perhaps it was better for the both of them to cut their losses sooner rather than later.

# CHAPTER TWENTY-TWO

IT SMELLED LIKE the sea and clean air. The volunteers who were clearing out the seaweed bloom had been working crazy hours since yesterday, and they'd already gotten most of it removed. It would be processed into fertilizer, which was wonderful for the whole community. The rest of the debris was still being worked on, but the Bay was mostly back to normal.

Cricket took her time walking to Ronny's, after seeing Wyatt off for his run. Since she'd given up her bedroom to her mother, she was staying at his place. And they'd taken full advantage of the situation, sleeping in an extra hour. They'd even managed to drink some coffee between dragging each other back to bed.

This third cup was much needed. Especially after watching Wyatt do his morning workout. God, what a body. She'd wanted him to do his routine in the buff, but he'd declined. After his run, he had stuff to do at the bar. Not only finishing up the railing, now that he'd gotten the right kind of wood, but he had to restock and do another inventory. The post-storm crowd had been thirsty.

She'd heard from Jade and Harlow, who'd wanted to know if Ronny's shack was still standing and how they'd weathered the storm. Cricket had been tempted to tell them about Wyatt, but what was there to say really? She wanted to stay, needed to leave, wasn't sure if there was a chance he was *the one*, but if she didn't find out, it might be the worst mistake ever.

Ginny was still out of town. She'd taken Tilda somewhere inland before the storm had hit, though Cricket had a feeling Ginny's need to get away had little to do with the weather. They'd promised to see each other before she returned to Chicago and Cricket figured she'd get the real story then.

Now Cricket was looking forward to spending some time with her folks. Just them. Ronny's minions were out in the surf, since the waves had been so much better after the storm. It wasn't easy for Ronny, but she knew her mother was keeping him entertained.

As she approached the shack, she heard them laughing. It was a little bizarre to see them getting along so well, and being so…well, chummy. Ronny's attitude wasn't a surprise, not after his admission that there would never be another woman for him, but her mom? She'd never been acrimonious but this was something else altogether. She looked happy to be with Ronny. And Cricket, of course.

Rapping twice on the door, she walked in to find her father at the stove, and her mom pressed against his side. She quickly stepped away and smiled.

Cricket quietly cleared her throat. "Pancakes? Again?"

"Yeah," Ronny said. "This time, no chocolate chips. Unless you insist."

"That's okay. If you've got blueberries, I could go for that. I'm starving."

Her mom, in a short sundress that showed off her great figure, looked as if she had never belonged anywhere but Temptation Bay. Her hair was swept up in a messy bun, she had a little color after just a day in the sun, and she was barefoot. Just like Cricket.

Glancing at her watch, she raised her brows at Cricket. "I'll bet you're starving. That Wyatt of yours is—"

"Stop right there, or I'm leaving."

"I was just going to say he's fit."

Cricket felt her face heat, but she simply sipped her coffee and turned to Ronny. "Did you hear about your appointment yet?"

"They had a cancellation. The doctor is seeing him in two days," Victoria said.

Ronny flipped two pancakes, then looked up. "I can speak for myself."

"I know, dear," she said, moving closer to the counter, where she topped up what looked to be a mimosa cocktail. "So you can see that everything is going to be taken care of, and you're free to go back to work. I promise I'll keep you up-to-date with every single thing that happens."

Why her mother was so anxious to get rid of her, Cricket didn't understand and it was really starting to bug her. The thought of leaving Temptation Bay for an indeterminate length of time made her ill. Especially knowing what she'd have to face once she got back home.

Although, to be honest, this run-down shack and this crazy town were more of a home to her than Chicago ever would be.

"Where is your handsome hunk, anyway?" Victoria asked.

"He does have a business to run, but I'm pretty sure he'll be able to join us for dinner. Sadly, his backup bartender is off tonight, so that means he'll have to go back to the bar afterward."

"I hope he joins us," Ronny said. "He's a good guy. I'm not crazy about the fact that he's been working so hard to get those storage shelves underneath the shack. I hadn't realized how old they'd gotten."

"He's happy to help, and so am I," Cricket said, debating making a pot of her kind of coffee, but choosing orange juice instead. "So, Mom, what's the judge got to say about you spending all this time here?"

"He's fine. Away at another one of his golf tournaments. I assure you, he won't miss me a bit. And as much as I do love Paris, I was getting a little homesick. This feels like a real family reunion, only better, because there are no pesky grandparents or other relatives to contend with."

"It's really lovely to see you." Cricket gave her mom a quick hug. "I've missed being able to come visit you so often."

"Since I came to Chicago last time, you owe me a Paris vacation."

"I'm using up all my vacation time here."

"Which begs the question…" Her mother gave her a look that was almost scolding.

"I'm going back after Ronny sees the audiologist. And even if I didn't, I'd still have enough vacation time to stay another two weeks if I wanted."

Her mother's brows arched. "You're not going to do that, are you?"

"No, I'm not. But I do have things to do here, aside from going with Dad to the audiologist." In fact, she needed to call Penny later. "After that, I should know when I'll be going back to Chicago."

"For heaven's sake, don't you trust me to take care of your father?"

"That has nothing to do with it."

Her mother gave Ronny a sly look, but Cricket decided she didn't want to know. So she didn't ask.

DINNER HAD BEEN WONDERFUL, especially since her mom had toned down the innuendos. Wyatt was so charming Cricket wanted to haul him back to his place, but she held steady. He won lots of points with her mother, including bringing her favorite wine. Her enthusiasm about Wyatt was understandable; he was great, and would continue to be great even after Cricket left. The thought made her sigh, and to hide it, she had another spoonful of pistachio almond ice cream he'd brought, yet another thing to love about him.

*Like*, she corrected. *Like far too much.*

Wyatt looked at his watch. "I'm going to have to leave in a few minutes, unfortunately. Everything was terrific. Victoria, Ronny, you outdid yourselves."

"It was wonderful having you here," Victoria said, smiling happily. "A military man wasn't anything I ever imagined for Jessica, but I think you two make a beautiful couple."

Cricket winced, but when she caught Wyatt's gaze, it appeared he didn't mind them being considered a couple, if only a temporary one.

"She's been great. Told me all about pirates, the local folklore and made me remember that I really do love the sea."

"I thought you were in the Navy," Ronny said.

"Yep. But I think in my case, it was difficult to equate the ocean with pure pleasure."

"I see. Just like fishing is the last thing I want to do with my time off."

"And yet," Victoria said, "a day without surfing is a day of woe."

"Well, that's different. That's me and water, doing our thing. That's like flying, like dreaming."

Cricket almost made a comment, but she didn't want to spoil the basic truth of what her father had said. Letting him wax on about it for too long would take him to a dark space, though, and that she didn't want. "Ronny, you mentioned someone was interested in buying the shack and land. Was it the people who own the resort?"

He snorted, which told her a lot. "Like I would ever sell."

"I spoke to Penny the other day. She asked me for some help defining the offers and contracts some of the elderly fish people have been given. I hope to be able to make things clearer for them, but it would help—if you wouldn't mind—for me to have some idea what these people are offering."

"Well, first time around, they offered me over a million bucks. The second time, it was another guy, and the price had doubled. Maybe that had something to do with me laughing my ass off at the offer."

"Huh. A million sounds low for all the land

you own, but two million, maybe. I wonder what the going price is for regular beachfront properties. Guess I'd better find out before I go see her."

Ronny frowned. "She can't be thinking of selling."

"I'm not sure. She implied she was asking for someone else. But since she's alone now, I think it might be worth her while to consider it."

"Penny?" Ronny sounded affronted. "Nah."

Cricket finished off her ice cream as she thought about it. "I don't know. That amount of money can change your life, Ronny. It could set you up for whatever comes your way, and you don't have to sell all of it. You could always keep a small plot along with the shack."

Ronny looked at her as if she'd just said surfing should be banned. But that was him all over. When she met her mother's gaze, it seemed as if she was just as aghast. Even Wyatt looked at her funny.

"I just meant that it wouldn't be a bad idea to have a nest egg for further down the road. It would give you options, in case of another Sandy or Perfect Storm, that's all."

"That's an interesting notion, honey, but do you really think Ronny could ever be happy away from his beach, his people? It's a huge part of what makes him whole." Her mom smiled. "I was going to mention that it's obvious even you do better when you're here. It's so clear in the way you look, the brightness of your eyes. How happy you are…"

Cricket didn't dare look at Wyatt. "I didn't suggest he'd have to leave."

"I know you mean well," Ronny added, "but that's not something I'm willing to entertain. So how about we drop it."

Her mom put her hand over Ronny's, and it sent up another flag, although Cricket's misstep, which she didn't think was so outrageous, had changed the atmosphere of the whole evening.

Wyatt stood up, lifting his and her bowls to take to the kitchen, but Cricket wasn't about to make him wait on her when he had to face customers until one in the morning. "Put those down, please, and tell me what time I should come meet you at the bar."

He moved right next to her, and she felt his big warm hand on the small of her back…sliding down. "Anytime is good. Don't hurry on my account."

"I actually thought that might spur you into leaving early, but that wouldn't be fair. I really have taken up most of your time."

"You had a little help from a tropical storm."

"True."

He leaned down to kiss her, and if they weren't with her folks, she'd have gone for the gold, but there were rules about such things. Instead, she walked him to the door and watched him for a long minute.

When she turned back, both of her parents gave her exaggerated hubba-hubba looks. "Real mature, you two. I swear, I'm the only adult in this family."

SOMETIME AFTER TEN, Cricket walked to the bar, still reeling from her latest discovery. Wyatt was serving someone, but Bobby Cappelli offered her his prime seat, and moved a couple of stools down. "How you doing?" he asked. Like a regular person instead of a sleazy pickup artist.

"Good, thanks. You?"

"Same old, same old," he said, then he was pulled into a conversation with the guy next to him.

Tiffy nodded at her with a smile, as did Lila and Viv. She knew some folks in the bar, but there were tables of tourists, too, and a table full of single ladies having a blowout. All in all, it wasn't that busy, which was good, because she needed to speak to Wyatt.

He arrived with two bottles in his hand. One was a cold beer, the other was the Lagavulin. She wanted the latter, but she chose the beer.

"You sure?"

"Yep. Although, I do need to get over a recent trauma."

He opened the beer and set it down, leaning closer to her, a look of concern on his face.

"I'm pretty sure my parents are...doing it."

"Doing what?"

"*It.* I had to go into my bedroom to get something, and the bed hadn't been touched. Then my mother, my married mother, walked into Ronny's room to get a clean dress after she spilled some wine. I swear, I don't know what to make of it. She said everything was fine between her and the judge, but I don't think she's ever been secretive with me before, not about divorcing husbands. Of course, she probably wouldn't tell me if she cheated, but it doesn't seem like something she'd do."

"Do you think your folks would ever get back together? They seemed very comfortable with each other, at least to me."

"I don't think so, but then, everything's been so weird lately. Ronny's accidents, my mother showing up out of the blue."

"Well, it must be Parents Being Weird Week because the admiral called me again, which is unprecedented. He asked me about the storm, even though it's been on the news that it wasn't much of anything here in the Bay. I actually considered that maybe he and my mother might be having problems, or getting a divorce. Tomorrow I'm going to call my brother, find out what he knows."

"Huh. You don't think it could be that he's heard about us? Maybe Becky or Adam's grandparents?"

"What? No. Even if he did, he wouldn't care."

She sipped her beer and watched him fill drink orders. Watched people, nodded at those who nodded at her. But by her second beer, close to midnight, Wyatt caught her yawning.

"Why don't you go on up? Get ready for bed."

"Yeah," she said as she stood and started to walk out, but he caught her at the end of the bar.

In a low voice, close to her ear, he said, "I'll wake you up when I get up there, huh?"

Smiling, she kissed him, and he kissed her back. It wasn't earth-shattering, but at least by now, no one paid them much mind.

When he leaned back, she didn't let him go. She hated for the night to end in a downer, so she decided to tell him the news now, before he came upstairs.

"Something up?"

She looked down, before she was brave enough to meet his gaze. "I'm calling Grant tomorrow, letting him know I'll be flying back by the end of the week."

Wyatt inhaled, and held it, his face going stoic in that way he had.

She forced herself to do the same. No use letting the bar staff know there was trouble in paradise. Not when they both knew this was inevitable. So why did the thought hurt so damn bad?

# CHAPTER TWENTY-THREE

THE FIRST THING Cricket noticed when she rolled over was that Wyatt wasn't in bed. Cranking an eye open, she realized it was late—the sun coming into his room was far too bright to be early morning. Probably on his run.

As she stretched her neck, a rush of pleasure filled her with the memory of their predawn lovemaking. The way he'd teased her until she'd begged, and how she'd returned the favor, glad no one had been downstairs to hear the noise.

Ah, she remembered now. He'd told her that he had to be downstairs by ten thirty to accept deliveries, and it was almost eleven. Cricket was due at Penny's at noon. Before she left, she had to call Grant. The idea made her want to pull the covers back over her head, but instead, she grabbed a shower and had a good strong cup of the coffee Wyatt had so kindly left her, along with a note hoping to schedule a nap for this afternoon.

Yeah, as if they'd get any sleep.

As soon as she saw her cell phone charging on the counter, she sobered. Grant was still her speed dial 2, which she would change, pronto, but her job at the moment was to get her head straight. Now was no time to botch her plan of action.

Unfortunately, she got his voice mail.

"Grant, it's Jessica. Call me back, please." She almost said more, but changed her mind quickly. She needed to hear his reaction live.

The scant time she had left was spent eating a bagel, doing her makeup—not the real deal, just some mascara and lipstick, and picking out the right sundress. This was business, after all.

It was only a few minutes' drive to Penny's, where there were an awful lot of cars parked just behind the seawall, bracketing the path to Penny's house. Shouldn't everyone be selling their wares at the fish market?

It took a minute for Cricket to find a space for Wyatt's truck, but her cell phone rang with Grant's tone as soon as she started walking. "Hello?"

"Thanks for the call," he said, the sarcasm evident. "Finally. So, when are you coming back?"

"Over the weekend. Sunday night."

"What? Why do you need to stay that long? Victoria's there to take care of Ronny. I thought she talked some sense into you."

She hadn't spoken to Grant about her mother's visit. So, what the… "Why would my mother need to talk sense into me since she knows nothing about what's happening at work?"

The weight of his silence slowed her step.

In fact, her mom and Grant had never met.

"Sorry, I have another call. But take the weekend, since we're still strategizing our defense so we don't need you for that, but be here on Monday. No later."

Grant disconnected and she stared at the cell phone as if it could make sense of the steamroller that had run her over. They didn't need her for strategy sessions? When she would be sitting at the table with the defendant?

No, of course not. She was just window dressing. How stupid of her to forget.

And her mother?

That was the real kicker. Cricket knew something had been wrong since day one. She should have said something the minute Victoria stepped out of the cab. But in her wildest imagination she never would have thought her mother had some connection to her work. It made no sense. None.

Putting her phone in her purse, Cricket hurried her pace. She couldn't afford to be preoccupied. Doing everything she could to pull herself together, she knocked on Penny's door.

The woman opened it, looking sheepish. "We've got some company," she said. "I should've warned you. Once they found out you were willing to talk to me, they all wanted to come. You're one of us. Everyone trusts you."

Cricket had to let that sink in. Because she'd just committed herself to leaving on Sunday, while the living room was standing room only. She knew a lot of the people there, but some of the younger people were strangers. Probably related to older folks who'd held the land forever.

Smiling at the hopeful faces, Cricket understood they'd all want to talk to her, get her to read their offers. Although it made her feel a little better to see half the folks were eating Penny's famous homemade cookies. There was a table set up with tea, water and an assortment of treats, but Penny led her straight to the small card table in front of the crowd. There was one contract laid out.

For the next two hours and fifty minutes, Cricket barely had time to swallow. Everyone seemed to have questions, and none of them were too keen to let her finish a thought before asking another.

She focused on a few key sections: the lot sizes, the extant structures, proximity to the beach and the offering price. The more she looked at, the more she could see why these people were so confused. It was clear that the resort's attorneys were taking other things into consideration—primarily the age of the owners. Lots of disparity between similar properties.

"The Gomeses live right next door to me, with their five kids," Mr. Jonas said, his voice wobbling with his Parkinson's. Cricket had known him and the Gomes family her whole life. "No offense, but their place is a mess, and even though our lots are the same size, they offered me two hundred thousand less. That isn't right. Can they do that?"

"Unfortunately," Cricket said, "they can. They're under no obligation to be fair. It's just business for the resort. I know these are big decisions to make, but the only thing I can tell you for sure is that you need a lawyer to represent you. Someone from Rhode Island, preferably, who knows this beach and how you all make your living."

"That's you, isn't it, dear?" Hetty asked.

The murmurs of agreement from the rest of the crowd didn't help things.

"I don't have a license to practice in this state. And unfortunately, I have to return to my job this weekend. There's no way I can look at all of your contracts. It wouldn't even help you, since I couldn't represent your interests."

Hetty stood up. "Can't you get one? A license, I mean?"

"Technically, yes, although not quickly. However, I really do have a job. And I can't just walk away from it."

"Now, hush up, all of you." Penny stood in front of the table. "I asked her for advice, knowing she wasn't an attorney in this state. I said that earlier, remember? Now she's given us the advice, and that's that."

"But can't you just take a look at my contract?"

Cricket wasn't even sure who asked that. She didn't dare, or it would end up with her in trouble. She simply couldn't help everyone. "I'm so sorry. What I can do is ask around, see who I might know who could be a good fit for you all. Just please, no one sign anything yet. Okay? I'll get back to Penny as soon as I can. Which won't happen until I'm settled back at my office next week."

Penny thanked her and led her out, shielding her with her smaller body, but it didn't matter. Cricket still felt like hell leaving them like that. Just before she said goodbye, Penny handed her a bag of cookies.

"I made your favorites," she said.

"Almond biscotti? You didn't have to. They take so much longer than the others."

"Don't be silly. Now go, before this bunch is let loose. Have a safe trip home."

"Thank you," Cricket said. What she needed to do now was go straight to Ronny's and have herself a little chat with her mother.

Victoria answered the door. She was having a wine spritzer wearing one of Ronny's T-shirts, and little else. "Darling. I didn't expect to see you today. I thought you were having your little meeting."

Ignoring every word, Cricket put her purse on the dinner table. "You want to tell me what the hell's going on? How did one of my work associates, whom you've never met, know that you had come here to help with Ronny? And how, exactly, is it that *you* were charged with talking some sense into me?"

"Oh, please. It was nothing. I'm here because I want to be here, that's—"

"No. Stop. That's not going to cut it. Not by a mile. I want to know the truth. Right now. All of it. Leave nothing out, because I will dig until I find out every last detail. You know I can and I will."

Looking pale despite the color she'd gained beachcombing, her mother went to the kitchen and poured herself a little more wine. When she turned to face the music, she at least had the decency to look chastened.

"You know Declan—as a federal judge he's crossed paths with everyone in the legal community. He knew two of the founding partners at your firm very well. Old, old friends from law school. Declan said something about you graduating from Yale to Scoffield at a cocktail party, and of course, he jumped on it."

"Oh, please. Do you know how many bright, ambitious attorneys Ivy League law schools graduate every year?"

"Of course, but how many of them are endorsed by a well-respected federal judge?"

Next to none. Judges tended to stay away from

that type of thing. Everything that had made Cricket uneasy felt infinitely worse. "Better give it to me straight."

"There's nothing more to it—"

"Like hell. Are you sure you want me finding out some other way?"

"Nothing. I—I may have asked Declan to put in a good word…"

"Christ." Cricket felt sick. "I'm not like you, Mother. I'm independent. I earned my way through school, even at Yale. I don't need to buy my way through life."

Victoria's eyes closed and she turned her head. Cricket knew she'd hit a sore spot, but she wouldn't take the words back even if she could. She felt like a first-class fool. Utterly humiliated. God, Grant must have known from the beginning. All the senior partners knew. No wonder they felt free to manipulate her into doing anything they chose. They figured they could pull any string they liked since she'd been a charity hire.

"Well, I'll give you an update so when you call Grant or Scoffield for your next check-in, you'll know what to say. Tell them I said screw them. Screw them all. They can shove the rape case. I'm a damn good attorney. Let them give me lousy recommendations, I don't care. I'll find a job without their assistance. Or yours."

Victoria seemed smaller with her hunched shoulders and pallid skin. No, it was her expression that had changed her. She'd never looked so defeated before.

"Please, Cricket, don't shoot yourself in the foot. This is how it works in big law firms, that's all. Everyone rubs everyone else's back. It's always been this way."

"It never was for me." Cricket wanted to weep, but she wouldn't, not here, not now.

"I was only trying to help."

Cricket shook her head. "I can't believe you didn't know me well enough to realize..." She swallowed hard. "Did Ronny know?"

"No. I never told him any of it."

"Did he just hear all this? You know the walls don't hide a thing."

"He's at the dock with Skip."

"Do me a favor, don't tell him. It would only break his heart, too." Cricket grabbed her purse and walked out the door.

She took off her wedge sandals, not even enjoying the feel of sand between her toes. The tourists were back at play, but with no swells, there were only a few kids out there, probably trying to learn to stand up on their surfboards. High tinkling laughter came wafting by, along with some kids shrieking in delight. Cricket couldn't decide whether to tell Wyatt or not. He'd comfort her, of course he would. But then he'd try to convince her that her mother's actions didn't matter.

She wasn't ready to hear anything kind about

Victoria. She also didn't want to drown her sorrows in booze, but if she'd ever needed a Scotch, now would be the time. When she got closer to the bar, she realized it wasn't even open yet. He wasn't going back to regular hours until the weekend.

*Perfect.* She sighed at the irony of finally being with a man who actually wanted to comfort her when she was too embarrassed to be comforted.

He might be upstairs, but the idea of climbing up to his apartment made her want to crumble right there on the beach. This was worse than being dumped. Worse than Grant's betrayal. This was as if she'd gone to work every single day naked, and everyone saw, but no one said anything.

Two steps from the side deck, she realized Wyatt was inside the closed bar along with several waitresses, and they were all kicking out like the Rockettes, but with only one leg. The self-defense classes started today. On her drive to Penny's, she'd imagined coming back to the bar, waltzing in and having a beer while watching everyone else sweat.

She stopped where she was, figuring she'd wait until they weren't looking her way to dash up the stairs. Behind her, a car pulled into the parking lot. Becky's Highlander. She didn't spot the children in the back seat. If they were there, they were probably hiding after Becky slammed the car door so hard it shook the SUV.

Oh, God, Cricket hoped she didn't want to talk about dinner tomorrow. The idea of socializing, and acting normal around anyone was the last thing she wanted to do.

Becky stomped up the first step, then came to a jarring stop as she saw Cricket off to the side. "You scared me."

"Sorry. I was just going up to Wyatt's apartment."

"Is he up there?"

Becky really looked steamed. Every time Cricket had seen her, she'd been well put together: hair neat, makeup on, clothes that flattered. But right now she was wearing jeans that looked a size too big, a navy T-shirt with a hole near the hem and her hair might not have seen a comb today. "No. He's inside, teaching some of the staff self-defense."

"That stupid man..." Becky tried on a smile, but it didn't work. At all. "He checked into Ned's background. And not just a quick internet search. Friends were teasing Ned asking if he was looking to get top secret clearance or something."

"What?"

"I'm so furious I don't even know what to do. Well, I know I'm going to strangle him, but after that, there are too many options. Treating me like I'm a child. For heaven's sake, I'm not his responsibility. He needs to let it go, already. Let me be free to move on with my life."

"Oh, man. That was a shitty thing to do. I don't blame you for being angry. I'd hate it if he pulled something like that on me."

Becky managed a brief smile.

"But," Cricket said, knowing it was a risk, "even though I don't know Wyatt all that well, it seems hard to believe he didn't have the best of intentions. And yes, it was wrong, but I don't think he would ever hurt someone he loved. Certainly not intentionally."

Becky took the next step until the two of them stood together, still not in direct eyesight of the girls. They both watched Wyatt demonstrate a move that looked intimidating. "Don't fool yourself," Becky said. "You probably know him better than anyone."

"No, that's not—"

"I mean it." Becky shook her head. "Wyatt's changed so much in the last week, it's crazy. Good crazy. I'd lost hope he'd ever let a woman into his life. I prayed it was the first step in finally getting over feeling responsible for Adam's death."

Cricket must have made a sound, because Becky stared at her, tilting her head with confusion. "You didn't know?"

"He never said what happened."

"I probably should let him tell you, but that

could be the next millennium. Wyatt was in charge of the unit during a mission that went very badly. The information he received from head-quarters was faulty, and even though he followed procedure, did everything right, including saving a lot of civilians, he lost the rest of the team. Including Adam. I'm sure you're aware Adam and he were like brothers, but then, that's what happens to SEAL units. They're all brothers, and they never leave anyone behind. This time, Wyatt had to, or more civilians would have been killed."

"Oh, my God," Cricket said, although the whisper was carried away by the wind.

Becky's eyes were moist. "To be honest, after that, I'd been worried he had some kind of death wish. In the beginning, I mean. Like going up in that chopper when it was too dangerous. When I confronted him about it, he denied it, told me he'd never been in danger. He claimed he was just helping out because the coast guard was bound by stricter protocols." Becky sighed. "I told him right then and there if he did anything reckless, he couldn't be around the kids, because they couldn't take another loss."

"What did he do?"

"He was devastated. I might as well have shot him point-blank. But I couldn't back down. He had to understand that the kids were the first pri-ority. He swore he was being careful, that he'd never endanger his life knowingly. He said he'd be hypervigilant, which was a bold claim to make for someone like him. But he's stuck to his promise. I firmly believe he told me the truth that day. He just needs to be there to help. To do whatever he can, for whoever he can. My guess is that it makes him think if he can earn enough ticks in the saved column, he'll stop feeling so guilty about his men. About Adam."

"I knew there was something of the hero in him, but I didn't understand until now."

"No," Becky said, "he's the real thing. It's not an act. But I hope he can let go of that scorecard so he can start his own family."

Overwhelmed, Cricket didn't know what to say. A quick look told her that the lesson was coming to an end, but that didn't help her decide what to do next. Running away seemed the best option.

"I'm sorry I dumped my frustration out on you." The anger had leached out of Becky's voice completely. "I'm not going to talk to him now. I need to think things through. I mean, I was ready to call off tomorrow night's dinner, but I don't want to make any hasty decisions. Would you tell him that I'll call him later? And do believe me when I say you've been so, so good for him. It's the most alive he's been in years." Becky gave her a quick hug, and with a genuine smile she turned back to her car.

Cricket didn't move. Not even when the bar

door opened and some of the girls started leaving. The thing was, if she saw Wyatt, she'd end up telling him what had happened and be mortified. And if she didn't see Wyatt, she'd fall apart.

## CHAPTER TWENTY-FOUR

SWEATING LIKE CRAZY, Wyatt walked out of the bar, Lila and Viv behind him. He was ready to head up for a shower and there was Cricket, on the way upstairs. She looked gorgeous in that green sundress that made her eyes look more gold than brown. "Hey, you."

She seemed a bit startled at his voice, even though she'd been looking right at him. He guessed she was lost in thought. Hoped that was it, because he was starting to get the impression that something was wrong.

Shit, she'd called Grant today.

"Hi, Cricket," Viv said, passing by them. "Did you see? We kicked his butt in there."

"Did you?"

"Yep. Tell her, Lila."

"Hey, she likes the old guy. Ease up."

"Old guy?" Wyatt made sure he sounded wounded to the core. "Who you calling old?"

"Maybe if you stopped taking it so easy on us," Viv said, as she walked backward to her old VW Bug.

Lila whooped loudly. "Yeah. Stop treating us like girls."

He shook his head, glad to see them in such good spirits.

"You look like they're not exactly lying," Cricket said.

"Honey, they whipped my ass. How about you come up with me and help me turn on the shower. I don't have the energy." He leaned over to kiss her, afraid if she got too close, she'd recoil in horror at how sweaty he was. "Sorry if I smell," he said.

"It's worth it. But yeah, you do need a shower."

Taking her hand, he led her up the stairs, still convinced she wasn't quite herself. As soon as they were both inside, he made a point of standing right in front of her before he looked her in the eyes. "What's wrong, Cricket? And how come Becky ran off? I don't understand why you two didn't come in out of the heat."

She shrugged. "We were just talking. Becky said she'd call you later."

"Okay." He wouldn't push. "But I really do need to shower, and I'm prepared to wash you and pay attention to all those special places."

"Thanks, but right now a cold drink sounds awfully good," she said. "Can I get you one?"

She'd never sidelined him like this. Not once.

He waited till she got her drink. "Did you speak to Grant today?" he asked, his chest tightening at the thought she might be leaving earlier. He wasn't ready yet.

"Yeah, I did." She hid behind her soda can. "Go ahead and shower. I'll tell you what happened after."

"You don't have to tell me a thing. Just come with me. Take off that pretty dress, and those tiny bikini—"

His cell phone went off.

"I'm not even gonna answer that, because I don't have to."

She picked up his phone and put it in his hand. "It might be important."

"It's a DC area code." Curious now, he clicked on the call. "Covack."

"How you doing, Earp?"

Wyatt froze. He knew the voice. The name from his past. "I haven't been called that in a long time, Commander."

"Yeah, but that's who you are. How's civilian life? Did you ever buy that bar you wanted?"

"Yes, sir. And no, it's not called Wyatt Earp's."

Freeman barked a laugh. "You been keeping yourself in fighting shape?"

"I do okay."

"I figured. Hey, I'm going to be in your neck of the woods tomorrow. Thought I'd drop by."

That stopped Wyatt cold. "You're coming here? Do you know where I'm living?"

"Rhode Island. On the coast, isn't that right?"

"Yes, sir." Wyatt rubbed his jaw. What the hell was going on? "I'll be at the bar most of the day, but I'm tied up in the evening. Need directions?"

"Nope. I'll find you."

"See you then, sir."

When he disconnected, Cricket was looking at him with eyes full of questions. He had too many of his own to know where to start. "That was my old platoon commander, Jefferson Freeman. He's coming here tomorrow."

"To see you?"

"He said he's going to be in the neighborhood, but that's just weird."

"Was he a friend of yours?"

"Nice guy, but I wouldn't call him a personal friend. And now he's all of a sudden dropping by?" He wondered if hearing from the admiral twice in one week had anything to do with tomorrow's visit. "He mentioned the bar, but I didn't come up with the idea until after I was four months out of the service."

"Does he know the admiral?"

"Yeah, I'm thinking he might be tied into this somehow. I just don't know what's up. If something was wrong with him, I'd have heard about it from my mother."

"Could he be coming to pull you back in?"

"I can't imagine that. I was damn clear when I left. I mean, to him directly." He stripped off his shirt, then, after toeing off his shoes, his shorts, said, "Come on. Take a shower with me. I'm worried about what's bothering you."

Sighing, Cricket leaned against the counter, as if standing was too much. "It's nothing to worry about, I promise. But I'll tell you later."

"You know I'm on tonight. I assume you're going to your folks' for dinner, but right after that, okay?"

She nodded.

He had to let it go, even though he didn't like it. On the way to the bathroom, he caught his reflection in the full-length mirror hanging on the door, and patted his belly. "Damn. I have kind of let myself go. Freeman's going to make a crack about it first thing." Sucking it in didn't help much.

"You're insane." Behind him, Cricket shook her head in utter disbelief. "Let yourself go," she mumbled, and then laughed. Really laughed. So that was something. "And they say women are vain."

He clenched his ass as he walked into the bathroom.

THE RHODY DINER hadn't changed much since the last time Cricket had eaten there. About fourteen years ago. But they were still really laid-back, and didn't care that all she'd ordered was a chocolate shake while she worked on her Surface Pro.

She knew she couldn't stay too much longer, or Wyatt would call, and she didn't want to lie to him directly. He deserved better than that, especially when he was only trying to help.

She got a quick message from one of her Yale classmates who worked at a Providence law office. Natalie said she didn't know of a contracts lawyer from or right near Temptation Bay, but she knew some from Newport, and she'd reach out.

After a quick thanks, Cricket's thoughts went straight back to her mother, and their earlier conversation. Ronny's call hadn't helped things. He'd begged her to come home and talk. Obviously her mom had opened her big mouth. Again. Despite knowing how much the blowup must've unsettled him, Cricket said she needed a little time.

She couldn't help wondering if Grant knew from day one that she'd been given her job right out of Yale. He hadn't been as high up in the hierarchy as he was now, and certainly didn't have dealings with the senior partners.

It didn't matter in the end. He probably knew now, and Grant Herbert wasn't shy about using any form of leverage he could get his hands on.

She sipped on her shake, and made that horrible noise that told her it was all gone. It felt like a personal betrayal. Maybe she'd order another one, to go. Or maybe she'd just admit to herself that she was dreading telling Wyatt.

Of course, she could just tell him it had to do with Penny's meeting. The thought lifted her spirits. Until she realized that alone revealed all the things Wyatt admired about her weren't true. He thought she was bright, independent, confident, principled.

Maybe she was once, but that person hadn't shown up recently.

"You want a top up?" the waitress asked. "It's on the house. Just take me a second."

"No. Thank you, though. I was just wrapping up my work. I'll take the check now, if I may?"

The distraction, plus hugely loud music, was enough to get Cricket out of the diner, and all the way back to the bar. It didn't matter that she'd come early. He'd be glad to see her.

The dope.

Looking into the visor mirror of Wyatt's truck, she said, "Knock it off. Stop the pity party. You know the situation, now work on what you're going to do about it. Starting with telling Wyatt the truth."

The speech bolstered her all the way to the bar door, where she made one small amendment: nothing that would make things worse.

She barely made it two feet inside and she heard, "Hey, Cricket."

It was Igor. Jim and Ted were sitting at the table with him, and so were two other minions. Victoria must've barred the door and windows. "We all heard what you're doing for the fish folks. That's very, very cool."

"I'm not, though. I'm not representing them or

anything like that." Oh, hell. She wanted to turn around and walk right back outside.

Ted held up his dark ale in a toast. "My mom said you're doing plenty. That's epic, dude."

They all clinked their beers, and in the middle of that, an older man who worked the fish market, joined in with, "You're a smart girl, Cricket. And we all appreciate it."

All she could do was smile, especially when she realized how many locals were in the bar, half of them nodding at her. Her best escape was heading for the empty stool at the end of the bar. Wyatt would steal bits of time with her. It made sense to tell him now, instead of after closing. They wouldn't be able to get too deep, and she wasn't likely to fall apart in front of a crowd.

He came by two minutes later, again offering her a choice of Scotch and beer. Although it wouldn't go well with the shake in her stomach, she chose the Lagavulin.

"Did you have a nice dinner?"

"Yeah," she said, right before she downed the shot.

"Okay," he said, drawing out the word. "That seems unambiguous. Want to talk about it?"

Nearly sighing in relief, she nodded. "Can you?"

"It's not all that busy. Mostly locals, who can sit on it and spin if I take a little longer than usual. And Viv or Tiffy can pour." He checked behind him, then leaned on his elbows so he was reasonably close to her.

Cricket gave him the CliffsNotes version of what had happened, in between him filling two pitchers and making a drink Viv had never heard of. Finally, when she got out all the salient facts, he bent closer one more time, in a way that told her he wasn't going to be darting away anytime soon.

"Admittedly, I'm clueless about your world, about lawyers in general, and in particular your firm, but I imagine you were pretty lucky to get that leg up."

Cricket stared at him, utterly speechless. That was his takeaway? "My mother went behind my back to have Declan ask one of the senior partners for a favor. Clearly Victoria had no faith in my abilities to get in with a good firm. Not to mention she made me into a charity case."

"Yeah, that's true. I mean, you went to Yale. You probably wouldn't have had any trouble at all."

"No. That's not… Lots of people who go to Yale and Harvard can't get into good firms. Or even medium firms."

The way he looked down at his hands woke her up to what he was trying to do. He wasn't wrong, exactly. She wouldn't have necessarily snapped up a great job on her own. But that wasn't the point.

"Okay, you know more about it than I do. But as for them taking you on as a favor, I suppose that's technically true, but do you think that meant they had to keep you on indefinitely? I mean, if you were a lousy lawyer, I doubt they would've handed you any important clients. Yet they did, right?"

She nodded, unable to figure out why instead of making her feel better it did the opposite.

"It would have been wiser for your mom to tell you before she made the move, but hell, I know you. I know your character, and favor or not, you're smart, sensible and admirable. No one could miss that about you."

Behind him, Viv tapped him on the shoulder. "You think you could step in for a little while? There's a birthday party…"

"Sure," he said, "Be right with you."

Viv went back to work while Wyatt looked torn. "You all right for a few minutes?"

"Yes, of course. Go."

Alone again, the penny dropped, heavy as an anvil. The truth about herself was far darker than she'd realized, and so much worse that she'd rather die than admit it to him.

What a hotshot she'd thought she was, acing a firm like that right out of school. She'd even pitied some of her old classmates who had struggled to find jobs that could cover their student loans.

Not Jessica Shaw. She was too bright, a shining star. Hadn't everyone always told her that?

The true horror was that *she* believed that. It was so much a part of her that she hadn't ever given it a second thought.

Beneath the praise there lived nothing more than an excuse. It gave her the illusion that it was fine to make fun of the prep school privileged, when the reality was, she had a lot in common with them.

Wyatt thought she wasn't like them, and she would have agreed with him to her dying day, but it was a lie. God, she'd taken so much for granted, and all with benevolent condescension up to and including her moral high ground.

And now, what was she doing? Letting Wyatt scramble to make her feel better. He had his own issues. That commander calling must have brought up a whole load of pain about Adam, about him being the only survivor on a mission he'd led. And all she was doing was thinking about herself. Nice. More proof that— "Stop," she said aloud, not caring if anyone was watching. It was time to be a decent human being to Wyatt, who deserved so much more.

When he came back, wiping his hands on a bar towel, he smiled at her as if everything was coming up roses. He offered her more Scotch, but she got a glass of water instead.

Once he was elbows to the bar, she spoke

before he had a chance. "You given any more thought as to why your ex-commander might be coming?"

"No clue. I even called Becky to ask her if she'd heard anything. She hadn't, but she sure as hell gave me a dressing-down that would have put a BUD/S trainer to shame."

She managed a laugh in response to his hang-dog expression.

"Hey, at least the guy checked out. And I know you defended me."

"I hope she also told you that I wouldn't appreciate if you did that kind of thing to me. Although come to think of it, maybe you could work a little black magic with Gr—never mind."

"I'd love to, believe me."

She just shook her head.

"Anyway," Wyatt went on, "Becky's calmed down and she's curious about this whole situation."

"Did she mention she told me more about how Adam died—" She cut herself off at the hard expression on his face. "I'm sorry, I should have stopped her right away."

Wyatt's demeanor had changed in the blink of an eye. Before she could try to make amends, Tiffy called him over to help her, and this time he left without comment.

Cricket felt terrible for bringing it up. She should have waited.

"Hey."

His voice, soft and not angry at all, made her look up.

"I promise," she swore, "I won't say another word about it. I hadn't meant to talk behind your back."

He shrugged. "I would have told you, you know. Maybe not next week or even next month, but eventually, I would have."

At that, her stomach clenched. She wasn't even sure how she felt about the implication that they were in this relationship, or whatever this thing was, for the long haul. Or what eventually meant to him.

"I was filled with guilt and that got mixed in with grief and anger and letting down my brothers. But I'm slowly coming to terms with it all. I know I did my job to the best of my ability. Adam's death wasn't the first casualty I'd dealt with…but it was the last one I could bear."

She wanted to jump over the bar and hug him for all she was worth. They quieted, each of them in their own way saying volumes. He wanted to help her, she wanted to help him. Yet, they each had to get there on their own.

Tiffy came back again, but she wasn't asking for help. "It's pretty calm now that the surfers and the birthday party have split. I've got no problem closing up if you and Cricket want to take off. Think about it. I need to go blend three piña coladas."

"How about we go upstairs and help each other forget our troubles?"

Cricket blinked, quietly cleared her throat. "Excellent plan." She stood up, and slung her purse over her shoulder at the sad thought that maybe, more realistically, sex was all their relationship would ever amount to. It was certainly more than she deserved.

# CHAPTER TWENTY-FIVE

THE URGE TO salute Commander Freeman was all but overwhelming when the man he hadn't seen in almost three years walked into the bar. Freeman circumvented Wyatt's dilemma by holding out his hand.

The shake was as tough as the man himself. Not a contest. A statement. The commander hadn't changed, except for a little gray creeping into his hair. He was stocky and short—five foot seven—but then a lot of military men were. Pilots, especially, but many SEALs were like Freeman. Made of muscles, grit and a determination to never give up.

"Can I offer you something to drink, Commander?"

"You got coffee?"

Although it was hot outside at ten, Wyatt had brewed a fresh pot, strong like the commander liked it. "Still black?"

"Yep."

His curiosity was the only thing hotter than the coffee he brought to the table.

After his first sip, Freeman said, "You're not looking too bad."

Wyatt didn't bother with more than a nod in reply. Small talk and his guest didn't go together.

"Right." Freeman set down his cup. He sat with his back straight, and even though he wasn't in uniform, he might as well have been. He reminded Wyatt of the admiral. No wonder the two had had such a long friendship. "One of your fire team, Alan Schumate, is alive." Freeman paused. Maybe he'd expected Wyatt's shock and wanted to give him a moment, or had just seen it in his face.

"We've got fresh intel from a reliable source. One of ours in with the CIA sent us a picture. It's blurry, but the computers all say it's Chopper. He's been held in the prison outside Sangin and it's believed he's about to be sent to Kandahar, where there's every chance he's going to be made an example."

Wyatt still couldn't breathe, couldn't think. Chopper, alive? It wasn't possible. Wyatt had seen all his men go down, one by one. They'd all been gunned down seconds after entering the village. Their bodies left on the road for hours. "It can't be him. It's not possible."

Freeman nodded with sympathy. "Like I said, our intel is very good."

"Why now? Why hold on to him for so long?"

"I don't have any answers for you, Earp. But

I do know he's not in good shape. Whatever the reason for keeping him alive, I think he's running out of time. One thing's for certain, he's been through hell."

Freeman didn't have to elaborate. They both knew what that meant. Unimaginable torture.

"He's likely been brainwashed, or hell, they might've been prying information out of him."

"He wouldn't give them anything. Never."

"Bottom line, son, is we need to move quickly, or we lose him. I've got an express pass on a jet at the airport ready to take off at fifteen hundred hours. It'll be a full twenty-four hours in DC to get through the briefings that'll bring you up to speed, then it'll take us twenty-hours to get to Kabul. The team will be waiting on you. They'll take you through the drill. The plan is for a night extraction. The helo's ready, the men are the best. But we need you to take 'em to the field where you were extracted."

"Me? I haven't been in country for almost three years."

"You know the terrain, and you know what didn't work last time. So do we. We aren't going to make those mistakes again."

"That's crazy. I've been away too long. I'm in decent shape, but a hell of a lot could have changed since I was last there. They could be moving Chopper as a trap."

"They could, but that's not what the chatter

says. The admiral thought you might want the chance to bring Chopper home. But I gotta know ASAP. I can give you till noon." Freeman stood up, and extended his hand one more time. "For what it's worth, I think the admiral is right. You can do this."

*Then why didn't the admiral tell me himself?* Wyatt thought as he watched the rock-steady man who'd had so many lives of his brothers in his hands. The commander wasn't responsible for the FUBAR that had taken out his team. He'd been spitting mad at the outcome, and done something about it. He probably did believe Wyatt could pull it off, just like the admiral did, but Wyatt wasn't that soldier anymore. Hadn't been for a long time.

The thought of leaving Chopper's extraction in anyone else's hands made him nervous, sure, but more nervous than taking the lead? He wasn't a lieutenant anymore. Or a team leader. He was a bartender who occasionally flew a chopper. A babysitter, a friend and a man who finally understood that for the first time in his life, he'd fallen in love.

CRICKET HAD BEEN sitting on the boulder that had been *hers* since she was eleven, although it wasn't so private anymore. If she turned her head to the right, she'd see a tour group walking toward the Treasure Cave, and to the left, there was a big family getting ready for a picnic. Straight ahead was her ocean, though. Crashing against a group of rocks that were as old as the Atlantic, that held its secrets close and tight.

She'd been on the boulder for an hour already, just thinking. Worrying about Wyatt's meeting, about her relationship with her mother. When Ronny had called her this morning, she'd told him she'd speak to him, but she wasn't quite ready for Victoria, which was true. She was, however, not as mad as she had been. Mostly thanks to Wyatt. He'd made some great points. Then he'd made love to her so slow and tender it made her cry. He didn't even say hush. Just held her close.

Ronny would be meeting her at any minute, though, and she wanted to be open to what he had to say. He'd defend her mother, of course, but who knew? Maybe he'd have some great points, too.

"Permission to come aboard?"

He was right behind her and it made her smile that he always asked if he could sit with her. Back in the day, she had turned him away, but more often, she'd loved his company.

He perched in his regular spot…not quite as roomy as it had been when she was a kid, but they were both comfortable. "How you doing, Baby Girl?"

"Better."

"Good. It's hard to listen well when anger's coursing through your veins."

"I'm pretty sure I'm more disappointed than

angry. All she had to do was ask me first. I don't understand why she needed to go behind my back."

"Well," he said, pushing back his hair. He'd worn his crazy blue sunglasses that made him look like a '70s version of an alien. "I figured it was time you knew a few things about your mother. First off, the only reason I was able to have primary custody of you is because Vic stood up to her parents. That wasn't easy for her to do back then. Hell, it's not easy to do now because those two are real tight-ass rich WASPs."

Cricket laughed. Ronny was irreverent, absolutely, but she'd never heard him talk about his ex-in-laws in such vivid terms.

"She'd already disappointed them by marrying me, and getting knocked up before she went to college. If they'd had their way, you would have been swept up into their Connecticut lives and I wouldn't have seen you again until you hit eighteen."

"Are you serious? Tell me, Ronny, because if this is just you speculating so Mom and I will patch things up—"

"I give you my word, Baby Girl. I only speak the absolute truth when we're on this boulder."

"I believe you. Just the thought of not being with you all those years makes me sick. It would have been unbearable."

"You'd have come out fine," he said. "Different on the outside maybe, but honey, you were you from the day you were born. No one could take that from you, I don't care who."

She wanted to hug him until the sun set, but she just moved her hand over his.

"Sending you to prep school was a concession, but an easy one because your mom and I always wanted you to have the best education in the world, and I never could have paid for that. And when you spent those summers and holidays with her or your grandparents, Vic had drummed it into their heads that if they said one word against me, she'd leave with you, and they'd never see either of you again. It meant she didn't get to see you as often as she'd wanted to. But she made that tough call, because she wanted you to stay with me. And for you to enjoy the freedom of living in Temptation Bay. But it wasn't easy for her. There were lots of times she felt like a terrible mother, but all she knew for sure was that she wanted you to chart your own course, and not become conditioned to the kind of life she had."

The tears had started the moment Cricket learned about the life with Ronny she'd almost lost. She'd like to say it was the ocean spray wetting her face, but nope. She was bawling like a baby. "What I said to her was awful." Her voice was all wobbly and broken, but Ronny had heard that all before. "I owe her so much."

"I know, sweetheart. We both do. You want to hear the rest, or you want to take a break?"

"You know what? I want to hear everything, but let's walk on the beach for a bit, okay? At least until I'm not sobbing all over myself."

He helped her down, and she let him. When they finally made it to the shore, he took her hand again, as they walked slowly, going around whatever was in their path, paying no one any mind.

"That struggle Vic had over being a bad mother? When she saw she had an opportunity to help you get a great job straight out of law school, she jumped on it. Even I knew the judge thought you were very bright and you worked hard. He was genuinely proud of you, as was your mother. And it had very little to do with you going to his alma mater. But he warned Vic that just going to Yale wasn't a ticket to a big firm. Even if you'd been his own flesh and blood, he only could have done so much."

"Oh, God," she said, sniffing hard, trying not to start the waterworks again. "I had no idea."

"'Course you didn't. Vic didn't want you to. She asked the judge to make it happen. Call in a favor, whatever he had to do."

"It would have been so different if I'd known all this before I went to Chicago."

"That would have meant your mother would've had to admit a lot of uncomfortable things to you. And much as she disagreed with your grandparents, she didn't want you hating them." He pulled Cricket back, when a rogue wave almost hit them. "Damn, I miss being in the water," he muttered.

Cricket smiled. "I know." Then she noticed someone waving from the sea wall.

It was Queenie's sister. "Thanks for what you're doing for us, Cricket," she called out. "Queenie's feeling better than she has in ages."

Sighing, Cricket smiled, waved and said, "You're welcome," then kept on walking.

Ronny grinned at her.

"I haven't done anything, not really." After another big sniff, she said, "It's a long story."

"So I've heard. I don't think it matters to them how you help. That you went to talk to Penny was a nice thing."

Cricket leaned over and kissed him on his weathered cheek. "I had good influences."

"You sure did. At least one. Now, let me finish up before you ask which one of us I meant."

"You know that I'm happier than I have any right to be because of both of you, don't you?"

"You have all the right in the world, Baby Girl," he said, stopping to pick up a pretty shell and handing it to her. "Shall I continue?"

"Please."

"So, Vic asked her husband to call in a marker. He agreed, but at the time the marriage was a little rocky. The man, whatever else you think of him, is a smart guy, and he knew about Vic's track record. But they'd gotten hitched after a short, impetuous romance. Meaning, it was just your mom being her wonderful self, but he neglected to get a prenup."

"Oh. That's interesting."

"His family didn't think so. Anyway, he told Vic he'd call in the favor but she had to promise to stick with him for five years, and work on the marriage. And to sign that key piece of paper." Ronny smiled, but he looked a little sad, too. "The judge is worth a lot, but your mom didn't blink. Didn't hesitate for a second. She wanted to give you a solid start. She has her faults, just like the rest of us, but when it comes to you, never question her intentions. She's never failed to do what she thought was best for you."

Cricket stopped walking just as a wave hit almost to her knees. She didn't care. It could have swallowed her whole and taken her out to sea, and she'd still be speechless and bewildered and embarrassed, not necessarily in that order.

She'd told Becky the same thing about Wyatt just yesterday. Talk about swift retribution. "I think it's time I go talk to Mom."

"I knew you'd see it my way."

"No one sees anything your way, Ronny. You are one of a kind."

"Ah, you know exactly how to butter me up.

I'm gonna go check on the boat. You take your time. Maybe give me a ring when it's the right time to come home."

AFTER ONE OF the most emotional days of her life, Cricket hoped things weren't about to get even worse as she walked to the bar. Wyatt had called her half an hour ago to come meet him. As she got to the door, she saw Becky standing all the way at the corner of the deck. She looked nervous, too, which didn't help Cricket relax. Becky joined her. "I was supposed to arrive in fifteen minutes, but I couldn't stand the waiting. I'm dying of curiosity about the commander. Wyatt wouldn't tell me anything."

"Me, neither," Cricket said, wishing Becky had waited. After her conversation with her mother, she'd spent the last hour wandering the beach, thinking. She'd actually come to a decision about what she was going to do, but now, that would have to wait until Wyatt told them his news. She opened the door, letting Becky walk in first.

Wyatt seemed to take Becky's early arrival in stride. In fact, he barely smiled at either of them, and that made her stomach roil.

Wyatt fixed another drink, Cricket didn't see what it was, and brought two drinks to the table, handing something blue to Becky, while she got a cold beer. Wyatt had nothing in front of him. He sat down and looked at both of them in such a way that if he waited another second to spit it out, Cricket was going to scream.

"One of my men survived. Chopper's been held by the Taliban all this time. The commander's asked me to go in country and lead the extraction team."

Cricket wanted to throw up.

Becky didn't look any better. "You said no, right? I mean, how dare he ask you to go back into that nightmare after so long? It's unthinkable."

"I wouldn't be going as a SEAL or an officer. I'd be away for approximately ten days, and I'm sorry, I can't tell you any more than that."

Cricket had no words at all.

Becky seemed to turn to stone in that moment. "Is that why you've stayed in shape? All those morning exercises, all the running. Were you just biding your time until you heard they needed you?"

"No," he said. "I don't want to go. I have to. You should understand that better than most people. I left a man behind, and now I have a chance to make things…better."

Cricket hadn't really believed things could get this much worse. Not knowing what to say was probably a good thing, because Becky was going at Wyatt like a wildcat.

"You promised. You gave me your word you'd be safe. You promised my children you'd be careful. I thought you were supposed to be honorable. Steadfast. What am I supposed to tell Josh and Rose? That the man they adore and talk about every single day is willing to risk his life? Just like their daddy?"

"Hopefully, you won't tell them anything, Maybe that I had to go out of town on business."

"Hopefully," she said, the sarcasm burning. "I trusted you."

"I'll be fine."

Becky stood up, sending her chair crashing into the table behind them. "How many times have I heard that one? Every damn mission. Every one. And every single time I lived in terror of what would happen. Of what *did* happen."

Wyatt looked eerily calm, but Cricket knew he had to be as crushed as Becky. The two of them were different portraits of the same anguish. As for herself? She was pretty numb at the moment, except for the gurgling in her stomach and the lump she could barely swallow past.

She'd known since the night of the storm that she'd fallen in love with Wyatt. The real deal, with all that came with it. The fear, the hope, the expectations... It had been swept aside for a bit by the twists of fate, but last night, she'd lain awake, watching him sleep, knowing that she wasn't the same person anymore. In spite of everything that had happened, her heart had been reshaped by the man next to her. And now, that new heart was being ripped from her chest.

"Look, I'm sorry, but I have to do this. And I'm sorry about the dinner," he said, looking more at Cricket than Becky, then back again. "But I'm looking forward to getting to know Ned when I return."

Becky shook her head, her stare, her whole being, wounded from the inside out. "I warned you, Wyatt," she whispered.

For the first time since they'd come inside, she saw the crack in Wyatt. It was subtle, but obvious if you cared about the man. "Let me ask you a question," he said, rising slowly, looking only at Becky. "What if it were Adam?"

Becky froze again. Her chest didn't move at all. Then her tear-streaked face got so pale, Cricket was afraid she'd crumble. Instead, she ran out of the bar as if she'd been lit on fire.

WYATT WATCHED THE door for a long time, although he knew Becky wouldn't come back. What he didn't know was if she'd ever come back again. Cricket walked up next to him, so quiet. As quiet as she'd been through this whole mess. He took her hand and pulled her close, hoping she wouldn't push him away...unbelievably grateful she didn't.

"This really is messed up. I hate the timing.

You'll have left for Chicago before I get back, and that kills me."

"Don't say that." Her voice came out as no more than a croak, but that might be what it was supposed to sound like. "Of course you know how devastating this is for Becky. And what it will do to the kids if something goes wrong. You just spoke to the commander, but please, can't you give yourself more time to think this through? You need to truly consider what this will mean, and I'm not talking about the admiral or the Navy or your old commander. Those kids love you. Becky loves you."

He pulled back enough to look into her eyes. Waiting, praying, for her to add her own name to the list.

"I understand you feel you have a duty," she said, "and that most of your life, duty has been the most important thing. Far above anything else. I don't understand the kind of agony you went through at losing your men, and the burden of what to do now. You're torn between honor and responsibility to the people who care most about you. You can't guarantee a safe return." Tears welled in her eyes. "For Becky's sake and your own, I hope when you do come home, that you'll have those same people welcome you back."

His chest constricted. He didn't have a clue what to tell her, how to explain that it was the cruelest choice he'd ever had to make.

She dashed away the tears that had spilled down her cheek. "What time are you supposed to leave?"

"Little less than an hour."

"Then you'd better hurry up and kiss me."

He gathered her in his arms, loving her, sweeping her into a kiss he never wanted to forget. Not as long as he lived.

# CHAPTER TWENTY-SIX

THE MOMENT WYATT climbed into the E-B4 Advanced Airborne Command Post, he was bombarded with visual images from several large monitors giving live reports from DC, CIA Central Headquarters in Langley and Kabul.

"Our situation has changed. We have new intel," Freeman said. "The mission has been moved up forty-eight hours so forget DC, we're headed straight to Kabul. You'll be briefed on the way there, and hit the ground running."

Wyatt's unhappiness with the update must have been obvious, because Freeman told him to go put his duffel in the last sleep cabin on the right, hit the head, get a drink then be ready because they weren't stopping until he knew every aspect of the plan to extract Chopper from the target, then burn that target to the ground.

Although his wasn't the only mission being orchestrated on this beauty, Chopper's extraction was priority one.

As he walked through the huge jet, the ratio of uniforms to civilians was about equal, although he was pretty damn sure the civilians were all

CIA. There were brass from the Army, Navy and Marines. Wyatt was probably the only person completely out of his element.

He took Freeman's orders literally, and by the time he was seated in front of a computer that was so advanced it made his head spin, he was already acclimating to the world he'd known for years. Now he had to catch up quickly on the operation.

"Earp, that you?"

He looked up at his screen, from where he'd been studying the map of the target. "I'll be damned," Wyatt said. "If it isn't Whiskey Eye himself."

"How you doin', bro?"

"Good. A little out of touch, but once you've been through hell—" he began.

"You're in hell forever," his old friend finished. "Chopper'll be real glad to see you."

"Yeah. I'm counting on it," Wyatt said, not at all sure that would be the case. Being held by the enemy for that many years without a ransom demand or a trade offered was rare as it comes. The last man left behind, that they'd known was alive, had been out for six long days in rough territory. Sadly, a couple of SEALs had fallen during that extraction. No one who'd been a SEAL ever forgot the creed. No Man Left Behind. But it was a special kind of agony to be the only one who made it. He wished he didn't have the experience to back that up.

And dammit, he could afford zero time dwelling on that.

The briefing, which should have taken a couple of days, was like a Hell Week all its own. He wasn't used to this shit anymore. Yeah, he could tell you the exact inventory of the bar, but what he had to absorb before they hit Kabul was almost crippling.

To make matters worse, he kept thinking about Cricket. About how she hadn't said anything about herself in her hard-hitting speech. He still wasn't sure he was doing the right thing. For Adam's family, for Cricket, or his own redemption.

Topping that off was his lack of confidence that Chopper really was alive. The photo was blurry. And nothing made sense about keeping him alive. Wyatt had a feeling Freeman might be in agreement.

An alarm went off, which got every last man's and woman's attention, but it was coming from Kabul, and it was quickly silenced. It had put the whole plane on edge.

When he looked at the screenshots of the target where he'd last carried out a successful mission with his team, it looked eerily the same. They hadn't been ambushed there. That happened as soon as they got into Sangin, the town the Taliban had since taken over.

He didn't dare go down that rabbit hole, because he wasn't sure he could come back out. Instead, he looked at every inch of the target, and after a couple of hours, he realized that something big had changed.

"Commander?"

Freeman joined him, and so did the rest of the group focusing on the rescue. "Those wires weren't there three years ago. Here." He pointed out two of the side buildings, close to the squat horror that was a holdout from the eighteenth century where the Taliban held prisoners.

That meant communication was inside the target. The only tech they had last time was in the leader's hut, on the opposite side of the courtyard from the guards.

Freeman changed the screen to the live feed from Kabul. A lieutenant saluted the commander and called in the SEAL team that Wyatt would be embedded in. Wyatt saw immediately that they were all SEAL veterans from DEVGRU, also known as SEAL Team Six. Every last one of them was well trained in explosives, tech, underwater maneuvers and High Altitude/Low Opening Jumps. They'd all mastered every skill, since there was no guarantee that every man would walk out of a mission.

"How long from approach to wrap-up?"

"Well," Lieutenant Wheeler, who was their team leader, said, "Osama bin Laden took thirty-eight minutes. We're not bringing back intel. We should be out in twelve."

"Be warned," Freeman said. "Better make it ten or less, because there are more eyes and ears than before."

"Yeah, we found that out, actually, and the last team that was there a week ago already laid down a pattern of explosives that will take all that juicy tech down and out. Including those in the hut."

"Roger that."

"Our welcome ain't gonna be pretty, but it'll be damn fast."

They proceeded to take Wyatt through the drill, every step from taking off in the Black Hawk helicopter, fast-roping down to the roof of the building where three men would set off the series of explosives, while the other four made their way into the target, taking out the guards, then harnessing Chopper to be lifted up via the blown roof. The Black Hawk would then land at the edge of the courtyard, where the rest of the team would evac.

Wyatt could see it in his mind's eye: all the practice runs, all the maneuvers, the night vision goggles that would turn the world green. He signed off, and didn't move an inch as the camera returned to overseeing operations.

It was past time he stretched his legs, so he got up and walked the length of the jet. A few doors were locked, not that he tried to open them, but he also shook hands with a number of brothers. And officers, too. But mostly brothers. In the tiny sleep cabin he stretched as much as he could, then worked his muscles with a quick hundred push-ups.

He was lucky he'd stayed in shape. But was it enough? It wasn't that he felt so out of touch, but these other guys, they were at the top of their game. They knew what they were doing.

Most important of all, he'd made a promise to keep himself safe. And damn, that was a hard pill to swallow.

When he stopped after ten more push-ups, he knew what he had to do. His body had just needed a little action to get his mind working properly. Walking back down to where Freeman was fixing a cup of coffee, Wyatt asked him to take it back with him, so they could have a private conversation.

Closing the door behind him, Freeman didn't even blink at how closely they stood together.

"I've made a decision, sir. I know my strengths and weaknesses and there's no question I shouldn't go in with this team. I'd only slow them down. Six is a badass machine that doesn't need an extra cog. I just gave the men the only intel I could help with. I'm not in sufficient shape, and I'm not mentally prepared for in-country warfare."

The commander was frowning heavily, but Wyatt wasn't going to change his mind.

"The only other way I know I can help and not

hinder is that after we get Chopper back to base, no matter what his condition, brainwashed or not, I should be the one who debriefs him."

Freeman, arms crossed over his broad chest, looked at Wyatt's duffel bag for a long silent couple of minutes. "I don't know, Earp."

"Sir, I mean no disrespect, but the first part is nonnegotiable. The second part is up to you."

The commander looked him square in the eye, then stuck out his hand. "I think that'll do just fine, Earp."

CRICKET LOOKED DOWN at her day planner and there were far too many question marks on too many days. No wonder.

It had been great seeing Ginny, and forgetting, at least for a short while, about her own situation. Her friend was in a really tough spot, and Cricket wasn't sure she'd been of much help.

Now that she was back at Wyatt's apartment, though, all she could think about was him.

She couldn't postpone returning to Chicago yet again, even though that's what she wanted to do. She simply couldn't put her whole life on hold indefinitely.

He'd been gone for five days, and every time her phone rang her heart just about stopped. Not that she believed he had any reason to call her. She hadn't given him one. She hadn't even told him she loved him.

It wouldn't have been fair. Logically she knew that, but it still hurt.

Still, she could've made a point of asking him to call. She knew he wouldn't have much opportunity, but dammit, he was a civilian after all.

Becky hadn't heard from him either, but she didn't expect to. She'd been awfully kind, trying to calm Cricket down, when she was just as worried herself. Worried and angry, and trying to keep it together for the kids' sakes. Cricket hated bugging her, but when she'd gotten a weird phone call from a weird number, she'd guessed that it was from a satellite phone. With all the static it had been impossible to tell if it was Wyatt on the other end before the call was cut off. Becky agreed it probably was a satellite phone.

Leaning back in Wyatt's favorite chair, she caught a glimpse of Josh's latest Lego project. She smiled first, and then her eyes filled. Wyatt's apartment felt empty without him, and so did she.

She had to wonder if she wouldn't be better off staying at the shack. Ronny's surgery was supposed to be in two weeks, but he'd gotten a summer cold and that had to be gone a couple of days before, or it would have to be rescheduled.

Her mom was being an excellent minder for Ronny, and they continued to enjoy the heck out of each other. Especially now that she'd admitted she and the judge were in the process of getting a divorce. Yesterday when Cricket had stopped at the shack, her mom had confided that she wasn't sure what she was going to do when Ronny recovered.

Cricket thought she knew the answer, but there was no use getting her hopes up, just because her parents were getting along so well.

The sound of a text had her straightening. It was just from Sabrina. She was going to be fifteen minutes late. Cricket had been helping out at the bar when she could, but she didn't know why they all treated her like she was running things.

Unless they knew something she didn't.

Of course all the customers had a million questions about Wyatt, where he was, what he was doing…and every time she'd dodged one of them she'd gotten the sinking feeling that after jumping back into the action, he'd want to go back to his old life. It wasn't rational. Maybe it was her brain trying to keep her from dwelling on the danger he'd put himself in. Being in the dark was torturous.

No. She had to believe he would come home. She had no idea what would happen after that. With Wyatt, that was. As for her job? She'd known before he left that she couldn't stay at the firm. Although it was important to be professional. Anything less would reflect on the judge and her own character, and while she didn't want to be a part of the rape case, she'd do what she could—without crossing a personal line. She'd given them a month's notice, and they could decide if it was worth putting her on the defense team. She hoped not, but it was their call.

Once she was in Chicago, she'd put her condo up for sale, and pack up all her things to be shipped back to Temptation Bay. Thank goodness Ronny's insurance had turned out to be excellent, covering almost everything, so she had some wiggle room.

A couple of other revelations had come to light after she and Victoria had forgiven each other. For one, she'd learned her mom was quite the wise investor and hadn't plowed through her trust fund as expected. Despite not getting much of anything from the divorce, she was doing quite well.

Another surprise was that Cricket also had a trust fund. Endowed by her grandparents and accessible once she turned thirty-five. Enough that her future would be fine—not extravagant—but fine when she passed the Rhode Island bar and hung out her shingle in Temptation Bay.

She heard a noise outside the door. Not a knock or anything, but even though she felt too drained to get out of her chair, she stood.

The door opened.

Wyatt.

Whole, alive, looking like crap, but still the best sight she'd ever seen.

He saw her and dropped his duffel bag. They

crashed into each other as if polarized, holding
on so tight they both were breathless.

When he finally kissed her, and kissed her,
and when she'd kissed him back, he suddenly
stopped. Held her at arm's length and looked into
her eyes. "I shouldn't have waited. I should've
told you before—but I've never been in love before and I messed up—"

"What?"

"See? Hell," he murmured, briefly closing his
eyes. "Cricket Shaw, I love you. I knew before
I left but I swear I'll make it up to you now and
every day. Even if I have to fly to Chicago every
damn—"

"You don't have to," she said, taking in a gulp
of air before kissing him again, reacquainting
herself with his taste. He smelled like way more
travel than showers, but that didn't bother her at
all.

"What do you mean?"

"I'm moving back here. Back home. I'll be taking the Rhode Island bar."

He had the oddest expression. "Where are you
planning on staying when you move back?"

"Well, I thought—" She swallowed. Hard.
While she screwed up her courage. "I need to
ask you something. And I promise there's no right
or wrong answer. Just the truth so I know what to
expect." She took a breath as he nodded. "After

being back in your old world, do you have any regrets about leaving the military?"

Shaking his head, he brushed a finger over her lips. "If anything, the experience showed me that I'd made the right decision. I'd already said goodbye to that life. I wish I could have told you sooner, but I was never in real danger. I decided while we were in the air that I wasn't going to set foot anywhere but Kabul headquarters. The team didn't really need me. I'd made a promise to Becky, and in my heart, to you. I had to make sure I came home. I had too much to lose."

Seeing the sincerity in his eyes, she could finally breathe again. "What about Chopper?"

"The mission was successful." His smile dimmed. "But it wasn't Chopper after all. It was a German reporter who had been missing for months. No one thought he was alive. So the mission wasn't a total loss. The man will get to see the wife and kids he never thought he would."

Cricket nodded. "I'm sorry he wasn't—" She stopped for a sniffle.

"It's okay." He touched her cheek. "I knew it was a long shot and made peace with it before I got on that plane. Look, I'll still grieve for the men I lost, but now I've got a life of my own to live for. I never want to be apart from you again, Cricket. And I missed Becky and the kids way more than I thought possible, so I hope like hell she can forgive me."

"She and I talked a lot, and I've got a feeling she'll be very forgiving."

The relief nearly poured off him. "I'll text her for now, let her know I'm home and with you." He pulled out his phone, but then just stood there, staring at her as if he'd never seen anything more wonderful in his life.

Cricket couldn't help it—she burst into tears. "You came back," she whispered.

"I did. Don't cry, honey. It's okay. I'm fine." He hugged her tight while she wept on his shoulder.

"I know. You're fine and you love me and—" She shuddered, trying to stop crying, but she couldn't.

Sweeping her up in his arms again, he carried her into the bathroom. "Want to take a shower with me? You know, while you catch me up on things?"

She laughed, nodded and, while she turned on the water, he sent a text to Becky.

"Oh, God. I love you, too," Cricket said as soon as he set the phone aside.

"Sounds like that's a problem," he said slowly, looking as if he was holding back a grin. "Is it?"

"No, it's just—I realized that I hadn't said it out loud."

"So, I guess we're both pretty bad at this love business, huh?" he said, as he lifted her shirt off.

Cricket unzipped his jeans. "Guess we'll have to muddle through it together."

"That's my thinking, too."

"Well, for a start, how about a little more action and less thinking?"

Wyatt laughed. "You got it, sweetheart," he said and picked her up and put her in shower.

* * * * *

# Get 2 Free Books,
## Plus 2 Free Gifts—
### just for trying the Reader Service!

**HARLEQUIN** SPECIAL EDITION

# Get 2 Free Books,
## Plus 2 Free Gifts—
### just for trying the Reader Service!

# Get 2 Free Books,
## Plus 2 Free Gifts—
### just for trying the Reader Service!